The Ultimate Romantic Challenge

KATHERINE GARBERA

BRAVA

KENSINGTON PUBLISHING CORP.
http://www.kensingtonbooks.com

BRAVA BOOKS are published by

Kensington Publishing Corp.
850 Third Avenue
New York, NY 10022

All Kensington titles, imprints and distributed lines are available at special quantity discounts for bulk purchases for sales promotion, premiums, fund-raising, educational or institutional use.

Special book excerpts or customized printings can also be created to fit specific needs. For details, write or phone the office of the Kensington Special Sales Manager: Kensington Publishing Corp., 850 Third Avenue, New York, NY 10022. Attn. Special Sales Department. Phone: 1-800-221-2647.

ISBN 0-7582-1243-7

First Kensington Trade Paperback Printing: December 2006
10 9 8 7 6 5 4 3 2 1

Printed in the United States of America

I want to thank my husband for being such a romantic guy and inspiring me to new heights with each hero I write. He really goes out of his way to make every day seem like our first date.

Acknowledgments

I'd like to thank Eve Gaddy, Beverly Brandt, and Nancy Thompson for always being there when I needed to talk about this story.

Also, a special thank you to Elizabeth Bevarly for taking time out of her busy schedule to read this book!

Lastly, to all the writers in the Slaving Away Café who gave me company and encouragement as I was working on this story.

Chapter One

Alexandra Haughton stood on a private balcony of her in-laws' mansion overlooking the water in historic Charleston, South Carolina. The perfectly landscaped lawn was a tribute to the garden staff her in-laws employed and Priscilla's determination to live in a type of paradise.

Since it was Friday night, she was at her in-laws' house for cocktails before they'd have dinner downtown at Circa 1886. But Priscilla had asked her to come twenty minutes early and had mixed martinis instead of their standard glass of chardonnay.

Something was wrong.

Even her father-in-law Burt's absence only underscored that something was amiss. Priscilla was the matriarch of their family, acting like a herald for all the decisions made by the Haughtons. It had been Priscilla who'd offered Alexandra a job when she'd wanted nothing more than to stay safe in her town house. Priscilla who'd informed her of the family's decision to offer her Marcus's seat on the board of directors. And Priscilla who'd told her not three weeks ago that it was time for Alexandra to start having a life again.

Whatever the hell that meant. She did have a life. A very busy one that was consumed with running Haughton House, one of the area's most prestigious hotels. She'd ended an affair just six months earlier, and she'd become a little driven when it came to work.

She wished that she could enjoy the dry martini and think of the spicy grilled shrimp over field green tomatoes that she'd eat as soon as they got to the restaurant, but instead she could only focus on the churning in her gut. Her instincts were screaming at her that the foundations of her carefully ordered world were starting to crack.

She never varied what she ate. Routine was everything in Alexandra's life, and she savored her schedule because it gave her life structure and meaning.

"I'm afraid there's been a change in plans for dinner tonight, my dear."

Alexandra refused to panic at her mother-in-law's words, though she didn't like the sound of that. "What kind of change? Are Daniel and Brad going to be able to join us?"

Daniel and Brad were her brothers-in-law. The twins were five years younger than Alexandra's own thirty-two years. They'd idolized Marcus and had transferred that hero-worship to Alexandra after his death.

"No, actually I accepted a dinner meeting for you and the Pack-Maur representative for tonight."

Alexandra's hand trembled and her drink spilled on the back of her hand. She hated that small physical betrayal. She was cool, confident. She ran a thriving business—it should take more than one little announcement to rattle her.

But it was more than a change in dinner plans, and Alexandra and Priscilla both knew it.

"Why? We're a family-owned destination resort, not the kind of place that belongs as part of a huge hotel chain."

She forced herself to take a sip of her martini and smiled at her deceased husband's mother. The fact that they weren't blood-related hadn't entered Alexandra's mind until this moment. She'd made herself invaluable to the Haughton family by running the resort the family had owned for generations. But in the back of her mind the same fear had always plagued her. She really wasn't a Haughton, and one day she knew that would be important. It appeared today was that day.

"I'm not so sure. Being a family-owned resort isn't going to last forever. The boys aren't interested in running a hotel, now that their computer company is doing so well, Burt's already retired, and I'm not going to be around forever."

Alexandra swallowed hard, ruthlessly pushing her emotions deeper, forcing her expression to be calm and cool. "It was Marcus's dream."

Priscilla took Alexandra's hand in her own. The older woman ran her finger over the platinum wedding set that Alexandra wore on her right hand. "Marcus has been gone ten years."

No one was more aware of that than she was. "I know, Priscilla."

"Maybe it's time for all of us to move on. Mr. Powell—the man from Pack-Maur—wants to speak to you about coming to work for him. They are all really impressed with the changes you've made here at Haughton House over the last few years."

Normally she'd be ecstatic about the praise; everything she knew about hotel and restaurant management she'd learned the hard way by working in the resort. "I'm not interested in working for a hotel chain."

What if they wanted her to move? And they would, she thought, as all the implications of what her mother-in-law was saying sank in. Any job she took with Pack-Maur would involve travel. She knew the company and had read about their groundbreaking innovations.

"You might not have a choice. We'll consider your opposition to the buyout, but right now we're leaning toward selling to them. Listen to him, Alexandra—give him a chance. You're too young to be a widow."

Alexandra took another sip of her martini, feeling the closest to out of control that she'd been since her husband had died just days before their first wedding anniversary. She struggled to keep her smile on her face. "Of course. I want to do what's right for the family."

Priscilla smiled at her. "You always have."

Alexandra nodded at her mother-in-law. Not wanting to think about how she'd made the choices of the Haughtons her own choices. "What time am I to meet him?"

"In a few minutes. We invited him to join us for drinks before he takes you to dinner. Burt is showing him around the gardens to give us a chance to talk."

"Is there more?" Alexandra asked before she could help herself. She gripped the smooth wrought iron railing that lined the balcony. The warm breeze off the river stirred her hair and she closed her eyes for a moment, letting it wash over her.

"No, dear," Priscilla said, walking over to stand next to her at the railing.

"Marcus loved the ocean."

"Yes, he did." Much of their courtship had been spent out there on Marcus's yacht, the *Golden Spoon*.

Alexandra finished her martini and held the glass loosely in her hand. Priscilla put her hand on her shoulder.

"Give Sterling Powell a chance, Alexandra. That's all I'm asking you. I think this is the best move for the family to make."

And that said it all. Priscilla was the head of the family and they all followed her wishes. "I will."

"I know this is hard for you," Priscilla said.

Alexandra doubted her mother-in-law knew exactly how she felt. Priscilla's husband was still alive and at her side. They were both healthy and had been married for thirty-seven years. Later she might appreciate Priscilla's sympathy; right now, she didn't.

For the first time in ten years Alexandra realized that the Haughtons were focused on a goal that she didn't share. Their paths where this man was concerned would differ, and whether

Alexandra wanted it or not, Sterling Powell was going to change their lives.

Alexandra understood what the other woman was saying. It was time to move on. It had been for a while but Alexandra had hoped . . . well, what *had* she hoped? That her life would continue on its path without any more upsets?

She knew better. Whenever she got comfortable and started to relax, something else jarred her from her routine. "I'm going to pour myself another drink. Can I get you one?"

"No, thank you. I'll go see what's keeping Burt and our guest."

Alexandra went inside to make another drink. Crossing the polished wood floor, she couldn't help but stand and stare at the wall of family photos. She was in the majority of them, as were the boys and Priscilla and Burt. She always felt the sense of Marcus's loss strongly when she saw the family together.

Especially tonight. Once at the bar, she poured the vermouth and gin into the shaker with the ice. She shook it harder than was required to mix the drink.

"I'll take one of those."

The deep masculine voice brushed over her senses like a warm breeze on a cool day. Sterling Powell. She recognized his voice from the phone conversations they'd had. She'd always enjoyed sparring with him on the phone. And she'd had one or two fantasies about what he looked like.

She glanced over her shoulder. He was taller than she'd expected, towering over her own five-foot-seven frame. His eyes were warm gray; his face wasn't technically handsome but there was something there that captured her attention. His jaw was strong and stubborn—she knew that from talking to him.

She stepped back to put more space between them and stumbled into the bar. He caught her with one sinewy arm around her waist. She pressed her free hand against his chest; the other one held the cocktail shaker like a shield.

"I didn't mean to startle you," he said, his minty breath brushing against her cheek.

She didn't believe that for a second. From the three conference calls they'd had to set up this trip, she knew he was the kind of man to find a weakness and take advantage of it. And showing up here on her home turf without letting her know was definitely a bold move.

He was too used to manipulating his opponents, and she knew that no matter the casual social setting, they were combatants. She pushed against his shoulder and he stepped back, letting her move away from him.

He was sexier than she'd expected him to be. His deep voice had played a part in her erotic fantasies since they'd first spoken, which annoyed her. She prided herself on making sure that no man got the jump on her.

"You didn't," she said. Going back to the bar, she busied herself putting some olives on a cocktail stick and arranging the glasses.

"I made the martinis a little strong—I hope that's okay."

"I'm sure I can handle it."

She doubted there was little that Sterling Powell couldn't handle. But she knew for all his strength he had to have a weakness and she was determined to find it. He'd set the terms for the battle by showing up unexpectedly . . . guerilla-warfare-style business. She would do the same, using whatever weapons she had at her disposal to find his vulnerabilities.

She set the cocktail shaker on the bar. God, his cologne smelled good. She wanted to give him one of her withering stares, the one that always made everyone jump to do her bidding, but instead she found herself breathing deeper and trying to figure out what scent he was wearing. Not a good idea when she was trying to find his weaknesses.

Damn, was this what came of one small change in her routine? A total loss of her common sense and the ability to function? She'd done business with enough men to know that even though it was a new millennium, they could still be distracted by a flash of leg and a little flirting.

Her business ethics were always at odds with manipulating men that way but if they allowed themselves to be led around by lust, then why shouldn't she exploit it? Men used the traits intrinsic to their sex in business. They could coldly detach emotion from a decision matrix, something she wished she could do.

She was always calm and cool—totally collected. The person who everyone else turned to in a crisis. This wasn't a crisis, she reminded herself. He was just a man who was . . . staring at her, at her mouth.

She licked her lower lip. His eyes narrowed as he tracked the movement. *Interesting.*

"Sterling Powell," he said, holding his hand out to her.

"I recognized your voice."

"And I yours. You aren't what I expected," he said. His gaze never left her, skimming down her body, lingering over her breasts and hips.

He was attracted to her. It had been a little less than a year since her last affair, and she wondered if Sterling might be her next lover. She was definitely attracted to him.

She turned back to making the martinis, refilling her own glass first and then pouring one for him. She poured a Scotch neat for Burt, who she knew had to be nearby. "What did you expect?"

"Someone . . . I'm not sure, but not a woman like you."

She didn't know what that meant, and wasn't interested in pursuing a personal topic while her in-laws were a few feet away. She handed Sterling his martini glass.

"I need to freshen up before we leave for dinner. The Scotch is for Burt," she said, quietly exiting the room.

Sterling watched Alexandra walk away, aware that his mind wasn't on business. It had been that way since the first time he'd called the Haughton House and heard her voice. He'd expected the soft, slow modulations of the South and, of course, she'd delivered that but she was also so fiery and hard-nosed on the phone that he'd expected her to look harder, to seem hardened by life. But instead there had been a hint of vulnerability in her eyes. He'd like to think at forty that the real reason for his attraction to her was her eyes, but he'd reacted to her like he was eighteen. Pure lust at the thought of caressing her curvy body and holding her in his arms.

He'd expected her hair to be pulled back tight from her face; instead, her dark, curly hair hung in soft waves halfway down her back and she'd been dressed in a slim-fitting sheath dress that left her arms bare. He wondered how her hair would feel sliding over his skin. Would it be as soft as it looked? Those springy curls would feel so good wrapped around his hand as he took her mouth with his.

She glanced over her shoulder, catching him staring at her. "Like what you see?"

"Yes, ma'am."

"Good," she said, and with an extra swish in her step, walked out the door. Damn, she was one feisty woman.

He took a healthy swallow of his martini to get himself back under control. He'd come to Charleston on business, but that didn't mean he wouldn't enjoy the pleasure of Alexandra. Picking up the Scotch she had poured, Sterling joined Burt and Priscilla on the balcony.

"Thanks. How'd you know what I needed?"

"Alexandra did."

"She always takes care of details," Burt said, lifting his glass. "To health, wealth, and happiness."

Sterling tipped his glass to Burt's and then took a swallow. The older man was fit, in shape, and knew a lot about the current hotel industry despite the fact that he'd been retired for five years. The Haughton House was a property that Sterling had his eye on for a while and he was glad they finally agreed to meet with him.

"Where's Alexandra?" Priscilla asked. She was smaller than her husband, only coming to his shoulder. She had honey-blond hair and green eyes. She talked in a slow southern drawl that made him think, however clichéd, of mint juleps sipped on a hot summer's afternoon. The slow pace of the South was in every move she made and step she took.

"She went to freshen up," Sterling said.

"I'm afraid this is difficult on Alexandra."

"What is?" he asked. In his experience, business was just that—*business*. Not a place for emotions. He liked it that way. In the corporate world he knew exactly how to act.

"The merger," Burt said.

Nice—he might not have to spend too much time here talking business. He was a little disappointed, because he wanted to spend more time with Alexandra. "We're going ahead with it?"

"If you can convince her, we will be," Burt said.

"Why is it so hard for her?" he asked, because he knew the rest of the family was ready to have a bigger company share the headaches of running the resort. It was a demanding enterprise. Burt had mentioned that he and Priscilla wanted to travel and enjoy their retirement years.

"Because she doesn't like change," Priscilla said.

Sterling couldn't understand that. He thrived on change, on adjusting his life and finding his balance in a world that was always in flux. He knew there was more to Priscilla's words but also knew that Alexandra wouldn't want to be talked about behind her back.

Besides, he wanted to find out the details of her life from her. "Pack-Maur isn't going to sweep in and start changing your resort overnight. We want to add Haughton House to our chain because of the things that make it unique and successful as a stand-alone resort."

"I don't see how those things will be possible once you start adding the Pack-Maur Standard."

Sterling glanced up as Alexandra walked out onto the balcony. She'd reapplied her lipstick, a dark, vibrant shade that accentuated her full lower lip. He stared at her mouth, unable to think of a response to what she said.

"She does bring up an interesting point. The Pack-Maur Standard adds ultramodern conveniences," Burt said.

He'd sent Alexandra a complete proposal of expected changes that would be needed to implement Haughton House into Pack-Maur's chain a week ago. From Burt's statement, he assumed she hadn't shared it with the rest of the board.

"True, but we add our conveniences in a way that emphasizes the theme of the resort. We're not going to remodel the rooms and take out the antiques that are there now and put in modern Danish furniture."

"That's good to hear, but what about—"

"Not tonight, Alexandra. You can talk business with Sterling tomorrow. Tonight let's enjoy our drinks while watching the boats go out to sea. What time is your reservation?" Priscilla asked.

Sterling saw Alexandra's eyes narrow, but she smiled smoothly and turned toward the railing where four Adirondack chairs faced the ocean. "Actually, I made an early reservation, so we should probably be going."

He put his hand at the small of Alexandra's back; she stiffened but didn't say anything. "Thanks for the drink and the tour. What time are we golfing in the morning?"

"Seven—Alexandra can give you directions to the country club."

Priscilla took their glasses and bid them both good night. He escorted Alexandra through the house and outside, where his Porsche 911 was waiting in the circular drive.

"Top up or down?" he asked, opening the door to seat her.

"Where are we going for dinner?" she asked, as she straightened her skirt, pulling the hem lower so that it covered her to her knees.

"The Ocean Room at The Sanctuary on Kiawah Island. Our reservations aren't until 8:30, but you looked like you wanted to get out of there."

"I did. Thank you. Are you checking out the competition? You know The Sanctuary is more like the other Pack-Maur properties."

"We're not interested in The Sanctuary."

"Just Haughton House?"

"That's right."

He walked around in front of the car and seated himself. He'd driven his car up from Atlanta, where he lived and Pack-Maur's headquarters were.

"Why are you so interested in my hotel?" she asked.

"I could give you a bunch of stats showing that Charleston is one of the top three travel destinations in the U.S."

"But . . ."

"We're interested because of the way you've changed the resort from a failing family enterprise to a moneymaker in a little over eight years."

"Are you saying I'm the reason why you're here?"

"Yes, Ms. Haughton, I am."

She bit her lower lip, wrapping her arms around her waist and glancing away from him. "What are we going to do for an hour?"

"I was hoping you'd show me around your town. I want to get a feel for Charleston."

"Top down, then. You won't be able to really feel the city with the top up."

He put the top down. "Where to?"

"Out of the driveway, take a right. We'll head through the city and then south to Kiawah Island. The City Market closes at seven so there's not much you'll be able to see tonight."

"I think I drove by it earlier. Lots of little stalls and shops?"

"Yes, that's it."

"It looked like it has been here forever. I still haven't adjusted to the historical significance of many of the places in the South."

"Where are you from?" she asked.

"California," he said, but he didn't want to talk about himself. If he'd learned anything living the last five years in Atlanta, it was that people in the South put a special importance on the past and where they came from.

"What brought you to the East Coast?"

"Work. Have you eaten at the Ocean Room before?"

"Yes, a few times. It's a very romantic place."

"You went there on a date?" he asked. Burt had intimated that Alexandra was single, but that didn't mean she wasn't seeing someone that her in-laws didn't know about. And she wore a wedding set on her right hand—what was that about?

"Yes, but also for business."

Which told him precisely nothing. "Are you seeing someone now?"

"I don't think that's relevant. You're here to buy out my resort, right?"

"I'm not just here for Pack-Maur business any longer."

"Really? One look at me and you decided . . . what exactly did you decide, Sterling?"

"I think I'll keep that to myself for now."

"Let me make something very clear, Mr. Powell. I'm not going to be swayed to sell out by a little romance."

"A little romance?"

"You know what I mean."

"I'm afraid I don't. Is that some kind of euphemism for sex?"

"No, it wasn't. Why are you thinking about having sex with me?"

"Answering that wouldn't be a smart move." He prided himself on his knowledge of the opposite sex and not making the kind of stupid remarks that got him labeled an asshole in the first few hours of meeting a woman he wanted to get to know better. And Alexandra Haughton was definitely a woman he wanted to get to know better.

"I read somewhere that men think about sex every few minutes."

"That's not necessarily true." He hadn't been thinking about sex on the drive down. Okay, so maybe he'd entertained one or two fantasies of her talking dirty to him, in that prim, proper tone she got whenever he didn't give in on an issue she wanted him to.

"Oh?"

"I only think about sex every few minutes when I'm with a woman I'm attracted to."

"And you're attracted to me?"

"I think we're both attracted to each other," he said, because he'd felt her interest earlier.

"That may be true but I don't sleep with men I don't like, Mr. Powell."

"Then I'll do my best to change your mind."

"A promise to return to Atlanta in the morning and stop your efforts to obtain Haughton House would work."

"That's not going to happen, Alexandra."

"Why not?"

"Because I want both Haughton House and you."

Chapter Two

Alexandra had dropped back into tour-guide mode after he'd dropped that bombshell. She could understand why he wanted Haughton House, even though she didn't like it. Fiscally it made good business sense for Pack-Maur to try to acquire it.

She tried to ignore the fact that he'd said he'd wanted her. Sex she could handle. She was a healthy woman who'd been single the better part of her adult life and she'd had a few short-term affairs. But Sterling had an intensity to him that was usually absent in her lovers. She preferred men who weren't looking for anything long-term—not that Sterling was long-term, but the way she felt around him differed from the other men who'd been her lovers.

Dammit, Sterling had rattled her more than she wanted to admit. Maybe he was just talking about sex. In her experience most men were happy with sex and talked of little else.

The valet parked the car when they arrived at The Sanctuary, and a short time later they were seated in the Ocean Room. She knew it was time to bring the conversation around to Haughton House and try to start talking him out of his plan. But she couldn't lie to him about the state of the resort. And if they talked business she was afraid she'd end up convincing him that his instincts were right on target.

"What do you want to know about Haughton House?" she asked, after the wine steward had left.

"Tonight I want to know about the woman who runs it," he said.

"What's to tell?"

"Rumor has it you're a workaholic who lives for the job."

She was. "I've heard similar tales about you."

He gave her a smile that was all teeth and not very comforting. "Been checking up on me?"

She shrugged, trying to appear casual when from the first moment she'd heard his voice, she'd wanted to know more about him. The behavior made no sense to her but she'd been unable to resist doing a quick Internet search on his name. "You are the competition. I wish I'd predicted you'd come here and not be content to continue our communication over the phone and through e-mail."

"Why?" he asked, leaning closer to her. They'd been given an intimate table for two that overlooked the dunes and then the ocean. It was the perfect romantic spot, and if she allowed herself for one moment to remember what it was like to be a woman—just a woman, not the manager of a resort—she'd sink down into despair that she was here for a business meeting and not a date.

"Then I would have done a little more research and had a plan to manage you in place."

"I wanted to surprise you," he said.

"You did."

The wine steward brought their wine and Sterling tasted and approved it. As the steward left, Sterling lifted his glass of merlot toward her.

"To getting what you want," she said, lightly tapping her glass to his and drinking. The wine was full-bodied and fruity on her tongue and she held it in her mouth as she'd been taught by Priscilla to do for a second before she swallowed.

"I have a feeling that soon we're both going to want the same thing," he said.

"I doubt that. And for the record, can the cheesy lines. I

know why you are here and I'd appreciate it if you stayed focused on that."

Their waiter arrived before he could comment, and they both ordered dinner. For a minute Alexandra almost panicked as she realized it was Friday night and she wasn't having her regular meal. But she forced those nerves aside and focused on the menu, ordering the first thing she saw listed for each course.

The waiter left and Sterling took another sip of his drink before leaning back in his chair, studying her with that intent gray gaze of his that saw too much. Dammit, what exactly did he want from her tonight? The entire board was meeting with him tomorrow.

Why had Priscilla and Burt insisted she have this dinner meeting with him? What detail was she missing so that this would make sense?

She needed to pull herself together and take control of the situation—and of Sterling. She could do it. "I believe we were discussing why you were interested in Haughton House."

"No, Alex, we weren't."

"My name is Alexandra," she said. The only person to ever call her Alex had been Marcus.

"No nicknames?"

"The twins call me Lexi, but everyone else calls me Alexandra."

An awkward silence fell between them and Alexandra hoped she'd annoyed him enough to send him back to Atlanta, but she knew she hadn't. In fact, she'd just made them both uncomfortable. As each course arrived she realized she'd made very poor food choices, selecting dishes she didn't like. She pushed the food around on her plate instead of eating it, drinking lots of water and eating more bread than she should.

She'd have to spend at least an hour in the gym tomorrow to work off all the carbs she'd consumed tonight. She hated exercise—she did it every day but she hated it.

"Why aren't you eating?" Sterling asked.

"Not as hungry as I thought." Of course he'd notice she was playing with her food. He was an observing type of man. She just wanted this night to end so she could figure out a plan for him and a way to find her balance.

Sterling put his fork down and reached across the table for her hand. "I'm not here to ruin your life."

"What makes you think that my not eating has anything to do with you?" she asked, struggling to keep her work mask in place. Insecurities and vulnerabilities that she'd thought she'd left behind long ago were suddenly rising to the surface.

"Let's have honesty between us, okay?"

She nodded. "I'm not lying. I have a thing about that."

"What kind of thing?"

"I just can't do it. Even to spare someone's feelings."

"Why?"

"Life's too short to have to keep up with stories," she said. She didn't want to think about the lies she'd told herself in the months after Marcus's death. "You are right. I was evading your comment about why I wasn't eating."

"Maybe we have more in common than meets the eye," he said.

He was urbane and sophisticated, clearly a man who knew what he wanted and went after it. She knew that she gave the appearance of being those same things, but inside she was a mass of insecurities and she doubted she had an inner core of strength to get her through the changes that were coming.

"Perhaps," she said, unwilling to show any more weakness to this man.

"You're a tough nut, aren't you?"

"It's a gift."

Sterling signaled for the check and led her out of the dining room and down toward the beach instead of to the car. "We're not on a date."

"Good thing . . . this one would go down in the record books as one of the worst."

"I wouldn't say *the worst*." He arched one eyebrow at her.

"Okay, so it wasn't that great. But if you had stayed on the subject—"

"Business?"

"Yes."

"Even though you ignored my comments earlier in the car, I did mean them."

"What comments?" she asked, stalling for time.

"That I'm not only here for Haughton House."

"Does that kind of cheesy line work with women?" she asked. Part of her—the one who'd once believed in white knights and fairy tale love—liked the thought of a man coming to Charleston for her . . . not for business or financial gain, but for her. And that part should have learned better long ago.

"I have no idea. You're the first to hear it," he said, in that deep voice of his.

She shook her head at him. "We're strangers."

"I'm trying to change that."

She wanted to laugh with him and pretend that some flirting was all this evening was about, but the truth was that Sterling wanted to take away the very sanctuary she'd created. The very thing that enabled her to get out of bed in the mornings. The essential energy that gave her life some sort of meaning and structure. And no matter how handsome or sexy he was, she couldn't for a second allow herself to forget that.

The ocean breezes were warm and the beach itself wasn't totally deserted. The moon rose over the water, full and bright. Alexandra paused to look up at the moon.

"Nice night to be on the water," he said.

"Do you sail?" she asked.

The water had been the one constant in his life from his childhood on the California coast to his career in hotel management that had started in Miami. "Not as often as I'd like to."

"Why?" she asked.

"There's always a crisis at the resort or something to keep me there. The only hobby I've kept up with is golf because business meetings often take place on the course," he said. Business had long been a constant in his life. The one place where he was confident and truly fit in. He'd carved a niche for himself that no one could infringe upon. Where the past didn't matter and the future was only what he made it.

Alexandra was unlike any other woman he knew. Burt had made it clear to Sterling when they'd discussed the merger that every Haughton had to be on-board for it to go through and that included Alexandra. He had no doubts that he could convince her from a business perspective eventually to agree to join the Pack-Maur team.

After reading over the report that had been prepared on Haughton House and the board, he'd noticed that Alexandra always did what was best for the resort.

"It's been a long time since I've walked on the beach."

"With a man?" he asked. He wanted to be the guy she broke her own rules with. She was his favorite kind of challenge. All mystery and intrigue bundled in a sexy feminine package. But he tried to keep that to himself. He knew that women didn't like it when a man thought of them and sex after only meeting a few hours earlier.

"Seducing me is not going to change my position on selling the resort."

"Do you honestly not feel anything toward me?" he asked. She was too straightforward to play hard to get. If she said she wasn't interested . . . then he'd back off.

"A spark of attraction," she said. "But chemistry is a weird thing."

He couldn't agree more. She said that the truth was important to her and he realized she used it like a shield to keep people at bay. He snagged her hand in his and slowed her pace. *Chemistry*. If only he could take what was happening between them and label it *pheromones*. Some kind of low-level attraction that could be analyzed, but this felt different.

This felt like him wanting her. Wanting Alexandra Haughton with her conservative clothes and hidden sensuality.

"What are you doing?" she asked, tugging at her hand. But he held it firmly in his grasp. Alexandra was used to everyone following her orders and backing down when she told them to. If he had any chance at winning this woman it would be to make sure he stood out from the pack.

Which suited him because being passive wasn't in his nature. She said nothing for a long while and he thought seriously about giving up, but to be honest it wasn't in his nature. Once he was fixated on a goal—and his goal was to have Alexandra—he never swayed from his course until he succeeded.

She was quiet and almost pensive as they strolled along the moonlit beach. Every woman he knew would find this moment romantic. His mom and both of his younger sisters had made sure that Sterling grew up knowing how to treat a woman.

She sighed, turning her head toward him. "I wanted to bid on some beachfront property out here, but the rest of the board thought we should stay focused on the main resort."

He groaned.

"What?"

"Business, you're talking business? Now?"

"Why not now? I thought that was the reason I was having dinner with you."

"It is, but being out here, in the moonlight with the sound of the waves washing up on the shore . . . I'm just surprised that hotel business is on your mind."

"Right, like it's not on yours."

He'd like to think at his age he'd learned to think of two things at once, but out here under the moonlight with a beautiful woman . . . business was the furthest thing from his mind. "No, it's not."

"Is this where you tell me you only have eyes for me?" she asked, tipping her head to the side.

"No, I'd never use such a clichéd line."

"Good, because I wouldn't fall for one."

"What about romance, Alexandra? Would you fall for that?"

She stopped walking, crossing her arms around her waist. "Romance is overrated."

"Really? Most people don't think so." Being single the better part of the last ten years had left him with the impression that romance was a very important element in all relationships. It was why Sherri, his ex-wife, had left him. Or, to be more exact, the lack of romance.

"Don't you mean most *women*?"

"Yes, I do. Every woman I've ever met would find this night almost a perfect romantic date." He couldn't help smiling down at her. She didn't pull any punches—she was the most honest woman he'd ever encountered. There was no room in her for subterfuge.

"I'm not like every other woman."

"I know," he said. Man, did he know. There was something ethereal about Alexandra and the haunted shadows in her eyes. She was fiery in the boardroom and on the conference calls they'd shared, she'd been a wily opponent who backed down for nothing, but here on this beach she was different.

Softer, somehow, and yet withdrawn. As if this was a place she didn't want to be. She fingered the wedding set on her right hand.

"Did I read the signals wrong?" he asked at last. No way was he pursuing a woman who wanted nothing to do with him.

"What signals?"

"That old chemistry we were discussing earlier," he said.

"No. I'm attracted to you. I think we would have one hot time in bed."

He knew they would, too, which surprised him. He hadn't come to Charleston to find a woman . . . but meeting Alexandra had changed all of that. There was something about her that called to him. He didn't like the feelings he couldn't control and hoped that this was just sexual.

"I knew I didn't misread the signs. Ready to head back to the hotel?"

"Why don't we go to my place? I don't like the staff to know about my personal life."

Alexandra had long since learned to separate her feelings from her body when it came to having sex. The first time she'd had sex with a man she didn't love had been two years after Marcus's death. It had been a hurdle she'd forced herself to get over. She'd been lonely too long and had been spending all of her nights watching movies where deceased spouses came back from the dead.

Feeding her own sick illusions that somehow Marcus would find his way back to her. Which she knew would never happen. Since she knew she'd had her one chance at happily-ever-after, she'd known that any kind of relationship with the opposite sex would have to be a purely sexual one. And she'd gone after a man who she knew wouldn't want more than a few nights with her.

He'd been a man who traveled to Charleston on business three times a year and always stayed at their resort. He always made a pass at her and she'd finally given in. Afterward she'd felt kind of numb and over time she'd made better choices of men.

Sterling parked his car on the street and followed her up the walk to her town house. She glanced over her shoulder at him. He had a quiet intensity that made her more aware of her body; she could feel his gaze on her with each step she took.

"Nice neighborhood," he said as she unlocked her door and stepped inside.

It would have been easier if they'd been swept away with passion, kissing frantically and making out in her foyer, the way frenzied couples always seemed to mate in movies, but they weren't young, impassioned lovers. They were mature—

Sterling caught her hand, drawing her into his arms as the door closed behind them. "Ah, that's better. No martini shaker to keep us apart."

He lowered his head, rubbing his lips lightly over hers as his hands slid lower on her back and drew her tightly against his body. She shifted against him, angling her head to a more comfortable position under his.

He teased her with nibbling kisses, but didn't kiss her full on the mouth. She waited for it, tensed each time he drew near, but he always pulled away. And the anticipation was driving her wild. She sensed he was doing it on purpose, making damned sure that she knew he was in total control here.

She plunged her fingers into his hair and held his mouth still on hers. Opening her mouth, inviting him to taste her. He thrust his tongue past the barrier of her teeth, deep in her mouth.

She was overwhelmed by Sterling. Held in his strong arms, one hard around her waist, the other smoothing a trail up and down her back. His scent surrounded her. Something raw and earthy—masculine and salty from the sea breezes. She tunneled her fingers deeper into his hair, holding onto him as if that would let her control him. Keep control of him. Make this crazy night about nothing but hot and wild sex.

She pulled back from him, caressing his jaw as she trailed her hands down his neck to rest on his shoulders. Her lips tingled from contact with him. Her fingers rubbed over his stubbled jaw. His dark hair was tousled from her fingers, his lips swollen. He looked like a fallen angel ready for sin, and she wanted to be the one to lead him down the path.

"That was . . . unexpected."

"I wanted to make sure that you understood why I was here," he said after a few minutes.

She doubted he knew why he was here. Maybe he thought the way to get her cooperation with the merger was to seduce her. Or maybe experience had taught him that dinner automatically translated into an invitation into the lady's bedroom. She didn't care what his agenda was. She had her own and she wasn't afraid to go after what she wanted.

What she needed. She needed to figure out what made this man tick and then use it to drive him away. Away from Charleston, away from Haughton House, and most definitely away from her.

"I had no doubts. Would you like a nightcap?"

"Only if you want one."

Normally she wouldn't but she needed time. Sterling had inflamed her with just one kiss and the feel of his body pressed to hers. Sex wasn't supposed to feel like this. Usually it was a pleasant feeling that built only after they were in bed and she was picturing some faceless lover in her mind. It had been a long time since a man completely dominated her thoughts.

"Cognac or Irish coffee?" she asked, pulling away from him and leading them into her living room. It was decorated with a loveseat and two side chairs.

"Cognac, please," Sterling said, walking around the room instead of taking a seat. He paused in front of the fireplace. On the mantel were Haughton family pictures but also a wedding day snapshot of her and Marcus kissing.

He didn't say anything and inside the tension built. Marcus had always been in a special category when it came to the men in her life, and Sterling had edged himself into that category without even realizing it. Time to force him back into the casual-sex-partner category.

"I have cigars if you'd like to smoke one with your nightcap." She tried to make him a guest. Maybe having sex with Sterling tonight wasn't the best idea. On one hand, it would distract her from the panic that was running through her mind, but on the other hand, he was causing even more chaotic thoughts and feelings.

"I can see why you are so good at running the Haughton House," he said, turning to face her.

"Really? Why?" she asked. She didn't like his perceptiveness. She didn't want him to realize that she was playing a role. She'd fooled everyone else into believing that her façade was the real woman.

"You think of everything," he said with a wry smile.

"I try." He had no idea how much time she spent making sure that she never forgot a detail. The devil was in the details, she'd heard growing up, and she'd never really thought about what that meant until she had to survive Marcus's death.

"I'm going to try to make you stop thinking."

She definitely needed to get him out of her house or make him realize that whatever power play he made wasn't going to work with her.

"I doubt that. I'm a pretty methodical person."

"Always? What about passion? You didn't feel methodical in my arms."

No, she hadn't, which wasn't in her plan. But after he left, she'd figure out that part, try to make sure that her reactions were simply physical. "Well, usually. You . . . I'm not too sure how to handle you."

"And you need a plan?"

"Yes," she said, crossing the room to a wet bar and pouring two glasses of cognac into snifters. "Did you want a cigar?"

"No. I don't smoke."

The mantel clock chimed the quarter hour and she glanced at it. Almost eleven—she had to make a decision. Was she going to take him to her bed and hope that sex would distract him in the coming days as the Haughton family and board of directors met with him?

Or was she going to send him home so that she could regroup and face him fresh in the morning. She didn't know and couldn't think as he took her hand in his and pulled her down to sit next to him on the loveseat.

He wrapped his arm around her and pulled her into the curve of his body. Saying nothing, he sipped his drink and Alexandra fought the urge to close her eyes and savor this moment with him.

Chapter Three

Mixed signals—that was what he was getting from Alexandra. She'd brought him into her home, kissed his socks off, and then relegated him to the couch with a cognac. But he was used to tricky negotiations and he hadn't expected anything with Alexandra to be easy.

Something wasn't right here with her reactions to him. She was an Amazon-goddess-warrior in the boardroom. The woman who knew what she wanted, the take-charge person who left no room for indecision wasn't here tonight.

Holding her in his arms on the couch made him realize how badly he didn't want to screw up with her. She should be nothing more than a pleasurable bonus to a business deal but somehow she was more.

He liked her. He liked the way that no matter how hard she tried to distance herself from the resort, it was still the most important part of her life. He meant to change that.

Her house was homey and comfortable. Antiques stood side by side with modern furniture. He catalogued everything he saw in the back of his mind to analyze later, maybe to figure out what made Alexandra tick, the same way he'd go into a resort that Pack-Maur was planning to buy and investigate it.

He stroked his hand down her arm, not sure if the night would end in her bedroom as he'd once felt certain it would. And that was okay—what he felt for her was too intense to be assuaged so easily. And he was well past the part of his life where he was all about a quick lay. He was a sophisticated man. A CEO, for crying out loud.

But he didn't feel like any of those things, and he'd trade them all for just a few more minutes in her arms. A few minutes with a real reaction, not this barrier she'd somehow put between the two of them.

The secret to getting around the wall had to be here in her home. He skimmed the walls, looking at the pictures.

"I noticed your wedding photo—are you divorced?"

She tipped her head back on his shoulder and looked up at him. Her gaze was probing and he had no idea what she was searching for, but hoped she found it. He hoped some of the substance he'd acquired after years of living showed on his face so she knew he wasn't just one of those men who moved fast through life, gobbling up women and leaving them behind.

"My husband died. I'm a widow," she said at last. There were shadows in her eyes.

"I'm sorry to hear that," he said, stroking her arm with his free hand. No one close to him had died—a few colleagues but no one he'd ever cared about. He thought about that for a minute, acknowledging that there were few people he'd let close to him.

"It was a long time ago," she said, closing her eyes. "He was Priscilla and Burt's oldest son."

She took a sip of her drink and then leaned forward to place it on the table. Her hips rubbed against his side and he took a long swallow to ignore the sensation of female curves rubbing against him. He pulled her back into his arms.

"Time goes by so slowly sometimes. A lot of days it feels like forever since Marcus was here and yet other times, just yesterday."

"You had a good marriage?" he asked. There was something in the way she talked about her deceased husband that told him the memories were happy ones.

"Yes. It was perfect."

"Perfect?"

"Like a fairy tale. Everything was just the way I'd always imagined that a relationship should be."

"Is this his ring?" he asked, lifting her right hand and holding it up.

She nodded, pulling her hand back and fingering the two rings. The last thing she wanted to talk about was why she still wore the rings.

"You were lucky, then," he said, not sure he wanted to hear about this perfect man.

"I was. What about you?" she asked.

"I was married once," he said, not sure why he was telling her.

"Good marriage?" she asked, taking his snifter and putting it on the table before settling back by his side. She turned so that they faced each other. She was so close that he could see that her brown eyes weren't really a pure dark color but more like hazel with flecks of warm yellow and green.

"Sterling?"

He couldn't remember what they were discussing. *Her first husband, brilliant Powell—get her talking about another guy. Great seduction technique.*

"You were telling me about your marriage . . . was it a good one?" she asked.

He cupped her jaw, rubbing his thumb over her full lower lip. Her breath caught. He wanted this conversation over. "At first, but after a year and a half we started to realize we wanted different things."

"What kinds of things? Kids?" she asked, sliding her arm around his waist and leaning closer to him.

He shrugged. He didn't like to remember his life with Sherri because it was the one failure he hadn't been able to fix. And he certainly didn't want to think about kids. "Money was an issue between us."

She didn't say anything else, but cupped his face in her cold hands and kissed him. It was a tender kiss. Soft and sweet. He wanted to take control, but the kiss ended before he could.

She pulled back. "I'm sorry your marriage sucked."

He laughed because no one had ever said that to him. His family had told him that he was better off on his own and his friends had just called Sherri a bitch and left it at that. "Thanks."

She traced the line of his jaw and he rubbed his face against her finger. He had a problem with five o'clock shadow and wondered if she liked the stubble. "You have yet to tell me about the job offer Priscilla suggested you'd be making."

"I think I mentioned that business is no longer my only reason for being here," he said. He didn't dwell on the fact that until their bodies had touched in her in-laws' house, his plan was simple and straightforward.

"Yes, you did. But you've been letting me set the pace since we got here."

"I was raised to respect a lady's wishes, and it feels to me like you've changed your mind." His father had always said to treat the women he dated the way he wanted his sisters to be treated by men. Because he'd seen Mackenzie and Colby both in tears after a boyfriend had played fast and loose with their emotions, Sterling had been careful never to do that with anyone he dated.

It had also made it easier for him to justify meting out a little brother-justice to the boys who'd hurt his sisters.

"Was that your mom or dad?" she asked.

"Both of them," he said, thinking of the way his father had always treated women. "I don't want to talk about my parents or our former spouses."

"What do you want to talk about?"

"Nothing. No more talking," he said.

He nibbled on her neck, shifting them on the loveseat so that her back was supported by one of the arms and he was cradled in between her legs. Bracing his arms on either side of her, he stared down into her eyes.

She traced her fingers over his face and down his chest, unbuttoning his dress shirt. He leaned down and took her mouth in the kiss he'd been waiting for all evening.

Her hands framed his face as he moved his mouth over hers, skimming his tongue along the seam of her lips and then pushing it inside. She tasted sweet and salty, uniquely Alexandra. He groaned deep in his throat and angled his head for a deeper penetration.

Her nails dug into his shoulders and she leaned up, brushing against his chest. Her nipples were hard points and he pulled away from her mouth, glancing down to see them pushing against the fabric of her dress.

He slid his hands beneath her body and lowered the zipper, pausing to see if she'd stop him. When she didn't, he caressed her back and spine, scraping his nail down the length of it. He followed the straps of her bra around to the front and felt her through the lace and silk of her undergarment.

She closed her eyes and held her breath as he fondled her through the material. Peeling back the cup, he ran his finger over her nipple. It was velvety compared to the satin smoothness of her breast. He brushed his finger back and forth until she bit her lower lip and shifted under him.

She moaned a sweet sound that he leaned up to capture in his mouth. She tipped her head to the side immediately, allowing him access to her mouth. She held his shoulders and moved on him, rubbing her center over his erection.

God, he hadn't been this hot since he'd been a teenager. He scraped his fingernail over her nipple and she shivered in his arms. He pulled the neckline of her dress down so he could see her. Her left breast was bare, the nipple distended and begging for his mouth. He lowered his head and suckled.

He held her still with a hand on the small of her back. He buried his other hand in her hair and arched her over his arm, so that both breasts were thrust up at him. He had his arms full of woman—a woman he wanted more than any other.

Her eyes were closed, her hips moving subtly against him, and when he blew on her nipple he saw gooseflesh spread down her body.

He pushed the lace from her other breast and bent to suckle her some more. He loved the way she reacted to his mouth on her breast. Her nipples were so sensitive he was pretty sure he could bring her to an orgasm just from touching her there.

The globes of her breasts were full and fleshy, more than a handful. He hardened as he wondered what his cock would feel like thrust between them.

He leaned down and licked the valley between her breasts, imagining his cock sliding back and forth there. He'd swell and she'd moan his name, watching him.

He bit carefully at the lily-white skin of her chest, suckling at her so that he'd leave his mark. He wanted her to remember this moment and what they had done when she was alone later.

He kept kissing and rubbing, pinching her nipples until her hands clenched in his hair and she rocked her hips harder against his length. He lifted his hip, thrusting up against her, and then biting carefully on her tender, aroused nipple. She screamed his name and he hurriedly covered her mouth with his.

Rocking her until the storm passed and she quieted in his arms, he held her close, her bare breasts brushing against his shirt front. He was so hard he thought he'd die if he didn't free himself and get inside her.

He held her in his arms, his erection still hard between them. She smiled up at him and he felt a clenching deep inside him.

"I guess you haven't changed your mind."

"I'm ready to have sex with you tonight."

The way she said it was out of character for the woman he saw here. Earlier he'd have agreed that she was the same driven businessperson that he was. But the woman whose home was full of photos of family and people who cared about her wasn't the type to engage in a summer affair.

"Just for tonight?" he asked.

"Don't tell me you have a problem with that," she said, lifting up to kiss him again. Her bare breasts rubbed against his chest. Thought left him and all he wanted to do was take her to the bedroom.

This time he took immediate control. Holding her head at an angle that enabled him to thrust his tongue deep into the back of her mouth, he tasted her thoroughly, savoring her mouth the way he longed to savor her body.

He caressed her neck with one hand, slipping it into her silky hair. When he lifted his head, her skin was flushed, her lips swollen and wet, and her eyes hooded.

"I do have a problem with one-night stands," he said, shifting her onto his lap and holding her against his chest, trying to get himself under control so he could make a decision with his head and not his cock.

"Why? It's just sex. We have no idea if this is going anywhere other than the bedroom."

Sterling pushed himself up and off her, his erection pressing against her center for a brief moment before he stood and walked toward the French doors that led to her small backyard. He stood there in the shadows of the lamplight and the moonlight. She knew so little about this man other than that he turned her on.

She pulled the bodice of her dress back over her bare, aching breasts. Despite the orgasm he'd given her, she still wanted more. Still wanted him. No other man she knew would be walking away now.

She didn't want to know more than that, because at dinner and on their walk she was already starting to come to know him and like him. He made her remember the dreams that she'd always easily pushed away with other men and she didn't like it.

She left the couch, struggled to zip her dress back up before she went to the small writing desk in the corner of her living room. Sitting, she jotted down the directions to the golf course where he was to meet Burt in the morning. In the corner of her desk was a paperweight that Priscilla had given her for her last birthday that said, *Beyond living and dreaming there is something more important: waking up.—Antonio Machado.*

She wondered sometimes if once she'd awakened to reality as she'd been, could she ever go back to dreaming. She doubted it. Anyway, dreams hurt too much when they were shattered, and she knew that Sterling represented a risk she didn't want to take. Not just personally and emotionally but also professionally.

He came over to her and put his hands on her shoulders. She didn't want to look at him, but part of living by the truth also meant not hiding from herself. So she tipped her head back.

"I don't understand you," he said.

She didn't understand herself when she was like this. She needed to get back to her routine. Go to bed, get up tomorrow at six and run three miles. Pretend that nothing was changing. Except that would be a lie. Would her life ever get back to the way it was?

No, she thought, it wouldn't. Especially if she let this man any further into it. Her life was complete with the running of the resort. The Friday night dinners with Burt and Priscilla and weekend phone calls from Brad and Daniel, Marcus's twin younger brothers. She had a life and if she didn't have full-out happily-ever-after, she still had a good one.

"I'm not that complicated," she said lightly, turning in her chair to face him.

She handed him the directions, realizing that a part of her regretted the fact that he wasn't a different kind of man. She knew that she was stereotyping by thinking all single men just wanted sex from women.

"Thanks," he said, folding the paper in half and stuffing it in his pocket. "Let's finish our drinks."

He walked back to the loveseat and she followed him reluctantly. "Aren't you leaving?"

"Not yet."

She picked up her glass. There were depths to this man she didn't want to think about. Her blunt behavior had driven away more than one man, and she didn't really know how to handle Sterling.

"What do you want from me?" she asked. For the life of her, she couldn't figure out why he wasn't running for the door. If she did get a fix on what would make him run, she'd do it. She needed him gone. He had rattled her more than she'd realized at first.

"Nothing you don't want to give me. Actually, I'm going to do my damnedest to seduce you."

She didn't understand him and frankly, wasn't sure she wanted to. He was different from the other men she'd known in her life. There was something solid and sturdy about him. Or maybe that was just the determination that she knew he had when it came to running Pack-Maur. Was she letting the business executive she knew color the man he was?

"I wasn't saying no to being seduced," she said, walking closer to him. She loved the way he smelled, that super-sexy cologne he wore. She wanted to touch him again, feel that stubble of his against her hands and just give in to the physical impulses, but he wasn't playing.

"Yes, you were. You want to keep this all about sex but I want more."

"Why?" she asked, needing to try to understand him when he was behaving in a way she couldn't comprehend.

"I wish I could explain it," he said, moving closer to her. Barely an inch of space separated them. She felt the heat of his body and breathed deeply.

"I can't believe I'm turning down no-strings-attached sex, but I want more than that with you," he said with a grin.

But the smile didn't reach his eyes and she had a feeling there was more to Sterling than the charming lover act he was peddling right now. She wondered if he'd give up his secrets for her.

"Don't tell me love at first sight?" She didn't buy it. What kind of game was this man playing? Did he think if he rattled her here in her home it would give him an edge in the boardroom?

"How about *like* at first sight? I think our lives are going to be intertwined for a long time, both business and personal, and I'm not willing to jeopardize that for a few hours of great sex."

She didn't want to think about lying naked with him, his muscled body moving over hers as she clung to him. Or maybe having him under her so she could be in control of every second of their time together. Yet those images ran through her mind. He'd be a thorough lover—she could tell that much from his kisses. His embraces weren't hurried, but intensely passionate. "So you think sex between us would be great?"

"I know it will."

He was a hundred percent cocky male, making statements and staking claims that he fully intended to back up at some later date and time. And the feminine part of herself that she buried down deep inside—the young-girl dreams she still held—wanted to run away from him. Only the fact that she'd given up running from anything that scared her kept her where she was.

"What exactly are you saying here, Sterling?" she asked. She wasn't going to second-guess him. She'd learned from running a resort that once she knew what someone wanted, she could manipulate them better.

"That I'm going to romance you, Alexandra."

"Romance me? Sounds like a challenge," she said, trying to keep things light. No man had romanced her. With Marcus she was so easy, because she'd loved him from the first moment they'd met.

"It is."

"Okay, then I'm going to seduce you. I'm not going to fall in love with a man again."

"I don't want you to fall in love with any man. I want you to fall for me."

"I can't, Sterling. I've already had a once-in-a-lifetime love."

"How old were you?"

"Twenty-one."

"You were still a girl with a girl's fantasies. I'm betting on the fact that you are a woman now with a woman's experiences and needs."

"I do have needs, which can be satisfied by going to bed with the man I'm attracted to."

"I share those needs but I want more with you."

"Back to the 'like at first sight' thing?"

"Yes. And I think you like me, too," he said, with that cocky grin she was beginning to despise.

"You're right. That's why I want to keep this all about sex."

"Let the best contender win," he said, lifting his glass.

It was a bet she couldn't let him win. If she let herself fall for Sterling, she'd end up losing, because if she'd learned anything when Marcus had died it was that life really was random. And there was no such thing as forever.

Chapter Four

Flowers and candy weren't going to cut it for Alexandra, and as he lay on his back in the suite that he'd been assigned at the Haughton House, his body hard and aching for Alexandra, he questioned why he'd left her.

But what would? He picked up his cell phone and dialed her number. He'd only left her house thirty minutes ago, so he doubted she was sleeping any better than he was.

"Hello."

"It's Sterling."

"How'd you know I wasn't sleeping?"

He didn't want to answer that. Had no real answer except the fact that he was hoping that what he'd felt pass between them wasn't one-sided. That perhaps she was as affected by him as he was by her. But of course, he wasn't about to let her think he had a moment's doubt about her behavior.

"I'm not. Why should you be?"

"This is part of that guerrilla-warfare style of business you practice."

"I have no idea what you're talking about." But he was glad that she'd paid close enough attention to him to know the kind of man he was. Because he did lead his life the same way he conducted business. Full-out-hundred-miles-per-hour.

She laughed; it was a deep, rich sound—another layer in the woman he was coming to know. "Yeah, right. You show up at my in-laws' house for dinner when you know I didn't expect you in Charleston until Monday."

"Oh, that. Once I talked to Burt and he mentioned golf—"

"*Liar*. Once you realized you could get the jump on me, you did it. I doubt you even like to play golf."

She was right. He played because deals could be brokered and closed on the course. But it wasn't his sport.

"What do you want?"

"*You.*"

"You could have had my body."

"I want more than that."

"I know. So why'd you call?"

"To talk."

"Just talk. Okay, what do you want to talk about?"

She'd shut him down if he asked anything personal, so instead he brought up the one thing he knew she'd talk about. "Why did you want to buy that beach property by The Sanctuary?"

"You called me in the middle of the night to talk business?"

"Yes. I think that's the key to unraveling your secrets."

"You have a plan?"

"Yes, but I can't reveal it yet. Are you going to tell me why?"

"The Sanctuary attracts a different guest than we do because of their remote location—they are isolated. At Haughton House we're central and that's great for the business we have now."

"You were looking to expand. Why?"

She didn't say anything for a few minutes and he heard the creaking of the bedsprings on the line. She was in bed—he could have been there with her if he'd been willing to break his own one-night-stand rule.

He pushed himself off the bed before he was tempted to stroke his own cock. Walking out on the balcony, the full moon spilled light on the beach and he saw a couple holding hands and walking along the shore. That was what he wanted. That bond. Someone who was his, someone he could belong to.

"I wanted a new challenge," Alexandra said.

He forced his thoughts back to their conversation. "Working for Pack-Maur will give you that."

He wanted to sell her on the job at Pack-Maur; she would have to move to Atlanta to work in their headquarters. His home turf. It would give him more time to court her.

"I'd have to move to work for them," she said softly, as if afraid of revealing too much. "I don't know that I'd like Atlanta."

"And that's a problem?" he asked, a picture of the driven woman that Alexandra was forming in his head. She was very determined to succeed in business. And she'd made some gutsy moves to make Haughton House the success it was today. Why would leaving Charleston be a problem for her?

"Not a problem so much as . . ."

He waited, letting the silence grow between them until it became obvious she wasn't going to say anything else. "Truth, remember?"

"I should have known you'd have a good memory," she said dryly.

Damn, he liked her. "To be fair, we discussed the topic only a few hours ago."

"I know. Why did I ever think you'd be like everyone else?"

"I don't know. You should have seen from the beginning that I was different."

"No ego problems with you," she said.

He'd always had a lot of self-confidence. His parents had cautioned him at times to prepare for defeat but since he didn't like to lose, it was never an option for him. Better that Alexandra understand that now than be surprised by his tenacity at a later date. "Nope. I know what I'm good at."

"What are you good at, Sterling?"

"Everything I set my mind to," he said, in a silky tone.

"Are we still talking about work?" she asked.

"Maybe. Why are you still hedging around telling me why

you don't want to leave Charleston?" he asked, because this entire jog of the conversation seemed to be a way of putting him off. Had he stumbled onto something more profound than he'd realized?

"Because I don't want you to know my weaknesses."

He swallowed hard. Truth was a double-edged sword and he understood that better than anyone else but he didn't want to wield it against Alexandra. He wanted to know her secrets, not to exploit them but to guard them. But he knew he'd frighten her if he said that. He'd sound like some kind of psycho stalker.

"Whatever you say, it won't go any farther than my ears."

"Ah, but you're the last one I want to know my secrets," she said.

He leaned against the wrought iron railing, crossing his arms over his bare chest. "Trust me, Alexandra."

"I can't—it would give you an advantage in any negotiations we have."

She was right. He used all the facts he could dig up on a business and the people involved to ensure he got the results he'd promised to deliver. In this case, he'd given the Pack-Maur board of directors his word that he'd bring Haughton House and Alexandra Haughton into the fold.

"Now I have to know," he said. "I'm not going to stop digging until I've figured you out."

"Thanks for the warning. Why don't you tell me something about you? Why is this deal so important to you?"

This deal was important because he'd given the board his word that he'd get Haughton House and his word was his bond. It was how he'd come so far in so few years. It was what separated him from the other men who would be CEO. He thought about pursuing the topic, about not letting her change it, but battles could be won by backing off. "I gave my word."

"I could almost like you."

"You do like me. You're just afraid to admit it."

"I'm not afraid of any man."

He wasn't too sure that her words were the truth. Unexpectedly the answer came to him. She wasn't afraid of a man or, for that matter, any person because she knew how to manipulate and negotiate for what she wanted from other people. "But you are afraid of intimacy."

Silence buzzed on the open line. "I have to go."

She hung up the phone and Sterling pocketed his cell phone, bracing his hands on the railing and staring out into the night, searching for answers to the mystery that was Alexandra Haughton.

Jessica Keller glanced up as the door to the coffee shop where she worked opened. Dan Haughton and his twin brother Brad walked in the door. Dan smiled at her and she felt butterflies in her stomach. Guys had always been kind of easy come, easy go for her. She'd dated her share of men but there was something different about Dan.

For one thing, he didn't have any part of his body pierced and he dressed like a Ralph Lauren advertisement. His blond hair was thick and a little on the long side; today it was windblown and tousled. She knew how soft his hair was, had tunneled her fingers through it just this morning when he'd kissed her before dropping her off at work.

As happy as she was to see Dan, she was less than happy to see his twin brother. Brad had been friendly and actually a lot of fun for the first six months she and Dan had dated. But for the last few weeks, since she and Dan had moved in together, Brad had been making snarky comments every time she saw him.

She started making a double-espresso for Dan and a latte for Brad. By the time they got to the counter, she had both of their drinks ready. She still couldn't believe that Dan was as into her as she was into him.

She was the manager of this shop and had worked here for almost three years while she'd been putting herself through school. And Dan respected the fact that she was a working girl.

A blue-collar girl who was doing her best to get ahead. Most guys she'd dated before Dan were more than willing to have her work hard as long as she was willing to support them.

"Hey, baby," Dan said, in that slow, sexy, southern accent of his, leaning over the counter like he was going to kiss her.

She shook her head, stepping back from him. If he started kissing her here she'd never get any work done. The rest of the day she'd be fantasizing about him making love to her on the counter next to the register. "Hey, Dan, what are you doing?"

"Heading over to the hotel to go out on the Jet Skis. Any chance you can come?"

"No, I'd probably get fired. I'm working."

"I'll keep this quick, then. How does dinner tonight at my folks' sound?"

Scary, she thought. *Really scary*. She was a small-town girl who'd grown up in a trailer park . . . a nice one, but still she wasn't the kind of girl that the Haughtons would expect their son to date. In fact, she had no idea what Dan saw in her. She'd met Priscilla and Burt a few months ago for the first time and they were really nice to her. They'd spent the day on a small island near the resort hotel they owned, just picnicking and snorkeling.

"Um . . . I'm not sure." Going to their house was way different from a picnic. And it would be the first time she'd seen them since she and Dan had moved in together. If Brad's attitude had changed toward her, she didn't want to see how Dan's parents treated her now.

"Can you take a break? Five minutes where we can talk alone?"

She didn't want to talk to Dan alone. He'd convince her to go to his parents' and then she'd be stuck. The same way she'd let him convince her to give up her apartment and move into his town house, though she'd promised herself she'd stay single until she was out of college. She didn't want to make the same mistakes her mother had.

Married at nineteen and two kids by twenty-one. If she went on a break right now with Dan, she'd find herself at some mansion on the water trying to fit in with her pierced belly button, tattooed back, and purple-streaked hair.

"I've got this, Jess. You can take five," Molly said with a wink.

"I guess I can take a break." She didn't want to be talked into spending the evening at his parents' house. They lived in a really exclusive part of Charleston that was all old-money and solid family connections.

He grabbed his espresso and walked outside. She followed him to the small tables set off to the side. It was a hot and humid day, typical for a Charleston summer. To be truthful, the heat didn't bother her—she'd grown up in Florida.

Dan pulled her down on his lap when she would have sat in one of the café-style chairs. He tipped his head back and drew hers down with his hand at the back of her neck. He kissed her slowly, his lips just moving over hers for a long minute before he opened his mouth and breathed into hers. The flavor of his espresso filled her mouth a second before his tongue did.

She tangled her tongue around his and held his face with both her hands while his mouth moved over hers. She pulled back a second later.

"That's better. Every time we see each other, you have to kiss me."

"I have to?"

"Yes. It's a new rule. Since we're living together, we have rules, remember?"

He was such a goof. She'd asked him to stop leaving a trail of clothing all over their town house—that was the only rule she had, and not walking around naked while she was trying to study.

"That's a silly rule."

"So is wearing clothes at all times."

She laughed. Dan made her want to laugh a lot. He was a serious and successful businessman—she knew that, but with her he was more relaxed. Since he'd entered her dreary world of work and school, she'd been happier. She was afraid she was falling in love with him.

Afraid because their lives were so different and she didn't see this relationship ending in anything but heartbreak for her.

"Okay, back to tonight. My folks are having a casual dinner. We're just grilling out and Mom said if you weren't there I'd be in trouble. You don't want to get me in trouble, do you?"

She rolled her eyes. Priscilla Haughton doted on her sons and their perfect sister-in-law, Alexandra—she doubted that he'd get into trouble. "Is this really important to you?"

"More than you can know."

That was all it took. She didn't want to disappoint Dan. "Okay, then I'll go. What time?"

"We'll head over after you get done with work."

A loud wolf-whistle made her glance over her shoulder and she saw Brad watching her with narrowed eyes. "If you're done with the ball-and-chain, we need to head out."

Brad put his sunglasses on and walked toward his brand-new Mustang convertible. Dan laughed at his brother's comment but she didn't like the way he called her that. Brad wasn't the nice guy he'd pretended to be in the beginning, and to be honest she had started to have doubts about Dan. Was there a jerk lurking under his sexy exterior?

Dan kissed her hard and quick, his arms wrapping completely around her body. He held her tight the way he'd been doing a lot lately. Like he was afraid she was going to slip away from him. She slipped her hands under his t-shirt, rubbing them over his back.

"Later, baby."

Alexandra never really had a day off. In the resort industry they were a 24/7 business and she was always available to her staff and her guests. When she entered the lobby just after noon on Saturday, her staff smiled warmly and she paused to speak to the Humphries, who made an annual trip to Charleston to celebrate their anniversary.

She made sure the details for their pontoon boat sunset cruise were set and then left them to their antiquing. They were repeat visitors who had been coming to the Haughton House every year since they married forty years earlier.

She entered the air-conditioned sweetness of the resort and stood for a minute to let the sweat from the summer sun dry on her body.

"Good afternoon, Ms. Haughton. Brad and Daniel are down at the marina and asked for you to join them there when you arrived."

"Thank you, Jane. How are things today?" she asked her duty-manager.

Jane was thirty-six, married, and had three kids that she fondly referred to as "the hellions." Jane's husband Marco was a trucker who spent more time on the road than at home but they had a happy marriage and there were days when Alexandra envied Jane her life.

"One small problem with the bathroom in 811, but maintenance took care of it and we moved the guests to another room. I'll send you an e-mail with the details."

"Thanks." Maintenance problems were the one thing they couldn't escape in a hundred-year-old resort. The newer buildings had a lot fewer problems but this main building was a constant struggle.

Alexandra left the lobby and walked down to the marina, keeping an eye out for Sterling—after their conversation last night she'd expected him to be waiting for her this morning. To push the advantage she'd unwillingly given him.

She was dressed in resort casual wear, a pair of wide-legged white pants that ended just above her ankles and her favorite turquoise sleeveless top. Charleston in June was steamy outside and she almost wished she'd worn a skirt so that her legs weren't so sweaty in the heat.

Daniel and Brad weren't waiting for her on the dock but were out in water on the Jet Skis. She waved when she saw them and they gestured to the wetsuit draped over the railing.

Hers. Even though she never used it, she kept all of her swimming gear in a locker near the marina, the same one the boys used. They had snorkels and scuba tanks. The boys were part fish, and until she'd taken over running the resort she'd spent a lot of time on the water with them.

This was something of a ritual, too. She used to love the water. She'd been the one to supervise the boys on the Jet Skis when she and Marcus had first dated and were married. She seldom went out anymore but every time they came to the resort, which wasn't as often as it used to be, they tried to get her out on the water.

"Going out?"

Sterling. She glanced over her shoulder at him. He wore only a pair of swim trunks and sunglasses. He held a life jacket in one hand and a Coke in the other.

"Not today. I'm meeting with the chef to discuss tonight's menu."

"When?" he asked, taking a swallow of his Coke. She watched his Adam's apple bob as the drink went down.

She was glad she had her sunglasses on so he wouldn't realize she was staring at him. He was seriously ripped—must put in a lot of time in the gym to get this kind of body.

"Not until three," she said, distracted by the remembered feel of his chest against her breast last night.

"Are you sure you don't want to go out there? Your brothers regaled me earlier with your skills," he said, putting his Coke can on the railing and pulling on his life jacket.

She could imagine what the boys had said. Though they were only five years younger than she was, they tended to hero-worship her. She knew it stemmed from the early days of her relationship with Marcus. She'd been so obsessed with spending time with him that she'd done everything he did.

"I'm sure they exaggerated. They're the daredevils—I just follow them with a first aid kit in case any of their crazy stunts result in blood."

"They said you taught them all they know," he said, a dare in his voice.

Or was she hearing what she wanted to? She couldn't believe she was having this discussion. At one time, life had seemed like one big dare and she had jumped waves, done stunts, and taken chances that she couldn't comprehend doing now. Yet a part of her longed for it, longed to let go of control and just do something that had absolutely nothing to do with running the resort.

"I might have shown them a few things a long time ago," she admitted. This was all Sterling's fault, the muddled feelings inside her. She'd been content in her routine and her boring little life. But one dinner and an incredible orgasm later she was contemplating actually giving in to the desires she was always able to overcome.

"You've forgotten?"

He did have a snarky way of talking, when he wanted to get a rise out of her. She tried to ignore it but it wasn't her nature to let someone—anyone—get away with teasing her the way he was.

"What is your deal? I haven't forgotten—I just don't want to go out there."

He held his hands up, but didn't back away from her. Instead, he took two steps closer so that only a few inches of space separated them. "I wasn't pushing."

"Yes, you were. Why?" she asked, trying to keep her eyes off his chest and her focus on their conversation. She should just walk away from him but she didn't want to. A part of her wanted him to goad her past her constraints. To force her to have to go out there on the Jet Ski.

He shrugged. "No reason."

"This has absolutely nothing to do with intimacy," she said, because she knew in her heart that it did. If she let go of this one thing she'd pushed aside, would it be the beginning of a crack in the wall she used to protect herself?

He didn't argue, and she would have felt better if he had because then she would have been able to defend herself. Would have been able to use anger or indignation to just walk away.

"Maybe I just want to see you in a bathing suit," he said softly. He traced a finger along the vee-neck of her shirt. She had used pressed powder to cover up the red marks left by his light beard last night. Chills spread out from where he touched her and her breasts felt heavier.

"Do you?" she asked, hating the catch in her voice.

"Hell, yeah," he said, pulling his hand away from her. "In fact, I put your brothers up to asking you down here."

"Why? We have a meeting scheduled for Monday."

"I want to see you away from work."

"You could just ask me out."

"I don't think that would work. After last night I had the distinct feeling that you weren't going to accept any more dates with me."

"Maybe," she said. Now she'd feel like she'd let him win if she didn't go out there. Oh, who was she kidding? She wanted to be out on the water, goofing around with her younger brothers and showing Sterling Powell that he didn't know everything about her. That he hadn't figured her out.

Please don't let him figure me out, she thought. She didn't want anyone to ever look at her and not see the confident woman she pretended to be. Mainly because she'd almost convinced herself that she *was* that confident person.

Grabbing the wetsuit, she stepped away from Sterling. "I'll see you out there."

Chapter Five

Sterling felt the impact of gaining Alexandra's attention as soon as she emerged from the changing room wearing the wetsuit. Unlike her clothing, which was discreet, the wetsuit clung to every curve of her body and he had to turn away to disguise his hard-on at the sight of her.

She gave him a knowing grin as she walked by him and down the dock to the Jet Skis. Her brothers hooted and hollered, riding in close enough to send a spray of water on the dock and right over Alexandra.

The water was cold. She tipped her head back, letting the sun beat down on her. She opened her eyes and looked at the boys, realizing how many little things she'd stopped doing because she didn't want to feel.

"Sorry there wasn't a bathing suit for me to wear," she said.

He hadn't stopped staring at her since she'd left the dressing room. She knew that the wetsuit clung to her body and it had been a long time since she'd been so aware of her own effect on a man. He made her want to preen and show him all he'd missed by leaving her the other night. By making this thing between them about some silly challenge instead of just two adults with a red-hot attraction between them.

In truth she relished the thought because Sterling usually made her feel so out of control. *But not now.* Now he was the one under her power. She liked the appreciation in his eyes when he looked at her. Liked it a little too much.

And that was the truth of the matter. She didn't want to feel anymore so she wouldn't be subject to the wretched pain she'd felt when Marcus died. And she'd done a good job of making sure she didn't, up to this point. But Sterling was different—he made her want to get a reaction out of him.

She climbed on the Jet Ski, plugging the safety ripcord into the unit, and started it. Sterling got on one as well, but Alexandra didn't wait for him. She roared out onto the water and away from the Haughton House.

And, for the first time, away from the past. Away from the problems that waited for her on the shore. The decisions which had to be made and the changes that waited for her, whether she embraced them or not.

She pulled back on the throttle, going faster and faster, trying to put distance between herself and her thoughts, but no matter how fast she went she couldn't escape them.

"Careful, Lexi," Brad said, coming up beside her and gesturing toward the boat lane.

She nodded and pulled back. "It's been a long time. I forgot . . ."

"Too long," Daniel said, coming up alongside her.

She hoped that he didn't say anything else. She hadn't been out on the water since Marcus's death. This was so stupid, these damned feelings that were swamping her.

"Where is that island you were telling me about?" Sterling asked, coming up alongside them.

"Follow me," Brad said, taking off. Daniel was a few feet behind him.

"I have a meeting," Alexandra said. She needed to get back to shore, change back into her own clothes, and go sit in her office. Work on a pro forma or approve the new uniforms for the recreation staff . . . anything but stay out here.

"Trust me, Alexandra. I won't let you miss your meeting."

"I don't need you to manage my life."

"No, but you do need someone to remind you to have fun."

With that he started after the twins and she was left to decide if she should follow him or go back to her safety net. Her routine. The sun was warm, the water cool, and the sound of laughter drifted over the waves.

She stopped thinking—for this one afternoon she was going to pretend that she was like other people. That she hadn't known the real truth of what the saying *who said life was fair*? was all about.

She caught up with the men as they neared one of the small barrier islands covered with rocks, shells, and dense vegetation. It wasn't that big—maybe half a mile wide. The resort had a small dock, and kept the beach on the resort side raked and clean.

She waded to shore, following the boys and Sterling. Sterling had a waterproof cooler bag with him. A small sign warned that this was private property and that guests of Haughton House were welcome. There was a rough-looking shelter with a couple of picnic tables, a phone, and a grill just off the beach. There was also a supply shed that Alexandra had the key to.

"What do you use this property for?" Sterling asked, as they settled at the picnic table.

Instead of catching her off guard, she was glad to talk about the Haughton House and how it worked. She'd spent the morning reviewing his bid on the property and knew she was fighting an uphill battle to keep Pack-Maur from buying it.

"Private beach parties and picnics. Our chef will prepare a box lunch for private events. Last spring we had a sunrise wedding ceremony out here."

"The beach parties are awesome," Brad said. "Dan and I usually deejay for the events."

"How do you get everyone out here?" Sterling asked as he pulled off his sunglasses and studied the landscape and the dock.

"We have pontoon boats that can carry fifteen guests at a time. Due to the space, the party works best for fifty to one hundred guests," Alexandra said.

"This place has great potential," he said. "Do you mind if I take some photos of the land?"

"I guess not. What's in the bag?"

"Lunch."

"I'll get everything set out while you check out the island."

Sterling took a digital camera from his cooler and walked off. He was all business and that threw her. She suspected he was doing his damnedest to keep her off balance.

Dan's cell phone rang and he moved away to answer it. Brad sat down next to Alexandra on the bench. "I think he's in love."

"Really? With Jessica?" she asked.

Brad nodded. "She calls every fifteen minutes and he doesn't care. Normally that kind of thing bothers him."

She slung her arm around Brad. "Falling in love isn't a bad thing."

"Yeah, right. I haven't seen you dating."

"I had my great love affair. But Dan hasn't. And neither have you."

Brad watched his twin walking down the beach and talking on the phone and then turned back to her. "I'm not sure I want that. He's so caught up in her. Last night she didn't call when she got home from work, so he called me in a panic, sure she was in a car accident or hurt or whatever . . . it was nearly midnight, Lexi. We had to drive the route she takes to work."

Alexandra hugged him close, not pointing out that Brad could have said no. He'd never deny his twin anything. She'd always envied them the closeness of their bond. "He's definitely got it bad. Was she okay?"

"She'd run out of gas and hadn't charged her cell phone."

"So you were her savior?"

"Yeah, I guess. Me and Dan."

There was something in her brother-in-law's voice that made her heart ache a little. Of course, he'd known loss and pain but he lived a pretty charmed life. Dan wouldn't ever really not be a part of Brad's life, but she sensed for the first time that Brad and Dan were really growing up and starting to have different lives.

Times change—she didn't say anything to Brad, just hugged him tight. He pulled back after a minute. "What's up with you and Sterling?"

"Nothing."

"Nothing? How come we beg you to come out with us every Saturday and you say no, but he asks one time and here you are?"

"It's not like that," she said.

"Then how is it?"

"I don't know. He is so confusing."

Brad laughed. "You sound like Dan."

"But unlike Dan, I'm not falling for Sterling."

"So you say."

Sterling walked back toward them. "Trust me, this is nothing like Dan and Jessica."

And a part of her wanted to weep at that thought. Not that she wanted to fall in love with Sterling but that she had no expectation of anything deep or meaningful with him. Because she'd had the fairy tale once and once-in-a-lifetime didn't come along twice.

Sterling uploaded the pictures he'd taken while they were on the Haughton House island into his PowerPoint presentation. He added his ideas for expansion and improvements and saved the document. Alexandra had rushed off to her meeting with the chef as soon as they'd returned to the resort.

He clicked through the pictures on his laptop, staring at the one of Alexandra he'd gotten when she'd been talking to Brad.

Several strands of hair from her ponytail had slipped free and whipped around her head. She had her arms on the table and she was in profile in the picture, one hand on her brother's arm.

From that angle she was part feminine mystique and part female goddess. He'd really wanted to go to her there on the beach and kiss her. To stake a claim in front of her family that she'd never be able to deny. But he hadn't. He'd gone back to snapping photos of the beach and focusing on his job.

He'd been cataloguing the assets of the Haughton House, but the only one he was really interested in was the beautiful woman who spent too much time in her office running the show. Everyone from the bellboys to the marina manager had nothing but respect for Alexandra. There was no bad feeling or gossip about her to be found.

Sterling had grabbed his laptop and sat on the veranda outside his ground-floor room. He glanced down at another of the pictures he'd taken of Alexandra. She had her arm slung around Brad's shoulder and the two of them looked so serious. It was a look he'd come to expect to see on Alexandra's face. He'd been surprised to see how motherly she was toward the twins.

He had another layer to the complete picture he was making of Alexandra in his mind. He picked up the phone and ordered a basket of gourmet snacks and herbal tea to be sent to her office. He knew she was still there.

He'd checked out her car in the parking lot before coming back to his room. His cell rang and he glanced at the Caller ID before answering. The last thing he wanted tonight was to talk to his mother. But she was a champion worrier and if he didn't answer this call after having not answered the other three she'd made today, she'd probably send his dad to Atlanta to try to track him down.

"What's up, Mom?"

"Hey, sweetie." It didn't matter how old he was, to his mom he was still her baby boy. She'd told him that when he'd asked her as politely as he could to stop referring to him as "sweetie."

But to be honest, there was a part of him that liked it. Liked the unconditional love she showered on him, no matter that he'd disappointed her a few times.

"Colby and Dylan want to get away next weekend. Can you get them a comp room in Santa Barbara?" His parents and sisters lived in the L.A. area. He'd been raised in Burbank, where his father had worked as an accountant for one of the studios. His sister Colby had married her high-school sweetheart, Dylan Parry, and they had two kids—thirteen-year-old Courtney and Lucas, who was eight.

His other sister, Mackenzie, was an intellectual properties lawyer for a big firm and was married to Garret Bashem. Garret was a director-producer. They didn't have any children.

"Sure, one of my hotels or another one?" he asked. His family had always been of the opinion that employee benefits could easily be extended to everyone in the family. Since he was the CEO of Pack-Maur, he was afforded at lot of latitude with things like this.

"Yours," she said.

"I'll see what I can do. This is one of our busiest seasons." He'd never say no to his family, but his mom tended to think that he could just book them anywhere at any time.

"Well, you know how Dylan's schedule is—they could really use this weekend away."

His mom was a master at using guilt on all of them. He felt a twinge now, thinking of his hard-working brother-in-law. He wondered if he'd ever outgrow the need to want to please his mom.

He accessed the Pack-Maur reservation system and checked availability. "There's a two-bedroom suite available—do they want to take the kids?"

"I'll just let you talk to her."

He heard the muffled sound of his mother talking to his sister and then Colby was on the phone. "Hey, Sterling."

"Hey, sis. Are you taking the kids on this getaway?" he asked.

"Which resort is it?" she asked. He heard the kids in the background and the sound of dishes clanking on the table.

"Cedar Bluff." As much as he liked his job and the life he had on the east coast, there were times like this when he wished he were closer so he could go to his parents' house and spend an afternoon surrounded by his family. Sometimes he was very alone.

"Yes, they love the pool there."

He finished booking the suite for his sister. "Why didn't you just call?"

"I get tired of asking you all the time. I wasn't going to call, but Mom insisted."

"I don't mind, Colby."

"I know you don't. But you never ask me for anything."

"Some day I will."

"Yeah, right. Do you want to talk to Mom again?"

"Nah."

"She'll just call back," Colby said.

"Thanks for the warning." Usually he felt a pang at what his sisters had. How they'd found mates and one had kids, while he'd drifted through relationships without ever creating a family of his own.

Colby laughed and hung up the phone. Sterling leaned back in the chair, his mind for once not on past mistakes but on the present.

"Who was warning you?" Alexandra asked from the edge of his veranda. Her curly hair hung in soft ringlets around her face. She wore her sunglass and she'd applied some lipstick.

"My sister," he said, concentrating on his laptop and not her lips.

"You must be the oldest," she said, crossing her arms over her waist.

"I am. How'd you guess?" he asked, saving his file and logging off the Pack-Maur intranet site.

"You're bossy," she said, cocking her head to one side.

True, but then, so was she. Which was probably why his bossiness bothered her. Brad and Dan had both done exactly what she'd told them to and followed her lead at the island. "I don't think birth order made too much difference there. Both of my sisters are bossy—might be genetic."

"Are you close to them?" she asked.

"I guess. My mom calls once a week and catches me up on everything going on in their lives."

"That sounds nice."

"What about your family?" he asked, because she seemed to be integral to the Haughtons and he wondered where her biological family was.

"You've met Burt and Priscilla and the boys," she said, fiddling with the ring set on her right hand. She slipped it off her finger, spun the ring around, and pushed it back on her hand.

"Yes, I have. Any siblings for you?" he asked, gesturing to the chair next to him.

"I'm an only child," she said, as she sat down next to him.

"And your parents?" he asked, when it seemed she wasn't going to say anything else.

"They died three years ago within six months of each other," she said.

"Were you a close family?" he asked.

"I guess."

Interesting answer that told him nothing about Alexandra. Why would she be reluctant to talk about her own parents when she surrounded herself with the Haughtons?

"I didn't stop by to talk about families. I had a message you wanted to see me," she said.

"I have some questions about the island and a few other properties in this area that I think the resort owns. If you're free I'd like to take a tour of them."

She glanced down at her watch. "I can give you an hour."

"Perfect," he said. He put his laptop away in his room and

locked it before joining her on the path leading away from the resort and toward the beach.

Sterling's questions were insightful and telling. He'd really done his homework before coming to Charleston, but then she hadn't expected anything less from him. He had a reputation for being thorough and dedicated.

She sensed that he was already making plans for the resort when it became part of Pack-Maur's chain, and to be honest, she couldn't see a way to block the sale. Dan and Brad had both asked him questions during lunch, and Alexandra's gut feeling was that the twins would vote for the sale.

"What areas did you want to see?" she asked, struggling to keep her mind on business. She wanted to ask him more personal questions. Ask him more about his sisters. He'd seemed so relaxed when he'd been talking about them . . . more open. She knew that if she had any chance of beating this man at his own game, she had to get her head together.

The problem with that was that when he was around, her thoughts were in flux. All of her instincts seemed to stop working and she focused on him. She wanted more of him. Not in the boardroom, but in her bedroom—and it ticked her off that he'd called a halt to things last night. Especially since he was still setting the pace for today and she'd never been much of a follower.

At least not since she reinvented herself after Marcus's death. And it was time to remember that. No matter how sexy Sterling Powell was or how much he tempted her. She didn't have time in her life for a man like him.

She had her hands full, worrying about the people she already cared for. The conversation with Brad had been bothering her because she feared for Dan and Jessica. What if they were only allowed a few brief years together?

"I read a report from two years ago where you mentioned property for a wedding pavilion," Sterling said, taking her hand in his. He rubbed his thumb over her knuckles but otherwise didn't give any indication that he was aware of what he was doing.

She didn't want to think about the plans she'd tried to get the board to go for that they'd ignored. Priscilla and Burt were willing to let her have the reins of the resort as long as she followed their directions.

His hand was bigger than hers and completely enveloped hers. He always took her left hand, never touching the right one where her old wedding set was. She saw him glance at it every time they met, though. "Why are you holding my hand?"

"Because I want to and we're alone."

"Do you always get what you want?" she asked, ignoring the shivers that spread up her arm at his touch. The sand was soft here, her shoes sinking down into it with each step. She had the feeling he got what he wanted more times than not and wondered if she wasn't in over her head with him.

That angered her a little because she refused to let any man intimidate her. She hadn't gotten to where she was today by backing down or backing away, and she certainly wasn't going to start now.

He stopped, facing her, his warm breath brushing over her cheek. "Not at first . . . but I never give up until I do."

He always stood close . . . too close. He was in her personal space and she knew that he was aware of what he was doing. "That's very admirable. The boys said you had some ideas for expanding the marina services."

"I do," he said, wrapping his free arm around her waist and drawing her into full contact with his body.

"Want to tell me what they are?" she asked, putting her free hand on his chest, pushing slightly.

"No," he said, not budging at her push. He was a strong man

but she knew that this time he wasn't moving to make a point—to let her know he wouldn't be pushed around.

"I don't understand you," she said at last, because she didn't know what to do to make him go away. That's what she wanted. If he left, then maybe life would return to the way it always had been. But a big part of her knew that wasn't the answer. That the changes were coming with or without Sterling. He was just here at the wrong time.

"Good. I don't want you to." He rubbed her neck with his hand and then dropped his arm away and started walking again.

"You're trying to figure me out, aren't you?" she asked, curious about what image he had formed of her. She had not been behaving as the character she'd scripted for herself today. Instead of being politely interested in him and keeping a cool professional distance, she was enjoying holding his hand as they walked together.

"Maybe."

"No maybe about it. Truth is a two-way street, Sterling."

"Okay, I am."

"What do you think you know about me?"

"I know that you are dedicated to your job and very good at it."

"You knew that before you arrived in Charleston," she said, because Dan had let it slip that he'd had drinks with Sterling when he'd connected through the Atlanta airport last month.

He nodded and she was pleased that he didn't pretend that he hadn't been scoping out her resort—and her. She hated that she'd missed the fact that he'd been snooping around.

She could only excuse it by . . . there was no excuse. She'd gotten so used to her safe, cushy little world that it had never occurred to her to look outside of it.

"I had my opinion reinforced when I talked to your staff. They are very dedicated."

Her staff was very loyal to the Haughton House because of the benefits and profit-sharing they offered. "Some of our staff are second generation. We've been a large employer in this area for a long time."

"What happened with the property you wanted for the wedding pavilion?"

She didn't want to tell him that she'd failed to convince the board to expand into weddings. "It was on the south side of the resort, but the property sold about six months ago. Burt knows the Hughes family really well. If we merge with Pack-Maur, I'd have Burt go with you to Macayah Hughes and talk to him about selling this property."

"This is pretty large for a wedding pavilion."

"I know—it's almost three acres. I would love to see a honeymoon retreat on the property as well. I think we could do four private bungalows." She had a rough idea in her head of what the property would be like. They'd have a separate kitchen for the units and a private lagoon-type pool to afford honeymooners all the privacy they needed.

"You have given this a lot of thought," he said.

She had thought of nothing but that special period in a couple's life. The period when nothing was wrong and everything was golden. Romance was still something that permeated every second of the relationship and not relegated to anniversaries and Valentine's Day. But she didn't say that. It was a sappy thought, and one she'd thought she'd put behind her, but just because she no longer had that kind of romance in her life didn't mean she had forgotten it existed.

"Well, there are two markets we're currently not performing well in."

"Weddings and conventions."

"Yes. Our convention space is outdated and I'm working with our convention manager to draw up a plan about what renovations need to happen and when."

"Is there enough of a market to support the renovations?" he asked.

"Yes, I have a pro forma on it sitting on my desk. Since we

have the property already, I'm in the process of approving the first phase of work."

They talked more about the honeymoon hideout she wanted to build before walking back to the resort. She tried to tell herself that she'd gotten what she wanted—he was all business. She wasn't disappointed by that. *Really*.

Chapter Six

Sterling pulled Alexandra to a stop before they entered the path that led back up to the resort. He was going slowly, trying to keep her off guard, but everything he learned about her made him want her more. He wanted to woo her with a carefully planned seduction but his instincts didn't want any part of taking things slowly.

He wanted to toss her over his shoulder, take her back to his suite, and make love to her until she didn't have the energy to lick her lips.

"What's the matter?" she asked, glancing up the path toward the resort.

Her hair was windblown from the ocean breezes, and she scarcely resembled the buttoned-down executive he'd first met. This was the woman he'd sensed she was at dinner when she was jumping between business and an edgy, aggressive sexuality that told him there was more to her than met the eye.

"Will you have dinner with me tonight?" he asked, because he knew that he wasn't going to be content to settle for having just a business relationship with her. He knew that he should do just that, but he couldn't. There was something about this woman that pushed all of his buttons.

"To continue our discussion?" she asked. She nibbled on her lower lip. "Sure. We can eat in the main dining room. I usually have dinner there—"

The last thing he had in mind tonight was business, but

she'd find that out soon enough. "I'll take care of the arrangements."

"That doesn't make any sense. You don't have the connections to get a reservation this late." She pulled her PDA/cell phone from her pocket. "Let me make a quick call and see what's available."

He took her phone from her hand and disconnected the call she'd started to make. "Leave it to me. Why don't you go home and get changed? I'll pick you up in an hour."

"Trust me—Saturday night is next to impossible to book at the last minute. Why don't we go to the concierge—"

"I will handle this, Alexandra. This is a date. All you have to worry about is what to wear."

"I don't worry over clothing," she said in a haughty tone.

He arched one eyebrow at her. "I have two sisters—I know all women do."

"Maybe you don't know everything about women, because I'm not like that. I'll be wearing a sleeveless dress."

"Is it similar to the one you wore last night?" he asked. He liked that dress but it was kind of traditional and conservative with its below-the-knee hemline. He wanted to see her in a shorter skirt and maybe a top with a neckline that revealed a bit of cleavage.

She flushed when he said it and didn't answer him. "Yes, it is."

"You have a uniform of sorts."

"There's nothing wrong with having order and organization in life."

"I didn't say there was."

"No, but you implied it. Spontaneity is highly overrated. As you will see when you can't get a decent reservation for dinner tonight."

"Order is a kind of prison, Alexandra. It gives you stability but it also leaves no room for the unexpected."

"Not all surprises are a good thing," she said, starting up the path to the resort.

He fell into step behind her, catching her hand and drawing her into his arms. "That's what makes them unexpected. Life is one big roller-coaster ride."

"Not if you play your cards right," she said, wedging her hands between them.

"How are you playing your cards?" he asked.

"In the most predictable manner possible. Taking the minimum risks and folding when the stakes get too high."

"It seems to me you want to fold your cards and back away from the table. That's not playing, it's hiding."

"I'm not a coward. I take a lot of chances with the running of Haughton House. Calculated risks."

"In the business world you take risks and they pay off. You have to admit that the bigger the risk, the bigger the reward."

"That's business. In my personal life I prefer a more cautious approach."

"So where do I fit in?"

"You don't," she said, pushing away from him. "I guess we'll skip dinner tonight and I'll see you Monday morning."

He caught her waist, wrapping his arms around her and pulling her flush against his body. Her hands caught his wrists as she tipped her head back against his shoulder and looked up at him.

"Not so fast. We're nowhere near finished."

She turned in his arms. "I'm not sure about that. You are rocking my world and not necessarily in a good way."

"How can you expect me to walk away when you say things like that?"

She shook her head. "I'm not ready for this. The changes with Haughton House are enough for me to deal with right now. I need my personal life to stay predictable."

"It's not going to work. I can't walk away from you."

"Why not? It's not about sex—we've already established that."

"Well, to be honest, part of it is sex. But another part—dammit, I'm going to sound like a sap when I say this—but you're like a hidden treasure, Alexandra. Something unexpected, and I can't leave it alone until I've fully explored everything between us."

He lowered his head to kiss her. Angled his mouth over hers and thrust his tongue as deep as he could. Tasting her and holding her to him. Showing her in no uncertain terms that he wasn't going to let her push him aside.

The Haughtons' home on the waterfront was even worse than Jessica had expected. Dan had insisted she looked good enough to eat in her dressy jeans that her last roommate had hand-painted with a magnolia and sequins down the side of her left leg. She'd paired it with a sheer, cap-sleeved blouse that buttoned between her breasts and then fell open to her waist.

But as soon as the door opened and the maid gave her the once-over, she knew she'd made a mistake. Inside she shrank just a little, feeling small and wrong again. Like she always was, but on the outside she put on a brazen smile and gave the maid a haughty look.

Dan's hand lingered on her backside as they followed the maid down the hall and out onto the veranda. He pulled her into the corner next to the French doors, wrapping one arm around her waist.

"Relax."

That was easy for him to say. He'd probably never walked into a place and known that he didn't fit in. In fact, he'd probably never been in a situation in his entire life where he didn't know how to handle himself. And she—well, she was over her head. Way over her head.

"I am."

"Yeah, right. You looked like you were going to give Marjorie a piece of your mind."

"You could tell I was—"

"Ticked off. You bet, baby. I've seen that look a few times, so I know what it means. What'd she do?"

"It's not her. It's me. I feel so out of place."

He rubbed the small of her back, right over the tattoo of a Mardi Gras mask. He loved that spot and caressed her there a lot. But it was that tattoo that really said who she was. The mask that she wore a lot of the time around other people. But in this house she couldn't be her full-out, in-your-face punk chick to keep people at bay.

"I can't believe you let me wear this outfit to your parents' house."

"I like this outfit. You were wearing it that first night we met. Remember?"

She did remember that night. She'd gone to a techno music club with a few friends from her chemistry lab and had spent most of the evening hanging around the deejay booth, talking to Dan.

"I don't think Marjorie likes it. She took one look at me and decided I wasn't the right girl for you."

"She wasn't judging you, I promise."

It was stupid to feel so vulnerable because of her clothing. She knew it and hated that she still felt like the hand-me-down girl that everyone else saw and judged. It was why she was so outrageous with her looks. She'd dyed her hair partially purple because she wanted people to stare at her hair and not her clothes.

"I'm being silly."

"Yes, you are. My parents already like you. They think you're too cool for me."

"Too cool for you? I doubt that they said that." Everyone who met Dan knew he had it together. She was the first to admit he had moments when he didn't always say the right thing, but otherwise he was as cool as they came and very sure of himself. She wanted that. She wanted that surety that no matter where she was, she could handle herself.

She'd gotten a little closer over the last few years but she still wasn't there.

"Yes, we did," Burt said.

Jessica looked up, meeting the older man's steady gaze. He was taller than Dan and didn't really resemble his sons except in the eyes. All three of the Haughton men had bright blue eyes like the ocean on a sunny day. "Dan's just about perfect."

"We're glad you think so."

She followed Dan and Burt out onto the veranda and soon she forgot that she didn't fit in with this picture-perfect family. With Dan's big hand holding hers, she felt like she was exactly where she belonged. Right up until Brad carried in a plate of tapas.

He was laughing and joking with his mother and looking very much like Dan until he caught a glimpse of her. He set the serving platter on the table and turned the conversation to the trip to Europe he and Dan had taken after graduating college.

Though she'd dreamed of a trip there, money was always tight and she hadn't made it yet. Dan lifted her hand to his mouth and when she looked over at him, he winked at her.

She felt small and out of place. Especially when Priscilla went back into the kitchen to finish fixing dinner and declined her offer of help. No matter what Dan thought, she couldn't see a time when his family would accept her.

After she left Sterling at the hotel, Alexandra drove to her in-laws' house. Her nature wasn't one that encouraged her to make friends easily. Normally that didn't bother her, but today, when she could really use another woman's advice, she wished she'd encouraged some of her co-workers at the resort when they'd invited her to have drinks with them.

Marjorie, the housekeeper, answered the door. "Hello, Ms. Alexandra. We weren't expecting you tonight."

"Is Priscilla entertaining?"

"Just family, ma'am. She's in the kitchen—Burt and the boys are out on the veranda."

"I'll announce myself, Marjorie."

"Yes, ma'am."

Marjorie disappeared down the long hallway that led to the laundry area and Alexandra went to the kitchen. Priscilla was alone at the island, chopping vegetables. A bottle of red wine sat on the counter next to her.

"I hope you don't mind that I dropped by without notice," Alexandra said before her mother-in-law could speak. This was a stupid idea. What was she going to say to Priscilla without sounding like an idiot? Was there any way to ask for help with clothing?

"You're always welcome here, dear—you know that. Are you here for dinner? Or is something the matter at the resort?" Priscilla asked, putting down her knife and going to the cabinet to remove a second wineglass. She poured a glass and handed it to Alexandra.

"Neither. I came to ask your advice."

"On what?" Priscilla asked. The older woman was very much at home in her kitchen. From the first time she'd met Priscilla, she'd realized that though the Haughtons spent a lot of time at the hotel, working to make it successful, they had always been really family-oriented. And when she'd first married Marcus, she'd wanted nothing more than to have the same goal. A family to surround them.

Alexandra wasn't sure she could ask for help now that she was here. She'd let Sterling rattle her and shake the things she knew about herself. But one thing was for certain—she wasn't going to let him be right. Not tonight. Not about her wardrobe or about her. "Clothing."

"Why? You're always well-dressed."

"Thanks." She forced a smile. Yes, she was well-dressed at work, but outside of work she always looked too buttoned-up. Too stiff. "It's been pointed out to me that I wear a sort of uniform."

"Oh? By whom?"

"Sterling Powell."

Priscilla started laughing, not in an unkind way. One thing about her mother-in-law—Priscilla had always treated her like a daughter. That was the only reason why she lifted her wineglass and swirled the liquid around instead of bolting for the door.

"It's not funny," Alexandra said, taking a swallow of the full-bodied merlot and leaning back against the countertop.

"I'm sorry, dear, you're right. I've just never seen anyone rattle you."

"I'm not rattled. The man thinks he knows everything." That was what really made her angry, that he'd assumed he'd figured her out after three conference calls and spending a day and a half with her.

Was she really that transparent? Was she really that predictable?

"And you're determined to prove him wrong?" Priscilla asked with a shrewd look in her eyes.

"Yes," she said. Now that she was here, she saw no reason to pretend her agenda was anything other than to best Sterling. He wasn't going to beat her at anything. Not at getting the resort to merge with Pack-Maur, not with this silly romance thing he thought all women wanted. Not with any damned thing that they could compete about. "And it has nothing to do with business."

"What do you want from me?"

She'd thought about it on the way over, remembered that Priscilla had bought her a new wardrobe to wear on a cruise not that long ago. "Where can I get an outfit to wear to dinner tonight that'll shock him? I shop on-line at Talbot's."

"I'm not really the best person for that kind of clothing. Dan's girlfriend might be able to help."

She swallowed hard. She'd only met the woman once—she couldn't imagine asking her for help. "Never mind. I'll figure it out."

"Alexandra, dear?"

"Yes?"

"This is what family is for. We help each other out when we're in a tight spot."

She smiled at her mother-in-law. She was too used to always being alone. Her own parents had been older when she'd been born and they'd been very much into each other and not at all interested in their child. Until she'd married into the Haughtons, she'd never felt part of a family. And the way the merger talks were going, she'd started feeling like she was on the outside again.

"I only have an hour," Alexandra said.

"Jessica's out on the patio with Dan. I'll go get her so the boys don't have to know what's going on."

"Thanks, Priscilla."

"You're welcome, Alexandra."

Priscilla came back into the kitchen five minutes later with Jessica, who was in her mid-twenties and dressed in a pair of tight jeans and a top that bared her belly-button, showing off a charm in her navel. Alexandra took another swallow of wine.

"You need some new clothes quick?"

"Yes."

"What do you have in mind?"

"Anything that doesn't look like this," she said, gesturing to her own outfit.

"I know the perfect place," Jessica said. "You are certainly in shape—there's no reason to wear these baggy clothes."

All at once she found that her plans of one-upmanship had changed and she was following Priscilla's Miata convertible into town, chatting with Jessica about what she thought her best body features were.

"You've got great legs—we should show them off—and nice tone on your arms."

Alexandra had no idea what her best body features were. She could honestly say she'd never really thought too much about her shape. She exercised, ate practically the same thing every day, and had worn the same size since she'd turned twenty.

"I can't wear something like you have on."

Jessica laughed, but in a kind way. "You think? Don't worry, Lexi. I promise you'll be comfortable in the clothes we find for you."

Alexandra couldn't help staring at the younger woman.

"Do you mind if I call you Lexi?" Jessica asked.

"No, I don't. The boys are the only ones who do."

"Dan talks about you a lot. I feel like I know you a lot better than I really do."

"Dan usually doesn't say too much," Alexandra said, realizing that Brad had been right and this young girl had changed Dan's life. She reached over and took Jessica's hand in hers, squeezing it for a second. "He's different with you."

Jessica nodded. "He's . . . just my everything."

Alexandra listened to Jessica talking about her brother and felt that wave of love and dreams for the future, and for once she felt that spark of excitement about being with a man, too.

Chapter Seven

Alexandra had been right—finding a Saturday-night dinner reservation anywhere in the area had been next to impossible. He'd had to use a little finesse to get everything the way he wanted it. He'd borrowed a yacht from the Charleston Yacht Club and had spent the last hour making sure that every detail was exactly to his specifications.

Alexandra had called and asked for an extra hour to get ready and it had suited him. He'd ordered a meal from the chef at the Haughton House, just the evening's specials. Their dinner was warming in the galley of the yacht.

They wouldn't leave the harbor tonight because Sterling didn't like to venture into unfamiliar waters for the first time in the dark. But he was a seasoned sailor, having spent summers with his father piloting their small twenty-footer up and down the California coast.

He parked his car on the street in front of Alexandra's town house. He leaned over to check his teeth and hair in the rearview mirror, something Colby had advised him to do when she'd started dating.

He picked up the long-stemmed white rose. The landscape lighting leading to her house clicked on when he was halfway there. As he climbed the two steps up to her front door, it opened.

"You're late," she said, through the open door. "Come in. I'm on the phone."

He caught a glimpse of her leg and her hair hanging loose to her shoulders before the door opened all the way and he heard the sound of her footsteps going down the hallway. He stepped inside the foyer, closing the door behind him.

He followed the sound of her voice into her kitchen. She wasn't wearing the same style dress as last night. Instead, she wore a pair of slim-fitting black pants and a strapless top that fit her curves. The top was a creamy color with rhinestones sewn into the material. Her neck and shoulders were bare. He hadn't realized how creamy her skin was until this moment. Her arms were long and graceful and as she hung up the cordless phone and pivoted to face him, he realized that she'd dusted some kind of glittery powder on her skin.

He couldn't speak for a minute, unable to reconcile the shy and tentative woman he'd held in his arms a few hours ago to this woman. She picked up her martini glass and took a sip. Unless he missed his guess, it was either a Cosmopolitan or a French martini.

He handed her the rose, which she took, brushing it against the bare skin of her shoulder. "Did you get a reservation? Or would you like me to cook dinner for us here?"

He glanced around—her kitchen was all chrome and steel, very high-tech. He had the feeling that she cooked the way she did everything else—with consummate skill. "You can cook for us another night."

"I'm not sure we'll have another date unless you work on your promptness." She gave him a look over her shoulder that would have brought a lesser man to his knees.

Since he was known for innovative, out-of-the-box thinking, he was glad he'd been able to pull this off without having to rely on her contacts. He had a feeling that a lot of men would have given up and simply called her.

And that would have set a tone for the evening that he didn't want. He wanted her to be damned sure that he was the kind of man who could take care of every detail.

"You were right—there wasn't a reservation to be had, and my plans took longer than I expected. I'm usually punctual."

She tipped her head to the side; a strand of her hair fell over the front of her shoulder. That long, dark curl contrasted invitingly with her pale skin. She shook her head and the strand fell back into place. "Time will tell."

"You're sassing me, aren't you?"

She shook her head at him. "No, not sassing, just enjoying this moment when you seem not to know the exact move to make."

"Why?" he asked. She was different tonight—more relaxed and at ease. Her clothes fit her in a way he didn't expect. They weren't casual at all, but sexy in an elegant way. But dammit, she still wore that wedding set on her right hand.

"It makes you seem more human."

He'd heard that before. Some of his staff at Pack-Maur had even gone so far as to call him an android because he usually functioned without a lot of sleep and made all of his decisions based on logic. He rarely, if ever, let emotion play a part in any of his decisions.

Which didn't exactly explain what he was doing here with Alexandra Haughton on a Saturday night. It sure as hell wasn't work and leaned toward pleasure but he was very aware of how complicated this was going to make things between them come Monday morning. And it was a complication he never would have allowed in the past. "What? You have doubts about my humanity?"

"Sometimes. You seem like this perfect automaton. Like nothing or no one ever really knocks you off your path."

He felt like he spent a lot of time planning and managing every little crisis that came up during the day or week that interrupted the flow of how he wanted things to go. But he didn't do it on any kind of automatic pilot. He wished that were the case because then he would have been better able to manage this night.

"Believe me, I'm not an automaton. I make mistakes." Hell, who didn't? He was glad she thought he was infallible but wanted to make certain she knew he was a flesh-and-blood man.

"And admit to them," she said, smiling at him. "Do we have time for a drink?"

"Sure. What do you have?"

"Girly drinks."

She gave him one of those looks that he'd seen on his sisters when they wanted to make a guy pay. He guessed promptness was a big issue with her and made a mental note to be on time from now on.

"What are girly drinks?"

"According to Brad, anything pink or mixed with fruit juice."

"Anything pink . . . I'll give him that. What are you drinking?"

"Cosmopolitan—want one?"

"I'm not sure—will my masculinity be called into question?"

"Since I'm the only one here, I think your reputation as a big ol' macho man is safe."

He doubted that. She could bring him to his knees with just one look. He'd scrambled and run around for the last two hours, making sure every detail was perfect for her. She had no idea the impact she had on him and he knew that it was important she never did.

Alexandra kept everything she felt or thought tucked close.

"Do you have any whiskey?"

"Yes, neat or on the rocks?"

"Neat."

She poured two fingers of expensive Kentucky sipping whiskey into a glass for him. She raised her own glass. "To buried treasure."

Damn, he knew he was going to regret saying something so sappy to a woman. "To smart-ass women."

She took a sip of her drink, winking at him over the rim of her glass. "Another toast?"

She was like a minx tonight. So different from the rule-following, orderly woman he'd come to expect her to be. Was it simply the change of clothes or was it something more?

"To mergers," he said, thinking of a more personal one than Pack-Maur's.

"To self-inflated egos being deflated."

He took a sip of his drink, walking closer to where she leaned against the countertop.

"To unexpected dinner invitations," she said, raising her glass to his.

"To beautiful women who like to toast." She smiled up at him.

They both took a sip of their drinks at the same time. She started to raise her glass again. He took it from her, placing it on the counter behind her, setting his next to it.

"No more toasting?"

He shook his head, pulling her into his arms and lowering his head to kiss her. She wrapped her arms around his waist and held onto him, and he felt something shift deep inside. Something that he hadn't realized was missing suddenly felt like it had found a home in her arms.

Alexandra had been to the yacht club a number of times in the past for parties and even dinner with one of the men she'd dated, but this felt different. She'd let go of the past a long time ago. Buried it deep inside where it could no longer affect her, but for the first time she realized that she'd put herself in stasis. She'd made herself a model perfect-looking woman.

Someone that Hollywood and the media would identify as a successful woman, a contented woman, a woman who needed no man by her side. She took her affairs where she wanted them and on her own terms. Something that Mr. Powell seemed not to have noticed.

He was intent on seduction. On treating her to the romantic fairy tale that she'd long since stopped believing in. And there was no way to convince him he was wrong, because he refused to buy into the role she'd been playing for the last ten years.

He refused to see the single, successful businesswoman she presented to the world as who she really was. Not that she even knew what was real anymore. She liked this new image that she'd created for tonight. The clothing that Jessica and Priscilla had helped her select had made her feel like a new woman. When she'd looked at herself in the mirror, she hadn't seen a woman she recognized.

Instead, she'd seen a woman with infinite possibilities. Then, in one brief, panicked moment when the time for Sterling to show up had come and gone, she'd realized that any changes she made had to be for herself and not for him. She refused to lie to herself and pretend that she didn't want Sterling. That she didn't want to see him working hard to impress her, because she did.

During their walk on the beach this afternoon, when he'd listened to her dreams for the resort, he'd made her realize that he was interested in every part of her. Not just a warm body with pleasing features to have sex with. Not just a worthy adversary to battle in the boardroom. But a fully rounded woman with desires and needs that went beyond sex and work.

That realization had been more empowering than the new clothing and wearing her hair down. It reinforced the things about herself that she'd always liked and those things she'd somehow forgotten in her drive to become a successful hotelier.

He led her to a luxury yacht berthed farthest from the yacht club. There were lights strung from the mast and along the railing. The time and effort he'd put into this dinner date was more than she'd expected. She tried to tell herself he had an agenda and not to be impressed, but she was.

"Is this yacht yours?" she asked, remembering he'd mentioned one last night when they'd talked about sailing. Being the CEO of Pack-Maur would enable him to buy whatever luxury toys he wanted.

He put his hand at the small of her back to escort her up the gangplank. His hand felt large and warm through the thin fabric of her silk shirt. His touch made her more aware of her body, and she deliberately slowed her steps.

"This one is a loaner, but I have one that I keep in Florida."

"Why Florida?" she asked when they were on the deck. The hardwood gleamed in the moonlight.

"It's easy to get down there for a few days and take a break. I've been overseeing the opening of Pack-Maur's newest resort, Pleasure Cai."

Her high-heeled sandals made her feel a little unsteady with the gentle rocking of the boat. She bent down and slipped her shoes off, staring for a second at the toe ring Jessica had given her to wear before she and Priscilla had left her.

"I'm impressed that you did all this for me." And she really was. She'd given the focused career-woman role her all for so long that most of the men she'd had affairs with didn't give a second thought to romance where she was concerned.

And while that didn't matter to her—*really, it didn't*—it made her feel good deep inside that Sterling had gone to all this effort on her behalf.

"Good," he said. "This is just the beginning."

He directed her onto the yacht. The night sky out over the water looked huge and filled with stars. The moon was only a sliver, and she closed her eyes because it had been too long since she'd been out on the water at night. "Have a seat while I take care of a few last-minute details."

"What details?" she asked. The breeze off the water was a little chilly and she shivered, rubbing her hands over her arms.

"Dinner and music. Lighting the candles on the table, making this evening something out of a dream."

"What are your dreams, Sterling?" she asked. He'd been careful to keep her focus and his on what he thought she wanted, never revealing what it was he was looking for. Something more than just a physical encounter—she understood that—but what else did he want?

"For tonight?" he asked, his voice low-pitched and sexier than hell.

"Yes, and for the future. You seem like a man who knows where he is going," she said, because she knew that he had his future planned out. That no matter what obstacles he encountered, he'd keep moving toward his goal until he achieved it.

"When I was younger I would have said they were pretty much like every man's. A job that I could make lots of money at and a pretty woman by my side."

"Sounds vague."

"It was. What about you? What were your dreams?"

"They were simple—find a husband who cherished me and then spend the rest of my days as his pampered princess."

He laughed, wrapping his arm around her shoulder and drawing her into the curve of his body. "What about now? I can't see you as the pampered princess."

She looked out over the darkness of the water, searching for an answer that she could give that wouldn't reveal too much of who she really was. "I guess I'd like to just be happy."

"Are you happy now?" he asked.

She thought about it. Her life was full with work and the resort. She defined herself by what she accomplished at Haughton House.

"Most days. You?"

"Yes. I wish I lived closer to my family. I envy you that. But I have a job that I love, and I'm in the company of a beautiful woman—what more could a man ask for?"

"Dinner," she suggested, taking a step away from him. He had all the right answers and she didn't want him to. She wanted him to make a slight misstep. Something that would convince her that he wasn't worth her time. But so far, she'd found nothing. Though she'd always believed she couldn't be seduced, there was something about Sterling that changed her mind.

After dinner, Alexandra helped him clear the table and volunteered to wash the dishes in the small galley. Which was not part of his seduction plans. He suspected she knew that and had suggested washing them as a way to give the night a sense of normalcy. A sense of the everyday, to make this evening with him just like any other Saturday evening.

He fiddled with his iPod until he found the play list he'd downloaded earlier. He'd asked Brad for some suggestions of songs that he knew Alexandra liked. Then he thought about the woman he knew and what impressions she'd left him with. He put the unit in the specialized Bose speaker system. The music started playing "You're Beautiful" by James Blunt.

"Nice," she said with that wry grin of hers.

"I know." Alexandra was used to men seeing her in one role and that was it. She liked the fact that it put her in the power position, but for tonight he needed her to understand that he couldn't care less about her skills in the boardroom. Tomorrow they could go back to being adversaries in the business world. Tonight was all about this woman who'd caught his eye without even trying.

He reached around her to take the dish she was rinsing from her hands. He canted his hips, rubbing his pelvis against her buttocks. She shifted against him, glancing over her shoulder at him. He danced against her subtly, caressing her body with his before moving away and putting the dish in the drainer. He came back to take another dish, this time brushing his fingertips against her shoulder and down her arm.

She didn't release the dish, just stood there holding it. He leaned over her and dropped nibbling kisses down her arm until he reached her hand. He tugged the plate from her grip, placing it in the drainer.

He wrapped his arms around her waist and pulled her back

against him. She relaxed into his body, her hands coming to rest over his. Hers were warm and wet from the water. He brought one of them to his mouth and licked the water from her fingers.

They finished the dishes together. He made sure that each touch lingered on her tempting body. Since he'd first held her in his arms, all he'd imagined was getting her into his bed. But on his terms. He wanted to prove to her that there was more between them than sex. He felt like he had done that today.

But tonight . . . tonight was for the both of them. Time to make sure she understood exactly what he had planned for the two of them.

The music changed to Marvin Gaye's "Let's Get It On."

"Not very subtle."

"It's a love song mix," he said, pulling her away from the small sink, leading her to the living area, which was large enough to dance. Circling her waist with his arm, he drew her closer, holding her loosely in his arms as he danced her around the room.

"I love Marvin Gaye. His music is so damned sexy. Did you know he was my favorite?"

As a matter of fact, he did. He'd asked Brad about her favorites earlier. R&B from the late 70s, early 80s were some of his favorite music, so it was a confirmation that they had more in common than being good executives. "Yes, I did."

She put her hands on his waist and tipped her head back as the rhythm of Marvin Gaye's sensual song played on. He moved his hips in time to the music and she did, too, mirroring his motions.

He spun her away from him and then pulled her back in his arms. Swaying together to the music, he lowered his head to hers, singing quietly in her ear as they danced.

He traced the line of her spine, caressing the smooth, bare skin above her top. Tipping her head back, she turned, catching his mouth with hers.

She sucked his lower lip into her mouth, creating pressure that he felt all the way to his cock. When she slid her tongue into his mouth, rubbing it behind his upper lip, he groaned. She was too damned sexy. He wanted to keep his mind on his seduction, but instead all he could think about was how hard she had made him. And how soft her body was.

Taking her head in both hands, he thrust his tongue deep into her mouth. She slid her hands over his shoulders, gripping his upper arms while he kissed her. Her hips moved against him. He stopped thinking of his well-ordered plans of seduction as his blood pooled heavily in the center of his body.

She turned in his arms, so that her back was pressed to his front. He held her loosely as they gyrated together to the music. She took his free hand in hers and kissed his palm.

The humid warmth of her mouth against his palm turned him on, especially when she pushed her tongue between his fingers. She drew his hand down her body in long, slow strokes over the fabric of her top. Rubbing their hands together over her curves.

He'd expected Alexandra to be a shy lover, someone who'd have to be coaxed along, but as he watched her dancing with him so sensually, he knew he'd been wrong.

The silky-soft fabric and rhinestones of her blouse abraded his hand. He changed the direction of her hand, bringing it down to her waist and sliding his finger under the bottom of her top. Her skin was cool to the touch. He spread his fingers wide, reaching the bottom of her breast with his forefinger. She wasn't wearing a bra.

He scraped his nail back against her skin. She drew his hand out from under her shirt. She cupped her breast with his hand, rotating his palm over it, while continuing to dance with him. He cupped her other breast with his own hand, but she drew his hand away from her other breast, back to his waist.

"You can only touch me when I say so."

She had that look in her eyes that told him she meant business, but he didn't take orders from anyone. Never had, which had led him to more troubles than he could count.

"Are you sure you're in charge?" he asked, biting gently on her neck.

She shivered in his arms and her hand tightened on his, squeezing her breast. She was wonderfully responsive. Finally he felt a crack in the shell that she presented to the world. The woman who was unaffected by anything or anyone. But she was affected by him right now.

"Yes," she said, her breath exhaling in one long sigh. She slid their joined hands down her body, her butt rubbing over his erection as she stroked their hands between her legs. She widened her stance and rocked back and forth. He held her close, rocking with her.

Turning again, she faced him, drawing their hands up the center of his chest. Wrapping her arm around his neck and tunneling the fingers of her free hand in his hair. She drew his head down to hers, nibbled at his mouth, and then backed away. She swayed away from him and he followed her as she danced around the room. He caught her close again, finding the zipper at the side of her blouse and pulling the tab down.

She stopped him from pulling the fabric from her body. As each inch of her skin was revealed, he went a little stiller. He watched her emerging from the clothing and knew that he wasn't going to forget this woman or this night for the rest of his life.

There was something almost magical about the moment and he wanted to make it last forever. To slowly love the both of them out of their minds. To make it so the feel and scent and taste of her was so deeply imbedded under his skin, he'd carry her around forever.

Her nails scraped over his chest muscles and down the center of his body, her fingers tangling in the thin arrow of hair that disappeared into his waistband. She scraped her finger lower. "Unbutton your shirt."

His fingers got tangled as he hurried to get his shirt off. He'd started this as a slow seduction. A kind of romantic fantasy, but he was on fire for her and he wanted—no, needed—to feel her naked breasts against his chest.

To have her legs wrapped around his waist. To plunge his cock deep into her humid center.

To find his home deep inside her body and not leave until he'd sated the hunger that had been growing inside him for this woman for a long, long time.

He wrapped one arm around her waist and lifted her off her feet. She curled her legs around his hips and he walked with her down the short hallway to the master bedroom. The king-sized bed dominated the room. He put her in the center of the bed.

Chapter Eight

Alexandra couldn't get the moody sensuality of Marvin's music out of her head or the feel of Sterling out of her arms. He carried her as if she were weightless.

She wrapped her arm around his neck and looked at the room over his shoulder as the music switched again; this time she heard the sultry sounds of Sade.

She wanted to close her eyes and pretend he was some faceless man. The one with the buff body that she thought of when she masturbated. Because she had been really selective of the men she took as her lovers over the years, there had been some long, dry spells.

But his mouth on hers was hot and real. The sting of his five-o-clock stubble against her skin was rough. She wrapped her legs around his hips as he came down on top of her.

"I like to be on top," she said, taking control now before this went too far. He'd set a mood that was trickling beneath her reserve, making things about more than sex. She wasn't ready for that and she couldn't—*wouldn't*—leave here tonight without sleeping with him. He'd think he'd won, that he'd found the chink in her armor, and she wasn't ready for him to find it. In fact, she planned to make sure he never realized she had any weaknesses.

"So do I," he said with a wicked grin, lowering his body over hers. His torso was hard with musculature as he rotated his shoulders. The light dusting of hair on his chest stimulated her nipples.

She traced her fingers down his bare back. He was hot, and sweat dotted his skin, especially at the small of his back. She drew her fingers through the dampness, pushing them lower under the fabric of his pants.

He reached between their bodies and unfastened his pants and hers. She slid her hands lower until she cupped his butt.

His touch moved over her breasts, rubbing circles around the full globes but not touching her nipples, which tightened in anticipation. Leaning back on his legs, he knelt between hers. Tweaking both of her nipples, then skimming his hands over her stomach, he explored every inch of her body, watching her carefully to see where she reacted.

"Lower," she said, not wanting this to be a drawn-out, soul-sex encounter.

"Not yet. I'm going to find every place that makes you squirm."

She reached out and stopped his hand from moving. He gave her a hard look, his gray eyes diamond-hard with warning. She knew then that any illusion she might have harbored of being in charge were false. He captured her hands, drawing them above her head.

She felt the wrought iron of the mounted headboard under her fingers. It was cold and hard. He wrapped her fingers around the bottom bar. "Don't let go or I'll have to bind you."

"I'm not interested in playing bedroom games—"

He brought his mouth down on hers, cutting off her words. She couldn't think as he thrust his tongue deep into her mouth and then lifted his head, biting at her bottom lip.

"You've been playing games with me since the moment we met, Alexandra. I'm in charge now."

She swallowed hard, more turned on than a liberated woman should be at the thought of following Sterling's orders. "Okay."

"Not *okay—yes, Sterling.*"

"Are you having some master-slave fantasy?"

"Yes, Alexandra. Any objections?" He drew his hands down her arms, and then slowly down her entire body. Pulling her pants from her legs and her shoes from her feet. She was left lying on the bed with her arms above her head, wearing only her tiny, lacy thong underwear.

She felt so exposed as he stood at the end of the bed, slowly drawing his belt from the loops and then pushing his pants and underwear down his body in one long movement.

His cock was fully erect, bigger than she'd anticipated when she'd caressed him earlier while they'd been dancing. He ran his hands down his own body, taking his cock in his hand and stroking it a few times. She saw a drop of pre-cum glistening on the edge of his erection and she licked her lips, wanting to know the taste of him.

She pulled her hands away from the headboard and came up on her knees, crawling toward him. She put her hand over his, rubbing at the moisture there, taking it on her finger and bringing it to her mouth.

He growled deep in his throat and lifted her off the bed. He sank down on the mattress, pulling her astride him, his mouth finding hers. Their tongues tangled and she felt overwhelmed as his hands roamed all over her body. His fingers rubbing and caressing every inch of her skin while he made love to her with his mouth.

"Kneel up for me, honey," he said, in a raspy voice that sent shivers coursing through her body.

She knelt with one leg on either side of his hips. He wrapped his arms around her and his mouth latched onto her nipple, suckling her strongly.

She gasped his name. Humid warmth pooled in the center of her body and she rocked against him, feeling the tip of his penis against her center. She wanted more. She needed him deep inside her. She needed it now.

She ached for his penetration. This was nothing like the sexual encounters she usually had. It was more intense, more real, and she forced down the emotions that threatened to surface and focused only on the physical.

His cock was hot, hard, and ready between their bodies. She rocked against him, finding her own pleasure as he continued to lick and suck at her breasts. He held her butt in his big hands, controlling the movements of her hips. Falling backward on the bed, his mouth never leaving her skin.

He rolled her beneath him and explored her entire body. Skimming his way down her sides, touching every inch of her skin. She felt raw and exposed, wanted to reach for him and turn the tables but she couldn't. His hands and mouth were everywhere, turning her on and making her crave more of his touch.

She laughed and jerked in his arms as he found her ticklish spots. He dropped a biting kiss there and then moved farther down her body.

His hair was silky smooth against her stomach as he licked the area around her belly button and then put his tongue in there. She arched off the bed, her hips rising, but his hands on her thighs held her still.

He put his face right on top of her mons, resting his chin on top of her clitoris, lightly, and looking up at her. She wanted him so badly. Wanted to feel his mouth on her and his tongue and fingers inside her.

"Sterling?"

"Hmm," he said, turning his head from side to side, caressing her with his entire face.

"Please . . ."

He moved back up over her body, stretching her arms over her head again. She gripped the headboard without him wrapping her fingers around it. He moved his body over hers in one big caress that brought every one of her senses to hypersensitivity. She wanted him. She couldn't take any more of this slow build to passion. She wrapped her legs around his waist and tried to impale herself on his cock but he pulled back.

He nibbled his way down the center of her body, squeezing her breasts against his face as he continued on his path straight back to her aching center.

She parted her legs, opening them wide for him, and he lowered his head, taking her in his mouth. First his warm breath caressed her and then his tongue. His fingers teased the opening of her body, circling but not entering her as his tongue tapped out a rhythm against her clit.

She gripped the headboard tighter and tighter as her hips rose and fell, trying to force him to penetrate her, but still he held his touch only at the entrance of her body.

"Please, Sterling. I need you. Now."

He caught her clit between his lips and sucked her into his mouth at the same time he thrust his finger deep into her body. She screamed as her body spasmed. She rocked her hips against his finger and mouth as he kept up the pressure, not letting her come down from her orgasm but building her up once again.

Sterling moved slowly up and over Alexandra. He was aching-hard and needed a condom fast. She tunneled her fingers through his hair and pulled his mouth to hers. She was languid as she moved against him, her legs tangling with his.

Her hands swept up and down his back, sliding around his hip to find his hard-on and stroke it. She reached lower, cupping his balls in her hand. Rolling them over her fingers, and he got so tight and so fucking hard he thought he was going to come before he could get inside her.

"Too much," he said, drawing her hand away from his cock. Though the feel of her hand on him was just this side of heaven. He was too close to the edge and it wouldn't take much to push him over. "I want to be inside you when I come."

"I want that, too. Do you have a condom?"

He fumbled for the drawer on the nightstand, grabbing one of the rubbers he'd put there earlier. She wrapped her arm around him, rubbing her hand over his skin. He loved the feel of her long, cool fingers on him. When she found the sensitive area at the base of his spine, tracing her finger in a small circle, awareness spread up his body in waves and a shudder went through his entire body.

He drew her hand away and linked their fingers together. Tasting her with long, slow sweeps of his tongue against her neck and her collarbone. She smelled heavenly . . . sex and woman—his woman.

He lifted himself away from her, kneeling between her legs as he dealt with the condom. She touched his thigh, the only part of his body she could reach, her fingers moving up and around to his hip, finding the scar that he'd had since he was eighteen and had done something stupid to impress his buddies and his girl.

She sat up, still caressing the scar that had been left by being dragged several feet over asphalt while car-skiing. Just one of the many stupid things he'd done in his youth. Back when he was still trying to prove he was a man, never realizing that men didn't have to prove their masculinity with dumb tricks.

She glanced up at him, a question in her eyes. No way was he going to tell her about his wild days. She saw a successful businessman and not a screwed-up youth with more testosterone than brains. He'd like to keep it that way. "Youthful indiscretion."

"I want to hear more about that . . . later." Her fingers were cool against his hip. She traced each one of his scars.

He nodded. Before he could say anything else, she lowered her head, her tongue tracing the rough skin. Each of the peaks and valleys where the asphalt had dug into his body and branded him. Her hair was silky and cool against his lower body.

She nibbled on his hipbone and then tongued her way across

his stomach, finding his belly button. She grazed her teeth lightly over his skin. Her fingers spread wide, caressing his entire body.

"Lay back on the bed. I want to explore," she said, her words spoken directly against his flesh.

"Another time," he said, his voice low and guttural with need. He wanted her under him now.

He cupped the back of her head, wishing he hadn't already put the condom on, and drew her up his body. She licked and caressed him. Lingering over his nipples. Kissing and sucking them into her mouth one at a time. Using her fingernail to abrade the one her mouth wasn't on.

His entire being ached to be buried in her. He didn't want to wait another second. Couldn't wait another second to get inside her. He tumbled her back on the bed. She held his shoulders as he slid up over her.

He tested her body to make sure she was still ready for him. He held his cock poised at her entrance, felt her silky legs draw up and then fall open. He held himself over her, less than an inch of space between their bodies, and waited. Anticipation made the base of his spine tingle.

She shifted under him, her shoulders rotating until the tips of her berry-hard breasts brushed against him. Her white-hot center brushed over his condom-covered cock and he wished they were flesh to flesh. He wanted to feel every inch of her.

He lowered himself over her, settling into place between her legs. She skimmed her gaze over his body, down to the place where they met.

"Watch me take you," he said, wanting her to see this moment when she became his for the first time. He wanted to be the last man who would claim this silky body for his own. Wanted to leave his mark on her in every way he could so that she'd never forget she belonged to him.

He lifted her hips and waited until her eyes met his and then slid into her body. She was a tight fit and he took her slowly, inch by inch, until he was fully seated inside her. She wrapped her legs around his waist, her ankles resting at the small of his back.

She closed her eyes for a minute, her arms closing so tightly around him that he couldn't breathe. He couldn't breathe anyway as he started to move over her, found her mouth with his. She turned her head away from him, kissed his shoulders and his neck, scraped her nails down his back as he thrust slowly, building them both back toward the pinnacle.

He caught her face in his hands, tipping her head back until she was forced to look at him as he rode her. Her eyes widened and he felt something shift deep within him. She lifted her legs, wrapping them around his waist, and he slid a little deeper in her body. Not as deep as he wanted to be. He wanted to go so deep that the two of them would never be separated again.

She gasped his name as he increased his pace, feeling his own climax rushing toward him. He changed the angle of his penetration so that the tip of his cock would hit the g-spot inside her body.

She shifted around on him as he grabbed a pillow and wedged it under her hips, then a second one so he could kneel between her legs, still thrusting. He could go deeper this way. Her eyes widened, her nails digging into his sides and her mouth opened on a scream that was his name as her orgasm rolled through her body. He continued thrusting, driving himself deeper and deeper until his balls tightened, drawing up against his body, and he came in a rush, thrusting until he was completely empty.

He fell to the side, next to her, pulling her into his arms as the sweat dried on his body. Her head rested against his chest and he swept his hands up and down her body, unable to stop caressing her.

When their heartbeats both slowed to something close to normal, he tipped her head back and kissed her. He wondered if she'd admit that things had changed between them. He went into the bathroom to take care of the condom and brought a damp washcloth back to clean her up as well. She said nothing as he tended to her; then he tossed the washcloth on the floor and pulled her back into his arms.

She leaned up over him—there was a sadness in her eyes he didn't trust, and he had no idea what to do with her. Sex had brought about all kinds of reactions from his lovers but never this kind of emotion.

"What are you thinking?" he asked, pulling her closer, running his hand down her back until he could cup her butt and draw her even closer to him. Sex was really cathartic, and he felt long-limbed and loose from making love with her. Now he could relax and figure out what move to make next. His mind was almost clear with a plan for the future. A future for the two of them together.

"That you are a great lay."

"What did you say?" Sterling asked.

She took a deep breath. She could pretend she hadn't said anything and then slowly creep away when he went to sleep. But she needed to wear out her welcome in a big way or she was going to find herself back in his bed again, having soul-sex and forgetting all about the careful plans she'd made for her life.

She took a deep breath, realizing she could mumble something else and never have this conversation, but she wasn't intimidated by Sterling. "You're a great lay."

The words were more a reminder for herself of what this was. No matter how real it felt to be in his arms, this was still about nothing more than sex. She almost hoped he'd get angry and tell her to get dressed. Maybe give her the cold shoulder for the rest of the time he was in Charleston.

"That's what I thought I heard. Are you sure you don't want to change your mind?" he asked in a stern voice that she was sure he used to get employees to toe the line at work. But she didn't work for him.

"Why deny it? You are a very thorough lover."

He started tickling her, his fingers moving over her until she was laughing without meaning to. She couldn't remember the last time anyone had tickled her. She was gasping for breath, trying to fend off his hands. Tears started rolling down her face and she started crying, really crying.

She rolled away from him and buried her face in one of the pillows he'd put under her hips when they'd had sex. She couldn't stop the tears and she had no idea where they'd come from. Oh, damn—she wasn't doing this. She had to get it together.

He put one hand on her shoulder and tried to draw her back into his arms but she fought him. She didn't want to be in his arms again. Didn't want to feel that sense of rightness and that feeling that she never wanted to move again.

He crawled over her, urging her onto her back as he settled over her. He lowered his head, slowly licking at the tracks of her tears down her face. She closed her eyes but that only intensified the feeling of Sterling. His chest against her breasts, his groin against hers, his legs twined with hers. His scent, that masculine cologne, and the earthiness of his body. The smell of sex was heavy in the room and her skin still tingled from everything they'd done.

"Open your eyes, honey," he said.

Honey. Why was he calling her honey? She didn't want to be his honey. She needed to be his hot number. His ticket for a vacation fling. Not his honey.

And she wasn't going to open her eyes. Not now when she felt so raw and stripped bare of everything. How come he was the man who'd made her feel like this? Why not any other lover?

"I'm not going to let you pretend that all we have is sex," he said.

She opened her eyes and met his serious gray gaze. She understood why he was so successful in business. He had that ability to completely focus on something, only this time it wasn't a business initiative, it was her.

"This is about more than sex. Why do you insist on trying to make this only physical?"

She couldn't tell him that she needed it to be physical. That on the outside she might look like other women who wanted families and connections to friends, but on the inside she was a shell. A hollowed-out shell of a woman who'd learned to survive that way.

And survival was the important lesson she'd carried with her since her twenties. If she'd learned one thing during that long decade, it was that at the beginning of each day simply getting out of bed and leaving her house was enough.

"Tell me, honey. You can trust me."

Of course she could trust Sterling—he was a solid man. *A good man.* The kind of man any woman would be lucky to call her own. "You're a good man, Sterling. Why don't you find a woman who can appreciate all of this . . . romance?"

He lowered his mouth over hers and kissed with so much tenderness that she wrenched her head to the side, breaking the kiss. She didn't want a tender lover. She didn't want Sterling to touch her with caring in his eyes. She didn't want him to make love to her. She'd have sex with him, but that was as far as it could go.

"I don't want any other woman, Alexandra. I can't explain and I'm not even going to try to. But you're the one I want."

"I'm not who you think I am." She'd give him a little bit of herself, anything to get him to stop looking at her. Anything to distract him until she could get out of here. Get back to her safe little house and her uniform clothing.

"You're not who *you* think you are, either. You've got the world fooled into thinking that you have it all."

How did he see that? She'd known from their dinner last

night that he was perceptive where she was concerned, and she thought she was able to see him more clearly than other people did.

But it didn't mean they had a deep connection. She wouldn't let it mean that. She'd had her soul mate. She'd had her chance at all that. She'd lived the dream and romance once and she didn't want it again.

"I'm used up inside," she said quietly, being as honest as she could be with him. She'd forced herself to be cold toward everyone, letting her only real intimate relationships be with Marcus's family—and then only because she'd made Haughton House her life. "I have nothing left to give a man."

He rolled to his side, pulling her into his arms, cradling her. *Cherishing her.* She didn't know where the thought came from, but when he pulled her into his arms she always felt cherished.

She heard the steady beat of his heart under her ear; it soothed the scared part of her. His arms were muscled and strong, his shoulders wide enough to carry any burden. But she didn't want to share her burdens. She didn't want Sterling to see her as she really was.

She pushed against his chest, trying to get up, but he held her securely in his arms.

"Why?"

"I'm not letting you go," he said. As simply as that, he made her objections seem silly and small. He made it sound like he was in charge of this relationship, and she was beginning to believe he really was.

"Please don't do this. I don't want to hurt you, but I know I will." This wasn't just seduction, which was what she'd initially thought it was . . . okay, what she'd hoped it was. This was a full-on romantic assault by a man who had plans for her in his life. Plans she had no intention of going along with.

"I'm a big boy. I know how to take care of myself. And I know how to win."

She knew he liked to win. If she'd had any doubt about that, tonight would have put them to rest. He'd had her favorite meal, her favorite songs, and he was looking at her like he wanted to be her favorite man.

"And I'm the prize?" she asked, trying for a lightness she didn't come close to feeling.

"Hell, yes. Tonight just confirms how good we are together." He caressed her back and hips, running his fingers lightly along the edge of her body. She felt so exposed in his arms, like she'd lost the outer layer of her façade.

"That was sex."

"Honey, that was so much more than sex. And I think you know it. That's why you're pushing so hard, isn't it?"

She couldn't answer him. She did know. He'd scared her when he'd held her body under his and she watched him take her. Watched him make her completely his. She'd felt it deep inside where she'd been alone for too long.

"I have nothing left to give a man," she said at last.

"I'm going to prove that you do," he said.

He didn't understand, and only the truth would convince him. "I made a promise to myself a long time ago that I'd never be vulnerable again."

Chapter Nine

Sterling couldn't argue with her anymore. Words weren't going to get the job done. The only thing that would convince her was action. He needed to know more about her past, what she was hiding from. He wanted to know the details but not tonight. Not while he had her in his bed.

He was going to use the physical bond between them to bind her to him. He was going to completely overwhelm her senses and keep her so satiated from making love that she didn't have a chance to think of getting away from him.

"I don't want you to feel vulnerable with me, honey. There are a few things I wouldn't mind you feeling while you are in bed with me."

"What are they?" she asked, shifting onto her side and resting her hands on his chest.

"Sexy . . . desirable, lucky that your lover is so ripped."

She laughed but the mirth didn't reach her eyes. "You are pretty buff."

"I like to work out."

"Why? I hate exercise. I only do it because I can't stand not to have control over every aspect of my life."

That was an interesting tidbit. She revealed pieces of herself in small increments, and he could do nothing other than gather them up and tuck them away. Add the pieces together and try to make them fit until he had her figured out.

To be honest, she was right. There were a million other

women who'd be easier to have a relationship with. But he was so fascinated by Alexandra Haughton he didn't care about any other woman.

"Sitting in an office all day makes me nuts. My mom says I never could sit still. And I guess that's true. We have a gym in the corporate headquarters building. I go down and work out twice a day."

"All that hard work has paid off," she said, skimming her hands over his body. His abs were delineated—something he'd worked hard to achieve, doing lots of crunches and sit-ups. He did them every morning as soon as he woke up, before he went for a run. He prided himself on being in top shape, physically and mentally.

"Tell me about your youthful indiscretion," she said, finding his scar. It started at his hip and went down the back of his left butt cheek and thigh.

He wanted to know all of her secrets and she was so good at hiding them. "You have to tell me something in exchange."

She lifted one eyebrow at him. Her breasts brushed his side as she leaned up over him. He reached down and caught her nipple between his fingers. He loved the velvet texture of her nipple.

He cupped her breast fully in his palm, continuing to stroke his finger across her nipple. She shifted around a little, pushing her breast more fully into his grasp.

"What if I don't want to make a deal?" she asked, stroking her hands over his chest. With each pass she came closer and closer to his cock but never touched him.

"Then I guess my dangerous scar will remain a mystery."

"Dangerous? You've got to be kidding."

"You'll never know." He knew the image he presented to the world and to women. They never saw anything other than the successful man he was. He didn't want to think about the mess his life had been until he'd finally gotten his shit together.

"Okay, you've got a deal. Now tell me about this scar."

"I was . . . I don't what you'd call it, but my buddies and I called it car-skiing." Just one more crazy stunt that they'd pulled on their skateboards. Life had been all about the adrenaline rush. Hell, most days it still was. With Alexandra in his bed he wouldn't have to look far to find that rush.

"What is that?" she asked.

"Where you have a towline attached to the back of a car and you are on your skateboard." He could still remember the heat of the day. The way the plastic tow bar had felt in his hands and the way his skateboard had felt under his feet.

"Sounds like stupid."

"Looking back, I'd have to agree—at the time, though, it was the ultimate in coolness. I think most of my friends and I thought it proved to our peers that we were bad-asses and not afraid of anything."

"Until you fell," she said. She kept caressing his hip as he told his tale. He liked the way it felt. Almost like caring, and that was what he really wanted with her. He wanted to wrap himself around her and make her forget that she thought she was used-up inside.

"Well, I'd fallen before. Only this time I didn't let go of the towline quick enough. I was dragged about fifteen feet on the pavement before my buddies noticed I was down."

"Didn't you have a spotter?" she asked, pushing him onto his side until she could see the entire scar. The back was worse than his side. Scraped his side and then rolled to his ass.

"Yes, she was distracted by Derrick." He'd never held it against Derrick. In high school he and his buddies had been all about getting a pretty girl in their car and touching and kissing.

"Ah, so your friends didn't see you fall. Did anyone else?" she asked.

He remembered that afternoon. The summer sun had beaten down on his chest, and he'd thought of taking his shirt off to impress Rebecca. Derrick had the top down on his Classic '69 Mustang convertible. Jenny had been sitting in the front seat next to his best bud, her arm around him.

"The girl I was trying to impress. I think I did a good job of convincing her I was a super-macho bad-ass until I passed out from the pain."

"Sounds very . . ."

"What?" he asked, as she tangled her fingers in the hair right above his groin.

"Stupid," she said.

He tweaked her nipple for that. "Well, teenaged boys aren't known for their intelligent decisions."

"Girls are," she said, skimming her finger along the side of his thigh. He spread his legs wider to accommodate her.

"You're right, Rebecca said I was a moron and wouldn't go with me to the prom. I learned that day that I would rather be healthy than a bad-ass."

"You let her go?" she asked.

"Yes," he said.

"That must have hurt," she said.

Rebecca had just been a girl. Someone that he'd wanted because she was pretty and popular but there had been nothing serious between them. Nothing that could rival what he felt for Alexandra some twenty years later.

"Not really. What kind of a teenager were you?"

He was curious about what had shaped the woman she was today. She said she was dried-up inside but he knew that she hadn't always been. At one time she'd had dreams. He wanted to know what they were.

"Way too smart for a cool kid like you to notice," she said.

He wondered if that were true—he doubted it. She was like a magnet where his attention was concerned. He couldn't imagine a time or place when he wouldn't have been attracted to her. He might not have known how to handle her. But he definitely would have noticed her.

She kept touching him and it was having a pronounced effect on him. She smiled up at him when his erection stirred, growing harder. "Or maybe you don't want to talk any more?"

There was no *maybe* about it. He skimmed his hand down her curvy figure. She fondled his erection, resting her head on his lower stomach. He felt each exhalation of her breath against his cock.

He put his hand on her head, wrapping his fingers through her hair and rubbing the back of her head. She shifted around until she was lying between his spread legs, looking up at him.

Having her between his legs, his hand on her head, he drew her toward his erection. She smiled up at him and licked the tip of him. His hips jerked up in reaction.

Stroking his length while she sucked on the tip of his penis, she had him in the palm of her hand. She took him into her mouth and he thought he'd die from the sweet ecstasy of her.

He drew her up his body before he spilled himself in her mouth. He reached for a condom with one hand and donned it quickly. He tested her and found her body warm, wet, and ready for him.

She straddled him and he entered her in one smooth motion. She rode him hard, her breasts bouncing with each movement she made. They both climbed quickly toward their climax, shuddering together and crying each other's names. Then she collapsed against his chest and he held her tightly, knowing he wasn't letting her go.

Alexandra woke in the middle of the night, startled for a minute at the feel of a man's arm around her. Sterling. His heat surrounding her completely. She skimmed her fingers over his arm down to his wrist, sliding her fingers through his until they were joined.

What was she doing still here? Nothing had been settled, and she knew that come Monday morning she was going to have to figure out how to deal with him in the boardroom. But tonight she waited for some divine intervention to tell her how to handle him in her personal life.

He'd made love to her two more times before they'd drifted to sleep. Her body ached in places she hadn't known it could. The room smelled of the sea and sex. There was no clock that she could see but the room was lighter—the beginning of dawn. She didn't want the night to end, but she'd stopped hiding from the dawn a long time ago and it made her angry to think that somehow she'd forgotten that.

That Sterling was changing her without her permission. She'd tried to make it all about sex but she knew it wasn't. He'd seen her crying and he hadn't said anything about it but he had offered sweet comfort in his arms. He'd offered her an escape when she needed it but she didn't kid herself that he was going to let her keep this relationship all sexual.

She had a decision to make. His hands tightened under hers. His cock hardened against her butt and he slid his hand up her body to cup her breast. She glanced over her shoulder at him.

He saw the questions and indecision on her face, but when he would have spoken, she turned in his arms and took his mouth with hers. Kissed him so that the words he would speak couldn't be heard.

She closed her eyes and held onto his shoulders, pretending that this was all a pretty dream. The kind of dream that couldn't exist in real life because it was too ethereal. He sucked her tongue into his mouth and nibbled on it. She liked the way he tasted first thing in the morning.

He fondled her breasts, rubbing his palms over her nipples until they were hard and aching for his mouth. She shifted her leg up over his hip, felt the roughness of his scar against her inner thigh. Remembered the craziness he'd told her about and the underlying determination never to make an idiotic mistake again.

His erection rubbed against her. She rocked against it, rubbing her wetness up and down his cock. He lifted his head for a second to smile down at her. There was something in that smile that she didn't want. A real tenderness and caring that she wasn't sure she was ready to acknowledge between them.

She leaned over him, reaching for the condoms on the nightstand. He bent and caught her nipple between his lips, suckling her sweetly, strongly. Drawing hard on her nipple until she moaned his name. Her hands holding his head, the condom falling forgotten in the sheets.

She rubbed her center against his hard-on, trying to get closer to him. Trying to assuage an ache that she was only now realizing was so much more than physical.

He switched to her other breast, then slid down her body, caressing her between her legs, his finger circling her opening. Dipping into her and taking her own moisture and using it to lubricate his fingers as he caressed her clitoris. She squirmed under his touch, reaching for his cock, drawing him closer.

Shifting around on the bed so that he was poised at the entrance of her body, he entered her, just the tip, then pulled back.

"Condom?"

Where had she dropped it? She rolled over to look for it. His hands massaged her back all the way down to her buttocks; then she felt the searing heat of his mouth on her. The warm, wet kisses that lingered over each inch of her skin. He nibbled on the cheeks of her backside and then tongued the crease between them. No one had ever touched her there and she wasn't sure where it would lead now.

She squirmed, needing more from him. She felt his hand at her entrance, dipping into her center and then tracing a teasing pattern over her backside. She shifted away from his probing fingers and found the condom, trying to turn over to hand it to him.

"Stay like this," he said. She heard him rip open the condom and turned in time to see him donning it. She tried to roll onto her back again. It might be better if she couldn't see his face. If somehow she could force him back into the sex toy category. As if he'd ever been there.

But he put his hand in the center of her back and held her still. Then he slid down next to her on the bed and drew her back in his arms. He pulled her top leg back over his hips so that she was open to him.

She felt his hand on her mound, his palm between her legs stretching her open to accommodate him. Then the tip of his cock was nestled at her opening. He rocked against her, teasing her with just that small penetration.

But she needed more. She needed him. Needed him deep inside her so that she could not think about the impact this night was going to have on her. She was desperate to have him inside her.

She reached between their open legs, circled her hand around the base of his cock and squeezed lightly, putting enough pressure on him that he jerked against her. Then he slid farther into her body. He rested his thumb against her clit and rubbed it up and down while he kept up the leisurely thrusting in and out of her.

His other hand came up to her breast, pinching her nipples lightly at first but then harder as his thrusts increased and the pressure grew between them.

She reached lower, scoring his sac with her fingernails. She felt his teeth against her shoulder, a small bite followed by a soothing kiss and his tongue against her neck.

He thrust harder against her and she felt everything inside her building toward her orgasm. She came fast and hard and heard him shout her name in her ear. She shook with the physical sensations rushing through her, but also with the emotional upheaval.

The fact was that no matter how hard she tried to make this all about sex, it never would be. Because his arms held her tenderly as he continued thrusting into her, riding out his climax and extending hers until another wave rose.

She gripped his thigh, her nails digging into his leg, before he turned her in his arms, kissing with long kisses that made it so easy for her to drift back to sleep with his arms around her. Made it easy to forget that she wasn't going to get used to his arms around her. This was for one night. But as she drifted off, she snuggled closer to him.

Sterling woke up to the sound of the shower running. He put his hands over his eyes to block the sun. His entire body ached, but he didn't regret a single moment of last night. Except for Alexandra's tears. He wasn't sure what had brought them on. He had been afraid to push too hard, even though in his experience the deepest secrets tended to come out in the middle of the night.

He got out of bed and rubbed a hand over his stubbly jaw. Alexandra was going to have beard burn this morning. He would make it up to her, he thought, soothing each red mark with his tongue. His stomach rumbled and he knew they were going to need breakfast first.

He crossed the room to the head, though calling the bathroom on this luxury yacht "the head" seemed derogatory. Like Alexandra calling him a great lay. He'd had a moment where he'd had to really struggle not to give in to the anger, but he knew she was fighting her own demons. And he wanted those reactions, so he'd swallowed his pride and found a way past that moment.

He rapped on the door before opening it. He saw the silhouette of her body behind the frosted glass enclosure. He didn't know what to say to her, very aware that a part of him wanted to try to fix her problems, even though he didn't really understand what they were.

He saw her turn toward him, put her gaze on the frosted door and just look at him. He went to the toilet to relieve himself and tried to act normal. Like he woke up every day with the woman he wanted by his side for the foreseeable future. Like this wasn't something he hadn't dealt with before.

He turned on the water and opened his shaving kit, taking out the gel he used to shave and lathering it up. The water shut off. He tried not to watch her in the mirror but he saw her draw the thick blue towel over the side of the glass enclosure and watched her dry herself off.

The shower door opened and steam wafted into the room. She stood there, one foot on the bathmat, one still in the shower, watching him. The towel was wrapped around her body and a bead of moisture dripped down her neck.

"I hope I didn't use all the hot water."

He didn't care. He could use a cold shower before he killed himself making love to her. No woman ever affected him the way she did. If he had to take cold showers the rest of his life to keep her happy, he'd gladly do it. "I'll make do."

He finished shaving, pretending that he wasn't hyperaware of her moving around behind him. He wanted to entwine her life so deeply with his that she'd never really know what was going on until it was too late. But that smacked of deceit and he didn't like that.

"Are you free today?" he asked. He wasn't ready to let her go back to her place on her own, where she'd no doubt reinforce her position and use it to wedge him further out of her life.

She stepped all the way out of the shower, watching him finishing up at the sink. He wished he could read her mind and see what was going on inside her head. "I'm meeting Jessica for drinks tonight but otherwise I'm free all day."

He wondered who Jessica was but didn't ask. He was doing the laid-back-guy thing. A man who wanted to spend the day with his woman without putting too much pressure on her. But damn, he didn't like it. "Want to spend it with me?"

She flushed, but didn't say anything. He was ninety-nine percent sure that if he pushed he could get the answer he wanted. But he was tired of pushing her until she responded.

He was tired of pretending to be someone he wasn't. He'd never really cared for that, even as a teenaged boy.

"Let me get a shower, then we'll grab some breakfast and I'll take you home."

"That wasn't a no, Sterling," she said, stepping closer to him.

"It felt like it," he said honestly. He needed to regroup, come up with another plan of attack. It was clear to him that surprising her was the only way he was going to make any progress. That feeling of everything being in flux was one that he usually liked but not with her. He wanted some sign that she wasn't going to slip out of his fingers if he made one misstep.

"This isn't going to be easy," she said carefully, and he realized that even though he thought he'd been doing the low-key thing, she'd felt pressured.

He knew that. He really did. But it didn't help that sometimes he was going to react like a man who was tired of moving carefully.

She moved closer to him. Another droplet of water followed the same course down her damp skin, disappearing under the towel. "I'm used to keeping everyone at bay. But last night it sounded like . . ."

"Like what?" he asked, forcing his gaze off her luscious bod and back to her face so he could pay attention to what she was saying. But when she was naked he didn't have the best attention span for conversation, unless she wanted to whisper directions for where she wanted him to touch her and kiss her.

"Like you wanted to try. That you weren't going to give up. Were you just playing some kind of mind game with me?" she asked. He caught a glimpse of the Amazon-businesswoman she was, but mostly she was just a vulnerable woman who'd made love to a man last night that she wasn't sure she wanted to get to know any better today. She was feeling her way around him, trying to see if he was worth the risk of starting a relationship.

"Hell, no," he said, drawing her into his arms. He wasn't playing mind games with her. "I'm not messing with you."

"Then what was that?"

He didn't want to have this conversation. To tell her that he had no idea what the hell he was doing with her. That each step in his planned seduction took him further off the course he'd thought they'd be on by now. "I'm trying not to move too fast, but I'm not used to it."

"I imagine you're used to locking on target like a heat-seeking missile, taking out the obstacles and hitting a bull's-eye."

"Something like that," he said with a grin. Because he *was* just like that. He thought he could use his laser focus to find the clear path that would bring her into his life and then he'd put her in the space he'd made for her.

"What do you want for breakfast? I'll fix us something while you shower."

"I don't know that there is any food in the galley," he said. He hadn't thought much beyond dinner. Hadn't wanted to stock up for breakfast and then face all that food by himself in case she'd decided not to stay.

She smiled then. "I can't believe you weren't prepared for me today."

"I didn't want to have to face a fridge full of food if you'd asked me to take you home last night."

"I'm not buying that."

"Well, that's the only thing I'm selling," he said, stepping into the shower and closing the door, effectively ending their conversation. He turned the water on and took a lukewarm shower. He dressed and found Alexandra sitting up on the deck, talking on her cell phone. He gave her privacy to finish her call, checking his e-mail on his BlackBerry and seeing a message from his vice-president about a problem at the Pack-Maur Summerlin Resort in Myrtle Beach.

He called James, hoping he wouldn't have to take a trip up the coast, but he was definitely needed there. He hung up with James.

"What's up?"

"How do you feel about a trip up the coast to Myrtle Beach?"

"If you have to work, we don't have to spend the day together."

"I want you to come with me," he said. And he did. He wanted to spend as much time with her as he could. To show her that there was more to their relationship than sex. Besides, he knew the perfect place for a picnic just outside Georgetown.

He wanted her to say yes. He wanted some sign that last night meant more to her than just sex. He always acted with confidence and rarely was that not rewarded by the results he wanted, but with Alexandra he knew he was treading in unfamiliar territory.

"I need to go home and change, but then—sure, I'll go with you."

Chapter Ten

Alexandra reached into her closet and pulled out her normal summer-Sunday clothes—a flower-print skirt and a white twin-sweater set. As she started to put the clothing on, she resented her strict wardrobe and the fact that she looked the same on the outside but she was changing inside.

She pushed her way to the back of the closet where she kept the stuff that she used to wear. There wasn't anything that would still be in style today. Ten years was too long for clothing to stay in fashion. But then her fingers brushed the hanging suit bag full of clothing that Priscilla had purchased for her last spring when they were going to take that cruise to the western Caribbean.

Alexandra had cancelled at the last minute when she'd realized that Priscilla had booked them on a singles cruise. But she still had the wardrobe. She unzipped the bag and saw the colorful summer dresses and skorts with halter tops. The slinky-looking sandals that didn't look like they'd offer very good arch support.

She glanced at herself in the closet mirror and she looked like . . . her mother. This outfit was exactly what her seventy-year-old mother would have worn on a Sunday. She reached into the back of the closet and pulled out the first outfit she found.

A white denim miniskirt and a white halter top with cherries on it. She opened the shoeboxes on the floor and found the ridiculous-looking little red sandals that went with the outfit.

She took off the flower-print skirt that fell below her knees and pulled on the white skirt. It ended at least three inches above her knees. She slipped her feet into the red shoes, and then, before she could change her mind, took off the twin-set and put on the halter top.

Her bra straps showed and she untied the top of the cherry-print blouse and quickly removed it. Staring at her bare breasts critically, she decided she could go without a bra. She wasn't that big and her breasts were still firm.

She tied the blouse back into place and stepped out of the closet. She wished for a minute that she had a pair of dangling earrings to wear but she settled for the ruby studs that the Haughtons had given her for her last birthday.

She wasn't changing, she reminded herself with a firm look in the mirror to make sure that she understood the message. This was only physical. Just clothing, but as she met her eyes in the mirror, she knew it was too late.

She put on her sunglasses and left without a backward glance. She wasn't going to analyze this. Sterling was a temporary man in her life. No matter what he thought or tried to convince her of, she knew the truth.

He was waiting on her front porch, sitting in the Kennedy rocker that Priscilla had found for her at one of the antique marts downtown. He was on his cell phone, and she stood in the doorway and just listened to his voice. Listened to the cadence of his speech, and remembered how the timbre rumbled last night when she'd had her head on his chest.

She stepped onto the porch and locked the door. Sterling looked up, smiled at her, and went back to his conversation for a split-second before glancing up again.

"I'll call you back," he said, disconnecting his call and standing. She didn't want to admit it, but he made her want to be a different person. He made her almost wish they'd met earlier, before she'd stopped believing in those silly dreams that all young girls have.

"Ready?" she asked.

"Definitely," he said. He came over to her, sliding his hand down her arm, briefly rubbing over the wedding set on her right hand.

She was amused with the way he was looking at her. She'd forgotten the power of allure. Of leaving just a little skin bare and how that could mess with a man's thinking. Since most of her affairs were conducted at night and with men who were on vacation, it was interesting to watch his concentration waver.

"Damn it, this really ticks me off. I wanted to spend the day with you, not putting out a fire."

She didn't really regret that he had to work today. It would give her a chance to kind of find her footing with him. To figure out the best way to go forward with Sterling and keep her emotions safe.

"I'm in the resort business—I know it's 24/7. What's the problem at the resort?" she asked. There might even be something that she could help with.

"One of the partners' sons and his girlfriend were involved in an altercation last night with some other resort guests."

"Shouldn't a lawyer be going to bail them out?" she asked. Maybe she should have worn her regular clothes. But no, these were her new clothes and they did nothing to change the woman inside.

"Yes. One is. I'm going because the resort guests are part of our elite club program and they are royally pissed. Nothing the general manager has done will satisfy them. Plus, there was some damage to several rooms."

"Sounds like one hell of a party." Luckily they'd only had one really bad partying incident in the last five years at Haughton House. And that had been the son of one of Burt's golf buddies, so she hadn't had to get too involved in it, though they'd called the police and there had been some illegal drugs in the room.

He rubbed the bridge of his nose and she saw some tension

in the line of his shoulders. She realized that he had at least twice the responsibilities she did with her job. It was odd for a moment, because he'd been so laid-back and easygoing that she hadn't considered how hard he worked.

"Yeah, something like that."

He couldn't stop touching her. He drew her closer to him. She arched one eyebrow at him. "Are you sure your mind is on work?"

"I know it isn't. This outfit—you're killing me. Did you wear it just to make me crazy?"

"Yes," she said, pulling her sunglasses on and staring down the walkway toward his car. "Glad it's working."

Sterling drove the Porsche with skill and speed once they were on the highway. He kept the radio station tuned to an oldies station and was on his cell phone most of the ride. She didn't feel neglected—instead, she had the opportunity to get an inside look at Pack-Maur. To see the way upper management handled a crisis and to see the way Sterling went to bat for his executives.

She was distracted when he disconnected the call and reached across the gearshift and put his hand on her bare thigh. He didn't say anything, just kept driving, but his hand was hot and heavy on her leg. Everything that had happened the night before, every inch of her body that he had touched and caressed, started throbbing in anticipation.

He skimmed his fingers over her skin in a light pattern that had her shifting in her seat. She put her hand on his wrist to stop him from going any higher. They were in a convertible on the highway—she didn't want some trucker driving by and getting a cheap thrill off seeing Sterling's hand up her skirt.

"What are you doing?" she asked, even though she knew darned well what he was up to. There was something innocent about the day and she'd forgotten what it was like just to spend a day with a man. What it was like to be outside with the sun on her face and the wind in her hair.

"Wishing we were heading up the coast for a private picnic."

"Is that what you had planned for today?"

He glanced over at her. "I thought we'd take the yacht up the coast. Anchor somewhere in the middle of nowhere and have lunch together."

She was glad that he'd gotten a business call. Being on the ocean wasn't something she was ready for. It wasn't that she didn't like the water. She lived in Charleston and was surrounded by it. But she wasn't ready for a boat trip out to sea. She wasn't ready to let go of those memories yet.

The therapist that she'd stopped seeing seven years ago told her that as time and life moved on without Marcus, she'd slowly have a lot of firsts without him. And she had. She'd learned to move around them and beyond them. But the ocean had been Marcus's favorite place to be. They'd spent so much time out there on his yacht, and she'd managed to avoid going out with anyone else. Even Priscilla and Burt.

Now a man who was changing her, forcing her to change the comfortable life she'd built, wanted to replace the last piece of Marcus left in her life. And maybe it was time to let go of it, she thought. But with the wind blowing through her hair and the sun falling warmly on her shoulders, she didn't think about Marcus or anything other than Sterling.

Sterling did a good job of ignoring the fact that Alexandra wasn't wearing a bra until he finished seeing to every detail at the Summerlin. He found her sitting by the pool talking on her cell phone when he was done. He had a box lunch stored in the car and wanted nothing more than to forget about work for the rest of the afternoon.

His job had always been his life and he never really minded the interruptions that it caused in his free time. He didn't really have any free time—he was always on call, always available for whatever Pack-Maur needed, but today he'd realized that he no longer needed work to fill his time. He wanted to fill the hours with Alexandra.

Oh, hell, he had it bad. It wasn't just about sex. Holding her in his arms, having the freedom to touch her whenever he wanted—these were all things that he wanted. It was the real thing. The kind of commitment he'd seen between his parents for years.

She caught him staring at her legs. Shifting them on the lounge chair, she ran her hand up one leg, smoothing her hand over the hem of her skirt and licking her lips. If they were playing a game of one-upmanship, he'd have to give her full props for pulling ahead. Way ahead. He wasn't thinking of anything but getting his hands on her silky-smooth legs.

"Alexandra," he said, but it sounded like a groan even to his ears.

"What?"

"Nothing." *Minx.* She knew damned well what she was doing to him. He almost regretted saying their relationship was about more than sex because she seemed determined to prove he thought of sex with her all the time. The problem with that was that he did think about sex around her, but it was tied up with so many other things. He thought about making love to her all the time, tightening the physical bond between the two of them until she couldn't get away from him. Until she no longer thought about leaving him.

"Ready to go?"

She stood up and picked up her purse, holding it over her arm in a wholly feminine move. "Yes. I like this resort. You know, it's very similar to Haughton House and less than two hours from there."

He didn't really want to talk about business with her right now. His mind had stopped functioning when she'd run her hand up the side of her leg. She took a tube of lip gloss from her handbag and applied it to her lips, her pink tongue darting out to smooth over her lower lip.

"I'm aware of the amenities and location. What's your point?" he asked, putting his arm around her waist as they walked. He really wanted to find someplace private and see how long it would take to kiss her lip gloss off.

"Pack-Maur should be diversifying. I did some quick research while you were in your meeting. Have you considered the Plimpton Seaside?" she asked.

It was clear to him that she'd done more than sit in the sun while he'd been working. And he had to admire the way she worked. If he'd been stuck at a resort, he'd probably have done the same thing.

Pack-Maur's development team had spent several months researching all the independently owned resorts on the coast. Places where property was hard to find and established, standalone resorts were in need of the financial influx that merging with Pack-Maur could bring.

"I don't want Plimpton's place." Frank Plimpton hadn't kept up with the maintenance of the main hotel, and while he had some nice new additions, it would take a lot of time and money to bring that place up to the standards of a luxury resort.

"Are you sure? I think you probably haven't spent the kind of quality time looking it over that you need to. We've got a little extra time now—what do you say we swing by there?"

"I want Haughton House." And the woman who ran it. Despite the fact that he hadn't concentrated on recruiting her for Pack-Maur's management team, he wanted her to be a part of it. He wondered how much work he'd get done if she was in the office down the hall from his.

"Have you looked at it? They have twice the acreage we do and they put in a new family pool with slide and lazy river. I know you mentioned that my leadership skills were part of the reason you wanted Haughton as part of Pack-Maur—I'd be willing to spend some time working freelance for you."

"It sounds very nice. We have a family resort in Hilton Head."

"This wouldn't be that similar. And it would be—"

"What's this about?"

"I don't know what you mean."

"Yes, you do. Why the hard sell on Plimpton's?"

"No reason. While I was waiting for you I had a lot of time to think."

"Well, stop it. Pack-Maur has checked out a lot of resort properties up and down the Southeastern coast, and the only one we're interested in is Haughton House."

She bit her lower lip and tipped her head to the side, studying him. "I can't figure out why. We don't have anything that makes us a better risk investment than any of those other places."

"Yes, you do."

She raised both eyebrows at him in question.

"You, Alexandra. You're the asset that those other resorts don't have, and working freelance for me isn't going to cut it."

She gave him a studied glance as they approached his car. She leaned back against the chassis, her arms around her waist. "I would be willing to continue our affair if you backed off acquiring Haughton House. It makes more sense for us not to be involved if we are going to be working together."

He braced his hands on either side of her hips and leaned over her. "Are you saying if I don't back off on the merger, we're over?"

She wedged her hands against his chest, but he didn't budge. He knew he was using his strength to keep her where he wanted her and he didn't care. There were some slights he could let pass. He knew he was pushing her beyond her comfort zone, but he wasn't about to let her think for one second that she could use sex to manipulate him.

"I just don't see how either of us can be objective in the boardroom after last night."

"I don't do one-night stands, honey."

"So you said, but I've been thinking—"

He covered her mouth with his, unwilling to listen to anything else she had to say on the subject. He suspected she was running scared. Running from him and whatever emotional barrier he'd pushed her past last night.

But suspecting that and wanting to be the caring, tender lover he knew she needed was hard when she kept pushing him. He was going to say something that he shouldn't. Something crude and rude, and he'd hurt her. He knew it. No matter how she acted around him or how blasé she sounded about having a one-night stand, Alexandra Haughton wasn't the kind of woman to have casual sex.

Alexandra knew she'd pushed Sterling until he reacted, but as his mouth moved over hers, she couldn't remember why she'd been pushing. She curled her hands around his shoulders and leaned up into him and his kiss.

She hadn't been herself since . . . hell, since he'd shown up on Friday night and thrown her life into chaos. When he was touching her, kissing her, it was easy to pretend there wasn't a world beyond the two of them. That this embrace was all that mattered.

She wished she had some kind of super power that she could use to protect herself from the power he wielded easily over her. She could only hope that he never realized how addled he'd made her.

Sitting in the sun by the pool at the Summerlin, she'd realized that she'd be happy to wait for him always. She couldn't go back to being the woman she was, the woman who'd built her life around one man. That was dangerous thinking. He pulled his head back, pressing hers forward to rest against his chest.

"I'm sorry." He spoke against the top of her head. She felt the warm puff of his breath against her hair.

"About?" she asked, still trying to figure out how she was going to get control of this situation. Fighting her own desires was hard. The men she'd had as lovers normally weren't so intense. She could think of no other way to describe Sterling. He was intense about everything he did.

But she had to get her head in the game today. Tomorrow morning at the full board meeting was going to be too late. Coming with Sterling this afternoon had seemed like such a good idea earlier. A chance to really check out the competition and see how he operated. But the more time she spent with him, the harder it was to remain objective.

"Kissing you to shut you up."

"You don't sound like it." He didn't. He sounded like he'd do it again in a heartbeat if he thought he could get away with it. And was she going to let him?

"Probably because I really enjoy kissing you," he said, tipping her head back and kissing her again, rubbing his lips over hers until she could hardly remember what they were discussing or why she thought it was so important, and that wasn't like her. Not at all like the person she was.

She was ruled by her head, not her emotions. She'd made a promise to herself when she'd finally rejoined the land of the living that she'd keep looking forward and not get mired down in these kinds of . . . emotional entanglements.

That was the problem the way she saw it. They both liked it too much. She'd come with him today . . . why had she come with him today? Sitting in the sun and thinking about Sterling, she'd tried to tell herself that she wanted to find out how he operated so she could use it to best him in the meeting they had scheduled.

She wasn't able to think of anything but the way he'd made her lips tingle just now. The man could kiss and wasn't shy about using his entire body to seduce her. She wanted to melt into him. To wrap her arms and legs around him and say to hell with the rest of the world and just disappear someplace where they could make love forever.

"Sterling—"

He put his finger to her lips this time. "No. No more talking. Not right now. I'm hanging on to my temper by a thread, and I don't want to say something I'll regret."

She wanted to push him until he said something that she could use as a reason to back away. Which ticked her off, because she was an intelligent woman in most situations. But not where he was concerned. She liked him—all of him, the man and the businessman. Liked the way he treated his employees with respect. Liked the way he kissed her and couldn't keep his hands off her.

"Not talking about it won't make it go away," she said. God knows she'd tried hiding from problems in the past and they'd never really gone away. They were always there waiting for you. And with Sterling she had the feeling that he knew this, too. That maybe he realized that they were going to have to face each other before they got to the boardroom.

"Won't make *what* go away," he said, opening the car door and gesturing for her to climb in.

"The fact that we can't work together and have an affair," she said carefully. She'd already given up on the idea that she wasn't going to have an affair with Sterling Powell. She wanted him too much to let him walk right back out of her life. But that didn't mean she wasn't going to set the terms.

"Yes, we can. We both know how to keep personal feelings out of the boardroom. I'm sure you've had to deal with issues regarding Brad and Dan or your in-laws. Haven't you?"

"Yes," she said. It had never been easy, but she'd had to actually reprimand Brad for leaving the front desk unattended while he made out with his girlfriend in the front-desk manager's office. That had been extremely embarrassing for her because Brad had denied he'd left his post and they'd had to review the security tape that had shown the eighteen-year-old and his girlfriend in a torrid embrace.

"That's not the same," she said, realizing that he was right. She didn't want him to be right. Not about this or about their relationship being about more than sex. She couldn't figure out which way to push to get a wedge between them. A wedge that she could use to protect herself from falling for him.

She already felt more for Sterling than she wanted to. It was insane—she'd only known the man two days, but he'd shaken her. She didn't like it but she didn't want to walk away.

"It's exactly the same. For the rest of today, let's just be a couple in a new relationship. Don't think about meetings and boardrooms."

She shook her head. She wished it were that simple but there were complications to any kind of relationship between them. And the sooner Sterling admitted it, the sooner they could stop this crazy affair. "I don't think that's wise. We aren't just a couple."

"We could be, honey. Stop looking for obstacles."

"I'm not searching for them," she said a bit defensively, and then realized she'd lied to him and herself. "Okay, I *am* seeking them out. This is happening too fast."

"But having a relationship based solely on sex wouldn't be."

They couldn't even have *that* anymore. Maybe that was what bothered her. Maybe that was why she was searching for something, anything that would make him say something to hurt her. Hurt her now, before she was involved any deeper than this first flush of attraction.

"Stop throwing that up in my face. I know the point you are trying to make and I'm not going to acknowledge it."

"Not acknowledging it and not knowing it are two very different things," he said softly, taking her mouth in a sweet kiss that felt like it would never end.

She realized he was right. She sat down in the car. The leather seat was hot under the backs of her thighs and she scooted forward to stop the burn.

This was what she was trying to avoid. She'd been burned too badly by love and relationships to ever want to go into one again. She knew she had to share the past with Sterling so that maybe he'd understand and just let her go.

Chapter Eleven

Sterling pulled off the highway just outside of Georgetown onto a two-lane road. Soon they were close enough to the ocean to smell the salt in the air. He pulled off onto a dirt road marked PRIVATE.

"What are you doing?" Alexandra asked.

It was the first thing she'd said to him since they'd left the Summerlin. He'd screwed something up with her earlier but he wasn't sure what. He only knew that when he kept his head in the game he was okay, but with Alexandra he wasn't sure that he knew what the game was.

"Stopping for lunch."

"I know that Georgetown is small and doesn't offer a lot of choices, but we can find something that's not this rustic."

"I don't want to share you with even a handful of diners in a small town," he said, meaning it. Salvaging the day was harder than he'd anticipated when he'd left Myrtle Beach. He felt certain that a quiet meal together would help that. He should never have brought her to the Summerlin with him.

"I'm not sure this is a good idea," she said. "I want to check in with the duty manager before I meet Jessica."

"Do you want to keep driving and go back to the Haughton where you can hide in your hotel?"

She shook her head, her silky hair sliding over her shoulders. "No. I'm not interested in hiding in the hotel today."

Finally, something was going his way. Since they'd left the

yacht he'd been off his stride, not able to figure out which move to make next with her. He continued driving down the road, stopping when they reached the dunes. He got out of the car and came around to open Alexandra's door. He offered her his hand, helping her out of the car.

He got the picnic cooler and a blanket out of the trunk. He took her hand and led her across onto the sand. She stumbled as her sexy heels sank in the soft earth.

"Here," he said, handing her the blanket and cooler and scooping her into his arms. She wrapped her arm around his shoulders and he felt like her hero. Like the kind of guy she could rely on and not just when it came to business.

She gasped as he lifted her and adjusted the blanket and cooler against her stomach.

"I won't drop you," he said. She was light, easy for him to carry across the sandy dunes that lined the coast in this part of the country.

"All that working out, right?" she asked, teasing him with her hand on the side of his neck.

"Exactly—this is another one of the perks that comes from working out." He was pretty sure that even if he didn't work out so much, he'd be able to carry her because she made him want to puff out his chest and prove he was the strongest choice when it came to the men in her life. He wanted to force her to see him as more than just another executive she battled with in the boardroom.

He set her on her feet and shook out the blanket. The breeze was pretty strong but he'd found a spot that was sheltered from the wind in the valley of two dunes.

Alexandra bent to take off her shoes and the hem of her skirt rose up the back of her thighs. He knew he should look away but didn't. She straightened and gave him a quick grin. "Like what you see?"

"You know I do." He'd been staring at her so much lately that when he closed his eyes, all he saw was her mile-long legs.

She settled in the middle of the blanket and started opening the cooler. Sterling sat on the edge of the blanket and removed his socks and shoes. She handed him a plate that had a cold salmon and Greek salad on it. She passed him the bottle of chardonnay.

"I can't find the corkscrew."

"It's in the zippered compartment," he said, finding it and opening the wine. He poured them both a glass. Picnics always ranked up there in the top-five list for women when it came to romantic dates. Since he liked to be outside, he didn't mind them much. The hard part about picnics was the food. He had certain standards, and a deli sandwich and chips didn't spell romance.

"This is really nice. Much better than a diner downtown."

"I thought so," he said. As they ate they talked about the small seaside towns on both coasts. When they were finished and the plates and trash were tucked away, he pulled out a small plastic container of chilled strawberries.

"What's that?"

"Dessert," he said, but held it away from her when she reached for the container. "Come closer to me. I want to hold you."

"What, no *please*?"

"Please."

She moved over next to him on the blanket. He lay on his back and drew her down next to him, leaning on his elbow so that he looked down at her. He opened the container and took out one of the strawberries. He rubbed it against her lips until she opened them, then inserted just the tip of the berry between her teeth. As she took a bite, juice dripped down her chin.

He caught it with his tongue, then drew her lower lip between his teeth and suckled on it. She opened her mouth on a sigh. "This feels like sex to me."

"Me, too, but we just had lunch and swapped stories. This isn't just about sex."

She started laughing. "Right now, I don't care."

He didn't touch that. He cared. He wanted her with a force that made a mockery of his lauded self-control.

"Untie your top."

She reached behind her neck and undid the knot, but left the fabric covering her breasts. He brushed the straps aside and ran the juicy berry along her collarbone, bending to trace the trail left by the juice with his tongue.

She reached between them and undid the buttons of his shirt, pushing it off his shoulders. He shrugged out of it, tossing it over the cooler. "You lie back."

He did as she asked and she leaned over him, the ties of her top falling down to reveal the curves of her pretty breasts. He rubbed the berry he still had in his hand over her nipples, then leaned up to lick the juice off of her. She moaned his name and arched her back. He wrapped one arm around her and continued to lick and suckle her breasts.

She shifted around on his lap until she straddled him. He lifted his head when she tugged on his hair. She put a ripe berry between his teeth and he bit down on it, juice slipping from the edge of his mouth into hers. Her tongue tangled with his. The kiss was sweet and hot.

She pushed on his shoulders, urging him onto his back. She used the berry in her hand to trace circles on his chest, around his nipples and then down the line of hair that disappeared under the waistband of his pants. She leaned down, rubbing her breasts against him, and then licked the juice off him.

He unfastened her skirt and pushed it down her legs with her top. She kicked it aside, coming back to unfasten his belt, and then unzip his pants.

"Lie on top of me," he said.

She lowered herself on top of him, but he stopped her. "On your back."

"What?"

"Trust me. You'll like this."

She moved around until she reclined on top of him. She nestled her head on his shoulder and he kissed the smooth skin there. He brought his hands up to cup her breasts and tease them.

"How does the sun feel? Not too warm?" he asked. He wanted every detail of this afternoon to be perfect. Absolutely perfect.

"No. It feels really good."

He reached between her legs and drew the crotch of her panties aside. She was already damp. He loved how hot she got for him. He dipped one finger into her and she shivered against him.

His erection was trapped between their bodies and he reached down with his other hand to free himself. He found the condom in his back pocket and sheathed himself with it.

Alexandra's waist came over his and she shifted her legs on top of his. He slipped the head of his cock into her body. He couldn't get deep penetration this way but it still felt good.

Alexandra shifted on top of him, one of her legs falling outside his. She put her right palm against the base of his shaft as she shifted up and then back down. He felt the metal of her rings against his hot skin. She moved slowly, building tension between them. He fondled her breast with one hand and fed her strawberries with the other.

They rocked together until the tension in both of them built, and then he felt her shuddering around him. He shifted her off of his body, pulling his erection out of her. Settling himself over her, he thrust deep, driving into her three times before his own climax rocked through his body. He cradled her close in his arms, knowing he was never going to let this woman go.

The last thing Alexandra wanted to do was go out to a club with Jessica, but she'd made the younger woman a promise and she always kept her word. Four hours after she'd made love with Sterling in the sun, her body still tingled and she still smelled strawberries with each breath she took.

She was glad to see her little town house when they'd returned to Charleston. Glad that she had a commitment that would mean she couldn't spend the evening with him. No matter what, she was glad that Jessica had asked her to have dinner and then drinks with her before hitting the techno-club where Dan moonlighted as a deejay.

She'd taken a shower as soon as Sterling had left but her body still tingled. She refused to even look at the cruise clothing that Priscilla had purchased. She didn't care if she had a uniform and everyone knew it—she needed the comfort of her clothing. Her plain, old, boring clothing and her ponytail.

She found her favorite Ann Taylor khaki pants and a twin sweater set in pale green. She felt more comfortable immediately. She sat down at her vanity and applied light makeup and pale lip gloss, then pulled her hair back into a ponytail. She looked like her usual self. Regular old Alexandra, ready for a quiet Sunday night.

Except inside she wasn't regular *or* quiet. Her emotions swirled around. Lust was a big part of it, but so were fear and excitement. Exhilaration at not knowing what would happen next.

Her doorbell rang and she put on her loafers before answering the door. Jessica stood on the other side, dressed in a form-fitting black micro-mini skirt and a shirt that left her midriff bare. Her black hair had a streak of purple down the left side and her eye makeup was heavy and dark. She looked like a Goth girl standing there.

It made Alexandra feel a lot more than ten years older than the girl, and so out of touch with the entire club scene that she questioned why she'd agreed to go. At the time she'd had some vague idea of proving to Sterling that she wasn't the boring little executive he had her pegged as, but looking at Jessica made her long to be that person.

"You're not ready, are you?" Jessica said with a critical eye.

"Yes. Just let me lock up and we'll go."

"Don't you have any jeans?" Jessica asked, walking into Alexandra's foyer and closing the door behind her.

She did have jeans, but she couldn't remember the last time she'd worn them. "Yes."

"Good. I'll help you change."

She didn't need any help changing, not from Jessica *or* Sterling. She was in flux already, and she wondered if it had anything at all to do with all the external things happening in her life. Or if it was simply part of some kind of awakening.

Yes, she thought, she was awakening after having been sleep-walking through life for too long. "My bedroom's in the back."

Alexandra put on a pair of skintight, faded jeans that she'd had for years, while Jessica went through the many shirts and blouses hanging in her closet. Then she started opening the drawers that contained Alexandra's scarves. She pulled out a large black square with brightly colored circles in various sizes on it.

"Here you go."

It's a scarf, she thought. Jessica wanted her to wear a scarf as a blouse. She knew that women did that all the time. She even had a scarf-tying book that showed her how to do it, but she just wasn't ready to wear that scarf as a blouse. "I don't think so. This top is okay."

Jessica tossed the scarf on the bed. "You can wear that top but only if you leave the cardigan here."

Alexandra had to laugh at the way she'd said it. She took off the sweater, which she didn't need on this sultry southern night.

"Are you this bossy with Dan?"

"Sometimes," she said. "He's a conservative dresser like you are but it looks better on guys."

"Thanks a lot."

"Oh, man. I think I've been hanging around Dan too long. I've forgotten how to think before I speak."

"You were right about the clothes. This looks more casual."

She heard the fax machine pick up in her office. Maybe there would be a business emergency and she'd skip going out with Jessica. She could spend a quiet Sunday night at home alone. Like she usually did. "Let me check that fax before we leave."

"Go ahead. I'm going to snoop around your living room."

"Snoop for what?"

"For pictures of Danny."

"Start with the album on the bottom bookcase—I've known him since he was fourteen."

Jessica's eyes lit up as she walked to the bookcase. Alexandra walked into her home office and over to the fax machine. The fax was from Sterling to the Haughton House board of directors—an agenda of what he planned to discuss at the meeting tomorrow. She set the fax in the middle of her desk when the machine whirred to life again, spitting out a second page.

This one was addressed only to her. Not typed as the first had been but handwritten.

Alexandra,

I enjoyed our day together—I hope you did as well. I'd like to see you again tomorrow afternoon. Meet me at the marina near the recreation rental desk at two.
Sterling

She found a pen on her desk and jotted back a note.

Sterling:

I, too, enjoyed our afternoon. I will see you at the board meeting. I'm afraid the rest of my day is spoken for. I'm out for the evening. Send me an e-mail at A.Haughton@HHResort. com.
AH

She punched in the fax number to his suite and pushed SEND. He was too arrogant. She'd known that about him from the beginning but everything he did just convinced her more strongly of it. He was making plans to buy out her resort, not her. And she'd never taken orders well.

She found Jessica sitting on the loveseat with the album open. She traced her finger over one of the pictures and Alexandra went to see which one it was.

Her breath caught in her throat as she saw Marcus, Brad, and Dan together. All three of them had their hands raised, holding up a twenty-pound marlin that Dan had caught but that Brad and Marcus had helped him reel in.

All three of the Haughton boys had their shirts off and wore only swim trunks. Brad and Dan looked like younger versions of Marcus, and Alexandra felt a pang at seeing him now. He would have been so proud of Brad and Dan for going after their dream and opening the software company.

She traced her finger over his beloved face and remembered how she'd felt that day. She remembered it because later that evening at dinner Marcus had proposed. Jessica tipped her head back and looked up at her. "Marcus was a total hunk."

"Yeah, he was. So is Dan."

"I know. Women are always checking him out," Jessica said, closing the album and standing.

"According to Brad, Dan doesn't even notice that anymore."

"Brad doesn't like me much."

Alexandra had no idea how to explain the complexities of Brad Haughton to Jessica. Brad had lost one brother and didn't want to lose another one. "I'm sure that's not true."

"He calls me Dan's ball and chain."

Alexandra made a mental note to talk to Brad tomorrow alone and tell him to back off on Jessica. She'd seen Dan with her and Alexandra knew if Brad kept pushing he was going to end up pushing Dan away.

"It's nothing personal. He doesn't like the fact that he and Dan aren't alone anymore."

"Really?"

Alexandra locked the front door and led the way to her car. "Where's your car?"

"I had my roommate drop me off. Dan said he'd bring me home."

Jessica didn't say anything else on the ride to the club and neither did Alexandra, but as she felt the younger woman's worry she realized that love at thirty-two looked really different from love at twenty-two.

Sterling knew he was bordering on stalker behavior when, just after midnight, he stopped the Porsche in front of Alexandra's house. They'd exchanged several short e-mails earlier in the evening. He was fairly sure he'd convinced her to join him tomorrow afternoon.

He glanced at the small potted plant he'd picked up after his dinner alone, and then back at her dark house. What kind of a man showed up in the middle of the night?

He didn't know. But he missed her. He'd only held her in his arms for one night and he knew that he wanted to do so again.

He pulled out his cell phone and dialed her number, then waited a full minute before he hit the button to connect the call. It rang three times before she answered. "Hello?"

No lights came on in her house. He leaned back in his chair, wondering where the hell she was. And knowing he had absolutely no right to ask her. She'd made it clear from the beginning that she wasn't pursuing a relationship with him.

He'd spent a miserable night working on his presentation for the full Haughton House board of directors and going out of his mind wondering where the hell she was.

"It's Sterling." Calling her was a class-one mistake. Normally, he never pursued a woman this way. He liked to tease and tempt and then let them come to him. But the feeling in his gut said that if he waited for Alexandra, it was going to be a long, cold night before she showed up at his door.

"It's after midnight—what do you want?" she asked, a teasing note in her voice that he'd never heard before.

He took notice of the music in the background but couldn't make out any other sounds. What if she'd had a date tonight? Though on Friday night she'd said she wasn't seeing anyone.

"I want you to let me in."

"Let you in where?" she asked, the volume on the music lowering. She said she wasn't dating anyone, so why should he be consumed with jealousy over where she was? They'd slept together once. But he knew that with her it felt like more than an affair. Had felt like that from the beginning and she still wasn't sure when every action he took with her was going to start being normal—for him.

He was feeling like a complete idiot and normally he wasn't like this around women but Alexandra was different. And that difference was starting to make him sweat. Because every move he made felt practiced and wrong with her.

"To your house, but I don't think you're home."

She made a little tsking sound under her breath. "I'm not at my house. Why are you there?"

He could sound like a sap and say he missed her or he could play it cool. "I'm looking for you."

"Yes, I know that, but why?"

Wasn't that the million-dollar question? He'd been asking himself the same thing all the way over here. And before he'd hit SEND on the cell phone and dialed her number. Why was he here? What did he want? Oh, hell, he knew what he wanted. He wanted to spend the night in her bed.

"I have a gift for you."

"At midnight?"

"What's your fixation with the time? It's not like you were in your bed sleeping," he said, which had been his fantasy. To come over to her place, wake her up, and then just take her back to bed. Make sweet love to her and hold her all night.

No talking, no debating if what they had was just sex or something more. Just holding her for one night.

"You sound cranky. Maybe you should be in bed," she said lightly.

"If you were home, I could be."

"Shouldn't you wait for an invitation?"

"If I did that I'd still be in my empty suite waiting."

"Maybe," she said. "Um . . . hold on. I can't hold the phone and turn at the same time."

Why wasn't she using a headpiece? He put her call on hold and switched the function on his cell phone to PDA and made a note to buy her a Bluetooth wireless earpiece for her phone. A car made the turn onto her street, pulling into her driveway.

He got out of his car, then snagged the potted plant and the jewelry box from the passenger side. She opened her car door and climbed out. She wore a pair of faded jeans that were so tight they should be illegal.

They made her legs look like they were miles long. Her sleeveless top was conservative-looking. High neckline and the hem fell to her waist. She looked so different than she had earlier in the day. But still so pretty that she took his breath away.

"What were we talking about?" she asked.

"Invite me in and I'll remind you," he said.

"Give me one good reason," she said carefully. She didn't look tired and cigarette smoke clung to her.

Where the hell had she been?

"What do you have there?"

"A gift for you."

She tipped her head to the side, studying him. Her pupils were dilated a little bit and he wondered if she was tipsy. "Have you been drinking?"

She smiled up at him and it was a sweet smile. One he hadn't seen on her before. She was definitely in a good mood. Where the hell had she been?

"Yes, but I stopped at ten. It's taking a while for my buzz to wear off."

Her neighbor's front-porch light came on and a shirtless man stepped outside. "You okay, Alexandra?"

"Yes, Paul. He's a friend of mine."

Sterling leaned against the porch railing of Alexandra's house. Her hair was pulled back at her neck and one small tendril escaped to curl against her cheek.

She nibbled on her lower lip as she studied him, trying to decide, he was sure, if she should tell him to go away or invite him to stay. She wasn't trying to seduce him, he knew that. But there was something sexy about her in that moment.

Hell, he always found her sexy. Which is why he was standing near her in the middle of the night instead of at his hotel suite. He'd missed her in his bed. He was a forty-year-old man and not an eighteen-year-old boy, so he didn't let his hormones rule.

Yeah, right. One month ago he would have sworn to the fact that he was well past the age where he'd react to any woman in a hormone-driven rush, but he hadn't been in the same room as Alexandra a month ago. And once he'd seen her up close and personal—all bets were off.

"You may as well come inside," she said, with a gamine grin that made him realize that there were way more layers to this woman than he'd first realized. And that he might never get to see them all.

"With an invitation like that, how can I resist?" he asked, putting his hand on her waist because he couldn't wait to touch her. Not another single second.

"Like you'd resist," she said, walking past him and climbing the two steps to her front door.

She was right. There was absolutely nothing about this woman that he could resist. However, that didn't mean he was going to be a pushover for her.

Chapter Twelve

Alexandra led Sterling into her house and knew that battle she'd been waging against herself for most of the day was lost. She didn't want to find reasons to keep this man at bay. She wanted to pull him closer to her. To wallow in the warmth that his arms provided after having been cold for way too long.

"What are you carrying around?" she asked, as soon as they were inside. She didn't want to admit it but she was so happy to see him. She'd missed him tonight when she'd danced with other guys—all she'd thought about was how wrong their arms felt around her. Or how strong their cologne was. Or how clammy their hands were on her arms.

"A gift for you," he said, putting the pottery flowerpot on the table in her entryway.

"You got me a plant?" she asked. She had no houseplants—well, that wasn't true. She had no *living* houseplants. No matter what she did, she couldn't keep them alive. She either overwatered, or underwatered, and in no time they were all dead.

"Yes."

"That's not very romantic, Sterling. This doesn't live up to the moonlight dinner on the water and the private beach picnic you had in your arsenal."

"You might change your mind . . . this is no ordinary houseplant," he said.

"What is it?"

"This is a strawberry plant."

She flushed a little, looking at the plant. She'd been trying to pretend like that sunshiny interlude had been an erotic daydream. "Thank you."

"You're welcome. I have one more present for you."

"I didn't get you anything," she said, not sure she wanted gifts from him. Actually, she was sure that she didn't want anything more from him. He was overwhelming her and making it difficult to remember exactly why she kept her distance from men.

"Let me stay the night and we'll call it even."

"See, this is about sex." But there was something in his eyes that warned her it was so much more. She'd missed him tonight. Which was utterly ridiculous because she shouldn't know him well enough to miss him. He was the enemy, she reminded herself, but she no longer bought that.

Sterling wasn't a ruthless corporate shark out to destroy what the Haughtons had built all those years ago. He wanted to keep the heritage they'd created and build it for future generations.

"Part of it is, anyway," he said with a wry grin.

"So what else did you get me?"

She left the foyer and moved into her living room, hitting the light switch as she entered. She saw the open photo album on the coffee table. Her first instinct was to hurry over and close it, but she didn't.

She kicked off her loafers and went over to the loveseat to sit down. Sterling followed her, toeing off his own shoes and then bending to remove his socks. She glanced at his very masculine-looking feet with a light dusting of hair on his toes. Her own feet looked so much smaller next to his.

He handed her a box wrapped in gold foil with a pink bow on top of it. From its shape and size, she suspected whatever he'd gotten her was jewelry.

"Nice bow," she said.

"I remembered you liked girly pink things."

She pulled the bow off and slowly unwrapped the package.

She didn't want him to have purchased her gifts. She'd never received a present outside of her birthday or Christmas. Also, on Boss's Day her employees usually gave her a massage gift certificate for the spa. But this was different.

"It's not dangerous."

Yes, it was. In ways he couldn't understand. All the men she'd filled her life with up until now had been plain vanilla. Boring and bland men who let her run the show and left her life alone. Sterling wasn't one of those men. He wasn't following the rules.

"Open it."

She was being silly and making a bigger deal out of this gift than she should be. He probably gave every woman he slept with some token. That's all this was.

She unwrapped the package and neatly folded the gift wrap, setting it on the coffee table next to the open album. She glanced over at the album page with the photo of Marcus and his brothers and she felt a sweet pang at what they'd once had.

"Is that your husband?"

"Yes. His name was Marcus."

"You already told me his name. What was he like?"

She glanced over at Sterling—no man wanted to know about the previous lovers his current lover had. But she knew that a lot of reasons why she was reluctant to be involved in more than a casual fling with Sterling stemmed from the wonderful relationship she'd had with Marcus.

"He was . . . I don't know how to describe him. He loved the outdoors and spent as much time in the sun as he could. But he was dedicated to Haughton House. To bringing it back to being a top-notch resort. We spent a lot of time together in the main resort."

"Is he the reason you don't want to see Pack-Maur acquire it?"

She shrugged. It was so much more complicated than what Marcus had once dreamed that Haughton House could be.

She'd taken the resort in directions he'd never dreamed it could go in. "There isn't just one reason."

"Tell me some of them."

He invited her to share her secrets with him and she was tempted to trust him. To trust that whatever she said he wouldn't laugh at as being too silly or judge it as being too small-minded. But she wasn't going to share that part of her soul . . . not tonight.

"I thought you wanted me to open the present you brought for me."

"Do you want to?" he asked, leaning back, stretching his arm over her shoulders.

"I'm not sure."

He took the box from her, removed the lid, and lifted out a silver charm bracelet with only one charm dangling from it. She reached for the bracelet, lifting it up to see the small strawberry charm. She fingered it gently and knew that she was way over her head in ways she hadn't even thought of before this.

She leaned back against his arm, tilting her head to the side so that she faced him. "Thank you."

"Give me your wrist," he said.

She lifted her hand to him and he put the bracelet on her. It was cold against her skin but his hands were warm. He held her wrist in his grasp, rubbing his thumb under the clasp. She shivered deep inside and it had nothing to do with sex or awareness. It was the shivering of a soul-deep coldness that she'd wrapped herself in long ago.

Preserving what was left of her wounded heart. But that shivering signaled an awakening and she knew it was too late to stop it. She'd realized tonight when she'd hung out in a dance club with Dan and Jessica that she no longer had that buffer she'd always counted on. That the buffer she'd used to protect herself was gone.

And this man was responsible for it. He was the one who had shaken the moorings of her life, first by making an offer for her resort—the one place she'd felt safe investing her emotions in because it was a building and not a person and could never leave her. Then, by making love to her like she was the kind of woman he'd always dreamed of. By making her his completely and leaving no room in her mind to doubt that she'd been marked by him.

She didn't want to be marked by him or by anyone. She wanted to go back to her quiet existence with its routines and safety. With no emotions. No emotions. That's what she wanted and needed.

Not these swirling feelings of hope, lust, desire. A longing in her for something more than the comfortable niche she'd carved for herself. She looked at the silver charm bracelet and felt swamped with so many things.

Sterling held her gently, as if he knew that he'd rocked her world, and she hated that. She didn't want him to be aware of the effect he had on her. Didn't want him to have any kind of effect on her. Didn't want him to ever realize that her life was no longer the safe refuge it had been before he'd shown up in Charleston.

Looking at photos of Alexandra's husband was about last on his list of ways to spend the evening. He flipped the album closed and then drew her into his arms. His gifts had made an impact on her. One that even he hadn't anticipated.

He hadn't figured her out, not all the way, but he knew that he was almost there. Hoped that he was almost there because while he'd been sitting alone in his hotel room, going out of his mind with jealousy, wondering where the hell she was and who the hell she was with, he'd realized that he was falling for her.

He'd probably known it from the first moment when he'd surprised her in the bar. Martini shaker in one hand, the other pressed against his chest. But this afternoon had brought it all home. Had made him realize that he wasn't going to let her go.

Whatever hoops he had to jump through to keep her in his

life, he was going to do it. And the strawberry plant and the bracelet were his way of reminding her that he was real. Not some dream man or fantasy lover, but a flesh-and-blood man who wasn't going to be happy until he'd claimed her, body and soul.

One tug pulled her into his arms. She wrapped her arms around his waist, holding him loosely. He liked the feel of her soft curves against him.

"I don't know what to do with you," she said, so softly he had to lean forward to catch her words.

That was quite a confession from the woman who always knew where she was going. Always knew what she was doing. Always had a plan of action. He didn't take it as a victory; in fact, he knew that only made her want to fight harder against him.

She needed to know, needed to plan. Part of it had to come from losing her husband. Goddamn it. He was going to have to ask her about Marcus. Was going to have to understand the man she'd loved and lost, because the key to Alexandra had to be buried somewhere in the past.

She didn't cling to the past, but she wasn't exactly embracing the future. It was like she was stuck in some sort of time warp and would be happy to stay there for the rest of her life.

Who the hell was he to nudge her out of it? He didn't have an answer, but he knew that he couldn't just walk away from her.

"Tell me about Marcus. Did you know what to do with him?"

She pushed away from him and picked up the photo album, unhurriedly paging through it. He saw a faint smile on her face as she traced her finger over Marcus's face.

"I guess so. Remember when we talked about what we wanted as kids and I'd said I wanted to be a princess?"

"Yes." How could he have forgotten listening to the faint hope left in those memories of her dreams? The fantasies that she'd had as a young girl had fueled her notions of love . . . first love.

Dammit, did he want her to love him? He knew in an instant that he did. He wondered if Marcus had any clue how much Alexandra had cared for him. How much he'd meant to her life. Because she'd dedicated the rest of her life to fulfilling his dreams.

"Marcus was my prince. We met when my mom and I came here for the summer before I started college. Kind of a last trip together before I went out in the world. Anyway, one of the teenagers I was hanging out with knew Marcus and invited me to go to a party. That was the first night of my vacation—the first night I was here. It was on the beach . . ."

As her voice trailed off, he realized he didn't want to know any more of the details. But a sick part of him did. He wanted to know just how wonderful her first summer love had been because he was her last summer love. He was the man who was going to take her from girlish dreams and fantasies into the reality of womanly dreams and real, live sexual fantasies.

"So you met your prince and then what?" he asked, because it sounded too good to be true. Didn't she realize that any guy looked good during a courtship, especially when they were so young that neither of them had any responsibilities? He knew better than to say that to her, but he thought it and realized what he was up against. He was competing for Alexandra as a flesh-and-blood man; he was competing against her feelings of great love and great loss.

"We lived happily ever after, for a year. My marriage only lasted a year. But we had it all in that time."

"All? A year is a drop in the bucket of life."

She pushed away from him. "Yeah, it is. When I'm feeling sorry for myself, I always have to remember that. The best year of my life was when I was twenty-one—everything seemed full of promise to us. Marcus was bigger than life, everything he touched turned to gold."

She faced him then. "I liked that, Sterling. I liked being part of that magical golden circle that was Marcus's life. And when he died . . . I had no idea how to function. No idea how to live without him."

He ached inside at her words. Felt the pain and confusion of what she'd gone through as a young woman. He remembered himself at that age, still half wild and running on adrenaline, his favorite drug. Hell, it still was, which was probably why he was so attracted to her.

"I'm sorry," he said, pulling her into his arms. "That must have been a rude awakening. But you've come a long way from that girl."

"I have," she said, leaning back so that she could stare into his eyes. "But I had to change a lot to get where I am today. And I've finally found that place where I belong."

He heard what she was saying—that he was rocking her boat and tearing it from its moorings, but it wasn't enough to deter him. He wasn't going to back down. "If you had even an ounce of the enthusiasm for life now that you did back then—"

"Don't say that. Don't judge what you can't understand. I can't live my life like that anymore because losing hurts too much."

She stood up, leaving the loveseat and pacing over to the window. "You know the main reason why I don't want the merger with Pack-Maur?"

He thought he already did know it. Knew he'd just figured it out while she'd been talking. She didn't want a merger because then she'd have to leave. She'd have to find her place in the world again. And as much as he wanted that place to be in his arms and at his side, he wasn't sure that he was the right man.

"Why?" he asked at last.

Needing her to talk so he wouldn't have to face his own inner demons. His own secrets. Those that he'd been hiding from her and, to be honest, from himself because he'd rather deal with and fix her problems than fix his own. And the biggest problem he had was that desire that always drove him to move on.

That the thrill of something new was all that had ever held

him, and with Alexandra, he wanted it—no, needed it—to be more, but he wasn't sure he had that kind of staying power inside him.

"I don't know who I am without Haughton House," she said at last.

He stood up and closed the distance between them. Cupped her face in his hands, stroking his fingers over her face and realizing that he'd pushed her too hard, searching for something he hadn't expected to find. But he'd found it anyway. He'd found that kernel of truth he'd been searching for and now he felt the impact of it deep inside.

He was responsible for stripping her to the bone and forcing her to acknowledge her vulnerabilities, and now he was going to have to protect that weak spot. He would show her how to rebuild her life and move forward from the morass he'd made of her existence.

"You are a sexy, beautiful woman. A businessperson with the acumen to take a small, family-owned business into the big leagues."

"I was surprised at how much I like running the resort."

"You've made some bold moves. I'm a little surprised at some of the risks you took."

"When you've lost everything that matters to you in the world, risks that involve money don't seem all that perilous."

Sterling lowered his mouth over hers, kissing her gently. He'd gotten way more than he'd bargained for tonight and he knew that they'd turned a corner in this relationship. He also realized that it was time for him to stop running from the past and come clean with Alexandra about who he was.

She'd never share her life with a man who couldn't be honest and he knew he hadn't been totally honest with her. Because he was a sweet and easy guy, just waiting for her to come to him. He was intense and passionate about her and he wanted her in his bed for the rest of their lives. And he wanted that damned wedding set off her right hand.

* * *

Alexandra felt raw from talking to Sterling about the past. She rarely thought of that time with Marcus except in a kind of hazy daydream. But tonight she'd been confronted not only with the dreamy parts of her life with him but also with the reality.

Watching Jessica and Dan at the club had reminded her of how intense emotions could be when you are young. They were the same age she and Marcus had been when they'd gotten married. And looking at Dan and his first real love, she realized that maybe she and Marcus had been too young.

She didn't really want to think about what could have been tonight. Sterling was way too real and too here for her to be thinking of another man.

Standing in the middle of her small living room, she rested her head on his shoulder and felt the strength implicit in the way he held her. Felt a kind of bond that went deeper than sex. Which scared the hell out of her. She could understand an attachment to him that came from great sex. But the potted strawberry plant and the way her heart had melted when she'd realized what he'd given her . . . *that* she didn't understand or know how to explain.

He had one hand in her hair, his fingers massaging the back of her neck, and the other hand at her waist. She tipped her head back, met his warm gray gaze, and realized that she wasn't going to hide anymore. Not from herself, or him, or the blatant sexuality that he brought effortlessly to the surface.

"Come to bed with me, Sterling."

He didn't say a word as she led him down the hall to her bedroom. She'd forgotten that she'd changed at the last minute and her khaki pants were discarded on the duvet. Looking at them, she realized they were a statement of the kind of life she'd carved for herself. A safe life. One where the risks were minimized in her daily life and maximized in her business life.

She'd let herself grow old and dead inside and she wanted

desperately to feel alive again. To feel alive the way she did in Sterling's arms. The way she had this afternoon with the sun beating down on her naked body and his arms wrapped around her.

The walls of her bedroom were painted a sunny shade of yellow and the windows were covered in a Laura Ashley floral print. Her duvet matched, and the queen-sized bed was covered with pillows in coordinating fabrics. There was a large black-and-white picture of Haughton House taken from the sea over the headboard. Her dresser held several candles and a small bookshelf was wedged in the corner.

"This room isn't what I expected," he said at last.

He looked out of place in the feminine bedroom. That should serve as a reminder to her that he was only in her life temporarily. But there were times, like now, in the middle of the night, when she was glad he was here. It didn't happen too often but every once and a while she really missed the feel of a man's arms around her.

"Like I wasn't what you expected when we first met face-to-face?" she asked, not really wanting to examine her psyche any more tonight. She wanted to forget about talking and just live in the moment with him.

"Kind of, but this is different. No uniform here," he said.

She'd gone out of her way to make this room the last vestige of the girl she'd once been. She'd tried to make it cold and sterile but she'd always believed a bedroom should be filled with flowery fabrics and rich, luxurious throws.

"Nope, nothing uniform about this room. What about your house? Is it *Architectural Digest* perfect?" she asked.

She could see him living in the ultimate bachelor pad. He probably had a cleaning service that kept it in tip-top condition. But she'd also wager he didn't spend much time in his home. A man like Sterling would be married to his job. Much the same way she was.

"Umm, yes, as a matter of fact, it is. I have a large place in the suburbs of Atlanta that I had custom-built." He unbuttoned his shirt as he spoke. Walking around her room.

"When you were married?" she asked. She really wanted to know what kind of woman he'd asked to marry him. What was that woman like? And what had gone wrong in their relationship? She couldn't imagine a man as romantic as Sterling not making his wife happy.

"No," he said, sitting on the edge of her bed and drawing her closer to him between his spread thighs.

"Why do you have a big house, then?" she asked. Even though her town house wasn't huge, there were times when it did seem too big for one person. Some nights, when the rooms were so stark and empty, she couldn't escape the feeling that the choices she'd made had left her alone.

He hugged her tight and she realized for the first time that he had secrets of his own. She'd been so busy protecting hers that she felt a little silly just now, realizing that there was a reason why Sterling was attractive and single.

What was it?

He rolled onto his back, pulling her down on top of him. She slid her hands under his shirt, against his skin. He urged her head back and kissed her like they had all night. Like he'd be happy to hold her and just kiss forever.

It was a sweet moment here in her flowery bedroom, and she let her mind drift away as a fire started to build inside her. She moved restlessly against him as he licked a path from her chin down the side of her neck.

He traced the neckline of her shirt with his fingertip as he kissed her there. She tunneled her fingers through his hair, holding him closer to her.

"Why do you smell like smoke?" he asked, pressing his nose against her neck.

"I went to a club with Jessica tonight. Dan's a deejay on the weekends." She pushed his shirt off his shoulders and down his arms. He tossed it aside. She wrapped her fingers around his arms, flexing her fingers in his strong biceps.

"Who is Jessica?"

"Dan's girlfriend—you mean he hasn't told you about her?"

"No, he hasn't. Did you dance with anyone?" he asked, flexing his muscles for her. She brushed her lips over his shoulder, licking lightly at his skin. She loved the salty taste of his skin.

"Jessica and I danced together, but only when Dan played one of my favorite songs."

"Not a Marvin Gaye song, I hope," he said.

Did he sound just a little jealous or was that her imagination working overtime? His hands were under her shirt, moving over her back and undoing her bra.

"Not in that club—they'd have kicked us out."

"What did he play?"

"Stevie Ray Vaughn's 'Look at Little Sister'."

"Stevie Ray? I never would have figured you for the hot-electric-guitar-loving woman."

"I guess you haven't looked hard enough." God help her if he looked any harder. But he didn't seem interested in the frivolous things that she shared with the Haughtons or with her co-workers.

He pushed her shirt up over her head and tossed it on the floor then peeled her bra down her arms. "I'm looking now."

He skimmed his hand over her torso before lowering his mouth and suckling at her breast. She squirmed against him, reaching between their bodies to unfasten his pants. His cock was hot and hard under her touch. She rubbed him through his boxer shorts until he grunted deep in his throat and shifted to his side.

He kept one arm wrapped around her waist and his mouth at her breast. She caressed his length, teasing him by alternating light touches and squeezing caresses. Cupping his sac in her hands, she rolled his balls against her fingers and then brought her hand back up his erection.

She felt a drop of moisture at the tip and rubbed her finger over it, smoothing it into him. She had never felt a man's cum hot and heavy on her body. She'd always had protected sex and no mistakes, and she wondered what it felt like.

She continued caressing him with her hand until Sterling pulled back, taking her hand in his and holding it over her head. "Enough. I'm going to explode."

"Good."

"I'd rather be buried inside you. I want to see you come while I'm inside you."

His words made her pulse speed up and her center even wetter. She reached for the snap on her jeans, but Sterling's hands were already there, unfastening her pants and pushing them down her legs. She shivered at the feel of his hands on her legs, so close to her center.

He pulled a condom from the pocket of his pants and put it on. He draped her thighs over his arms and lowered himself over her, pushing her legs open and entering her in one long thrust. She held onto his waist and felt the fire building inside her. The same fire that she'd felt before, but this time, now that she knew she wasn't fighting him as fiercely as she had before, it felt stronger, more intense.

This time she didn't hide from what he made her feel; instead, she reveled in the feeling of being alive. Because she'd been sleeping for so long, going through the motions of pretending to be alive, she needed this moment.

She didn't care that tomorrow she'd probably regret letting him in tonight.

Chapter Thirteen

Jessica eyed Brad warily when he came into the coffee shop alone. Her assistant Molly smiled and flirted with him—he was too much a charmer to really resist Molly for long.

Jessica kept her head down, filling out the paperwork for the order that she was submitting for sandwiches and cookies for the rest of the week.

"Got a sec, Jessica?"

She glanced over at him. He was the absolute last person she wanted to spend any time alone with. But when she'd mentioned to Dan last night that she didn't think Brad liked her, he'd asked her to give his brother another chance.

"Um, is it important? I'm kind of busy."

"I wouldn't have asked if it wasn't," he said.

She put the pen and paper down. Maybe she'd misjudged him. Maybe there was something she'd done without realizing it that had offended him. Maybe she could smooth this out and then have one less thing to worry about with Dan.

"Then I guess I have the time."

She smoothed her hands down her hips, wishing for a second that she had on her own clothes and not her coffee shop uniform, black pants and a black shirt with a java-colored apron with her name on it. She just didn't feel like she was as confident as she needed to be with Brad.

"What's up?" she asked as soon as they were outside.

"I just wanted to apologize for leaving you out of the conversation the other night. I had no idea that you'd never been to Europe."

Yeah, right. He knew she hadn't been because not two days earlier when he'd been at their house he'd heard her tell Dan she'd always dreamed of going to France and exploring the places she'd been studying forever.

"No big deal. Was that all?"

He took his sunglasses from his pocket and put them on. No matter how much he physically resembled Dan, they couldn't have been more different. Whereas Dan was all relaxed charm and open affection, brad was buttoned-down corporate bulldog and guardedness.

"Listen, I know this isn't going to sound right, but I think you're out of your league with my brother."

She was surprised by his words. "Dan's a big boy, Brad. He can take care of himself."

"That's just it, sweet cakes. He can't take care of himself when it comes to girls playing up to him."

"I'm not playing up to him," she said. "He's the one who pursued me."

He pulled his glasses down on his nose and gave her a shrewd, knowing look over the rim. "You don't expect me to believe he'd go after you."

"Why? Because I was raised in a small town and lived in a trailer park? Your brother isn't the snob you are. He sees past all that."

Brad pushed his glasses back up his nose and turned to leave. She watched him walk away, feeling more insecure about her relationship with Dan than ever.

She pulled her cell phone from her pocket and dialed his number.

"Hey, baby. Miss me already?"

"Yes," she said, so glad to hear his voice. "I've been thinking more about that idea I had for a dinner party tonight. Let's forget it."

It didn't matter that she'd spent more money than she really had in her budget on the food. Ever since she'd gone shopping with Priscilla and Alexandra, she'd begun thinking that she might fit in with the Haughtons but Brad was never going to accept her.

"No way. I know how much you're looking forward to it."

"I'm not anymore."

"What's the matter, baby?"

She doubted he'd believe her if she said his brother was—what? What could she say, that Brad didn't like her? That sounded lame even to her ears. "Nothing. I just don't want to disappoint you."

"There's no way you could."

Sterling walked into the Seaside conference room just a little before eleven. Brad and Dan were seated in the corner, talking, but broke off when they saw him.

"Hey, Sterling, man. Did you get back out on the Jet Ski Sunday?"

"I wish. I had a work emergency I had to take care of." It would have been nice to spend the day playing with Alexandra, though he had no qualms about the way the Sunday had played out.

"Too bad. Jessica and I spent the morning out on the ocean. It was gorgeous yesterday."

Sterling had no regrets about yesterday. He enjoyed his time with Alexandra. He'd covered more ground than he'd expected to and really felt like they were making progress. Holding her last night had just reinforced the fact that he never wanted to sleep without her again.

"It was a nice day. I hear you're a deejay," Sterling said. Maybe he should have asked Dan for some music tips instead of Brad. Not that Brad had steered him wrong.

"No need to ask who you heard that from," Dan said, unabashed.

Both of Alexandra's brothers had been openly matchmaking for him. They seemed to think that Alexandra needed to lighten up and live a little. He heard the door open behind him and turned to catch Alexandra entering.

She wore the same red business suit she'd had on this morning. Her hair was twisted up in a complicated do and one curl had escaped to hang down to her cheek.

She'd worn off her lipstick and had two assistants following her into the room. One of them went to the head of the table and started setting up a laptop, connecting it to the presentation screen. The other went to the antique sideboard on the left of the main conference table and began assembling food and drinks on the surface.

"What can I do to help?" he asked Alexandra, walking to her side. He wanted to bend down and kiss her, to soothe the tiny worry line between her eyes and pull her into his arms.

"Nothing. I've got this under control," she said, giving him a pointed stare.

A lesser man would have backed down for fear of being singed, but then he wasn't a lesser man. And he knew that her bark was worse than her bite. Or was it that he no longer minded the way she bit?

"I didn't think you hadn't."

She took a deep breath. "I'm sorry. I'm just a little tense about this meeting."

"Hasn't anything I've said over the weekend helped to ease your worries?" he asked her. He'd really done his best to show her that he'd take care of her resort. That Pack-Maur didn't plan to acquire Haughton House to make a quick buck.

"All you've done is convince me that I've got some tough competition," she said. From the sound of things, competition was the key word. Was she ever going to get to the point where she could just sit back and enjoy the relationship he was trying to build between them? Or was it always going to be this rivalry to see who would win?

He took her arm and led her out in the hallway. Away from her brothers-in-law, who were watching the interaction between the two of them with too much interest. Sterling had never been interested in publicly declaring, *Don't make this a battle between us*.

"You assured me that business has nothing to do with us," she said, giving him a tight smile.

His gut said that if he pushed too hard right now, he'd drive her away for good. And that would be playing right into her hand. She wanted him guarded and on the run so she could have the true power in their relationship but he wasn't willing to give that up.

"Business and pleasure are what we're all about," he said, reminding her of the facts he couldn't shake.

"That's not convincing me."

He couldn't figure out if she was teasing him or not. This was the Alexandra Haughton he'd expected to meet on Friday night. Totally prepared and professional, a modern-day Amazon warrior ready to take on any man foolish enough to stand in her way. He shouldn't be turned on by seeing her in business mode, but hell if he wasn't.

"And I meant it. What happens between us in our personal lives stays there, right?" he asked. He wanted to just tell her but knew orders didn't work with her. This meeting would be very interesting. If everything went the way he expected it to, Alexandra would be working for him as soon as the paperwork could be prepared. Which wasn't going to work.

"Of course. Why are you asking me that?" she asked.

"I don't want you to be mad at me when the family votes to merge with Pack-Maur." Pack-Maur had a very open fraternization policy, so dating her wasn't going to be a problem from the company's perspective. But Sterling didn't know if he'd be able to keep his mind on business when she was in a meeting.

"I'm not going to be mad at anyone, Sterling. I know exactly who's to blame for this."

"That's what I'm afraid of. Dammit, I should have waited—"

She shook her head. "Not you. I'm the one to blame. Obviously I did my job a little too well."

"You couldn't do it any other way," he said, wishing they were somewhere private and not about to go into a meeting with the board of directors. He wanted the merger out of the way so he could finish wooing her.

"I know. I've been thinking about things a lot this morning."

"What things?" he asked. It wasn't like her to be vague, and he could only guess that she was now because she was going to give him the brush-off. Wouldn't that take the cake? Now that he almost had their business dealings wrapped up, she'd decide that he'd pushed too hard and it was time to move on.

"Life things. It's like I needed to make the resort my life for a while and I have to wonder if a higher power isn't saying maybe it's time to move on."

Sterling had never believed in a higher power that controlled his life. He knew that he was where he was today thanks to his own determination and his own screwups. He'd learned more from his mistakes than he'd have expected. But if she believed in some kind of fate and it brought her into his company and to Atlanta, he was all for it.

"You should listen to this higher power."

"Yeah, right. I've got to go get ready for the meeting."

"What else could you possibly have to do before the meeting?" he asked, because she had copies of her presentation and her electronic stuff all set up now.

"I need to fix my lipstick so I can distract the Pack-Maur guy. What do you think—a nice, deep red or just something shiny?"

"Don't bother with anything on your lips—just lick them one time and he'll be sucked into a wet daydream."

"If only you were really that easy," she said, tucking that stray curl back behind her ear. "I'm not going to be pulling any punches in the boardroom. I've been known to really tick people off in the meetings."

"No matter how ticked off I get, I'm not going to let you back out of your promise to spend the afternoon with me." He'd made arrangements for them to shadow the children's recreation program. When he'd learned that Alexandra rarely left her office, he'd decided to change that. He knew that she was aware of what was going on in her hotel, had learned that she'd sat in on some of the craft sessions, but he wanted to see her outside with the wind in her hair and the sun on her face.

"Are you sure?"

"Positive."

"What's that all about, anyway?" she asked.

"You'll see," he said, stepping away from her as Priscilla and Burt Haughton came around the corner. He went to chat with Burt, very aware that she was still watching him.

Alexandra knew she'd gotten the boys', and maybe Burt's, attention with some of the things she said during the meeting. But Sterling had been prepared to counter most of the concerns she'd raised, and in the end she'd been stuck with a blatant appeal of familial obligation and the fact that there had always been a Haughton in the front office at the Haughton House.

"Do you have a minute, Alexandra?"

Priscilla. Her mother-in-law was dressed in a pants suit in pastel blue that really made her look professional but still very feminine. Burt had even changed out of typical golf pants and shirt for the meeting, wearing a black suit and tie.

"Of course I do. Let me grab the laptop and we can talk in my office."

"I'll meet you there," Priscilla said, leaving the room with Burt. The boys lingered for a few minutes and she saw Brad stop to talk to Sterling.

Dan broke away and came over to help her finish cleaning up.

"Hey, Lexi, are you free for dinner tonight?" Dan asked.

"We have an anniversary party scheduled for tonight, so I

was planning to work. The conventions manager is new and these clients are too important to risk any kind of screwup. But I can probably get away for an hour or so."

"Great. My place, seven. Jessica wants to start entertaining as a couple."

Brad said something under his breath that Alexandra didn't catch but it hadn't sounded very complimentary. Dan ignored his twin, giving him the finger before leaving the conference room. She caught Brad's sleeve when he would have walked past her.

"What?"

"You have to stop this."

"I don't know what you're talking about. Dan doesn't give a crap about dinner parties. You know it and I know it."

"Yes, I do. But he does care for Jessica and apparently she does like them."

There was a look in Brad's eyes that she recognized. It was the same fear she faced every morning lately. Fear of change. Fear of the world around her changing. She wrapped her arm around him, hugging him close to her, because at that moment he looked so much like the teenager she remembered who'd been lost when his older brother died.

He hugged her back. Holding her like he had when he'd been young and his older brother was gone. She wanted to tell him that Dan wasn't going anywhere. But she had no right to make statements like that.

"Have you ever considered that you might like Jessica if you give her a chance? Dan isn't a fool."

Brad gave her hard look. "I'll think about it."

"So I'll see you at Dan's later?"

"Yes," he said, walking out of the conference center.

Sterling picked up the papers left over from his presentation and put them in his briefcase, a sleek black leather case that looked as well put together as Sterling did.

"I'm impressed. I think you should know that I'm prepared to offer you the position of vice president in charge of development for the luxury line of Pack-Maur hotels."

Job security. God, she wished that was all this was about. To be honest, she knew she could get a job with any hotel company in the world. Her qualifications were good enough for that. "Thanks, I'll consider it. Could I stay here in Charleston?"

He shook his head. "You could visit. You'd be in the corporate headquarters to start with but you'd probably travel a lot."

Traveling didn't appeal to her. She didn't want to see new places and new things. Was that right, she wondered, or was she simply letting her fears rule her?

"I'm not much of a traveler."

Sterling closed the conference room door and walked over to her. She watched the way he moved, all casual, masculine grace, and remembered the way he'd moved over her in bed last night. She was afraid, she realized suddenly, but not of going to a new place or leaving Charleston. She was afraid of the chain reaction that Sterling had started in her. The way he'd enabled her to forget the rules of safe living that she'd established for herself.

But that wasn't the really scary part, she thought as he brushed his hand down the side of her face. The really scary part was that she minded it as much as she did. She knew the penalty for caring about someone. Someone who wasn't in her close inner family. She didn't want to visit that place again.

But time had dulled her pain and her remembrances of it. She only had a scarce recollection of what she'd felt in those dark months after Marcus's death. She turned away from Sterling.

"I have to go. Priscilla is waiting." She wasn't running away. It didn't matter if he thought her leaving the conference room was a retreat—she knew that it was just a strategic realignment. Time to pull back and regroup.

"You're not leaving here until we get this settled. There's an entire world out there waiting for you, honey. Don't let life pass you by."

She heard what he didn't say. *Don't let this chance at a relationship pass you by.* "I'm not letting you slip by, Sterling. No matter how much my self-preservation instinct says this guy is dangerous, I can't help myself. But my job is different."

He pulled her into his arms, cradling her gently against that wide chest of his, and she wanted to stay there forever. To just melt into him, but Alexandra Haughton melted for no one. She carried the weight of her world on her own shoulders.

She pushed away from him, but each time he held her it got harder and harder to pull away. She was getting in over her head with Sterling. No matter how much she thought she had him under control she knew she didn't. "I've got to go. Priscilla is waiting."

"We're still on for two, right?" he asked, catching her right hand and rubbing his finger over her wedding set. He never said anything about the rings but she knew he noticed them. Knew he wanted an explanation for them, and she also knew she wasn't going to give him one.

"Where should I meet you?"

"At the lobby exit to the beach," he said, reminding her.

She nodded at him, picking up her laptop again and leaving the conference room. As she walked down the hallway she didn't look at the walls and the old daguerreotype photos of the Haughton House while it was under construction before the turn of the last century. She didn't look at the first Haughtons who'd opened their seaside inn, but she stopped in front of the portrait of Burt and Marcus.

She paused there to look them both in the eyes and search for the answer to the question she didn't even want to acknowledge she'd asked herself. If she left Haughton House, would she lose her family, too? She wrapped an arm around her waist as she realized that her real fear in selling to Pack-Maur had nothing to do with her job, her career, but everything to do with the family that she'd made her own. And the fact that she wasn't a blood relative.

Sterling's arm snaked around her waist and he stood behind her as she stared at the portrait. He was so solid and strong that sometimes he made her realize that her fears made her weak. Made her seem like a pale shadow of the woman she could be. Made her want to revisit the secrets and the shames she had hidden deep inside her.

"What's going on in that beautiful head of yours?"

She didn't want to tell him and wasn't going to. He'd already witnessed enough of her weaknesses to realize she wasn't the woman she'd always tried to present to the world.

But Sterling didn't say anything and a few moments later when she pulled away from him, he let her go. She wondered at that, that he always let her go. She had the feeling that was more important than she'd realized. That there was something more here that she should be paying attention to, but she had to get through her meeting with Priscilla first.

Chapter Fourteen

Alexandra sat behind the desk in her office. The one that Priscilla had helped her decorate when she'd first taken over the CEO position at Haughton House.

"Sorry for the delay. Are you going to Dan's tonight for dinner?" Alexandra asked, keeping things normal. She wasn't exactly sure why Priscilla wanted to see her alone.

"We can't. I'd already committed to the Parsons for dinner and bridge."

"That sounds like fun," she said, glancing at her watch. She had to meet with the housekeeping manager in thirty minutes to discuss some loss-prevention measures that his staff wanted to incorporate into their existing policies.

"I know your day is busy," Priscilla said. "Thanks for giving me the time."

Alexandra rubbed the base of her neck where she felt a headache starting. "I always have time for family."

"Good. That's exactly what I wanted to see you about."

"I'm not following."

"In the boardroom while you were giving your presentation you separated yourself from the family. You made it sound as if you weren't part and parcel of Haughton House."

"Technically, I'm not a Haughton." And that was the rub. After all the years she'd spent feeling like she'd found a family and had a home, she'd started to realize that she hadn't been born a Haughton. Part of that realization had come from

Sterling. Dating him, sleeping with him, hearing him talk about wanting something more had made her understand how tenuous her position in the Haughton family was. Would they still be her family if she had an affair with Sterling and moved to Atlanta?

"You carry the Haughton last name, my dear. You hold shares the way the rest of us do. You are definitely a Haughton, Alexandra. Why are you doubting that?"

She leaned back against her desk, wrapping her arms around her waist, and searched for something to tell Priscilla that would make some kind of sense. Something that she wasn't sure she understood herself. Everything was morphing around her. The twins weren't the same peas-in-a-pod they'd always been. Sterling was definitely not just the corporate rival he'd been only a week ago. And she wasn't the woman she'd been just three short days earlier.

"I'm not ready for this change."

Priscilla leaned on the desk next to her, putting her arm around Alexandra's shoulders. The warmth of that embrace, the smell of Chanel, and the feeling of acceptance she felt from Priscilla made tears burn the back of her eyes. She was so glad she'd misread her mother-in-law. She wasn't ready to lose her and Burt and the boys.

"Do you think you'd ever be, my dear?"

Alexandra gave Priscilla a rueful grin. Priscilla was one of the few people who really knew her. They'd shared a lot of grief and pain, and that kind of bond left each of them with an intimate knowledge of the other. "You have a point. I'm not sure what's right for the resort anymore."

"What about Sterling Powell? What do you think of him?"

"He definitely knows his way around a resort. I had a chance to see him in action yesterday at the Summerlin in Myrtle Beach. He has a really great way of dealing with guests."

"Will he keep the promises he made?" she asked.

For one minute, Alexandra thought about lying. Thought

about telling the granddaddy of fabrications, because it would give her what she wanted. Priscilla would pull her support of Sterling if she thought he wasn't a man of his word.

But Alexandra had never cheated to win and she wasn't going to start now. "Yes, he will."

"Don't sound so unhappy about it. Nothing will change if we accept this merger."

"He offered me a job in Atlanta. That's a big change," Alexandra said.

"You don't have to take it."

"What would I do?"

"We all stand to make a significant amount of money once the deal goes through. You could become a lady of leisure."

At one time she'd wanted nothing more than that, but she'd changed. She could never be happy with nothing to do.

"I don't think I'd be too happy."

Priscilla stood up, staring at her with an expression in her eyes that Alexandra couldn't read. "Are you happy now?"

"Yes. Yes, I am."

Priscilla didn't seem any more convinced about that then Alexandra felt herself.

"Did Sterling like the outfit that Jessica helped you put together?"

"Yes, I think he did. What do you think about Jessica? Is Dan serious about her?" Alexandra asked, needing to change the subject.

"I like her. She's not Dan's usual type of girl," Priscilla said.

Thinking of the belly button ring and the purple-streaked hair, Alexandra had to agree. "Dan looks like he's not sure how he got her."

"Yes, he does. He keeps bringing her by the house. I think he's making a point about accepting her. Not that we'd ever not make a girl Dan loved feel welcome."

Brad wasn't above trying to drive a wedge between them, Alexandra thought. Did Priscilla not realize how threatened her son was by his brother's new relationship? "I wish Brad would find someone."

"He said the same thing about you," Priscilla said with a laugh.

Brad had always been close to his mom. "He's a busybody. Did you know that the twins set me up with Sterling on Saturday?"

"They mentioned something about that. It's been a long time since you went out on the water."

Her life had been defined by time on the water at one point. She'd spent her days in the sun, with the ocean spray on her skin, sailing, Jet-Skiing, and swimming. She'd been more at home on the water than she had on land.

"It's not fear that keeps me off the water, it's work. Running the resort takes a lot of time and energy."

"That's why you need to take time for fun," Priscilla said, walking over to the guest chair where she'd left her purse and picking it up.

Alexandra arched one eyebrow at her mother-in-law. "Fun? Since when do you care if anyone has fun?"

"Since Burt retired, every day he plans something different for us. Not a huge time thing, just something little that he thinks will be fun. He said we'd missed out on too much when we were running the resort and raising the boys."

Alexandra wondered how much of Burt's philosophy was behind Priscilla pushing her so hard to make some changes in her life. Whatever the reason, she was in the middle of making life-altering decisions, and she didn't feel so uneasy about that anymore. Now that she knew she still had her family beside her.

Sterling watched Alexandra working a few feet away from him with a group of eight-year-olds. They both wore Haughton House polo shirts and khaki shorts that had been issued from the Haughton House wardrobe facility. Taking over the children's group for the afternoon had been a risky venture. Some women didn't particularly like kids, and he'd heard more than once from the single women he dated that they didn't all have a maternal instinct.

He'd gambled that Alexandra would enjoy the time, and watching her help a little boy read the color-coded map that had been provided for the scavenger hunt revealed she didn't have an aversion to being around children. The afternoon passed quickly and soon the parents came to pick up their kids.

The wind had blown Alexandra's hair from her ponytail and it curled around her face. She smiled at him when the last child left and walked over to his side. The problems he had in the past, always walking away once he got what he wanted—well, he hoped it would be different this time. That with Alexandra he could lay to rest those feelings, but he wasn't sure.

Seeing that he'd pushed her out of her shell and that she'd changed in he last few days was a good thing.

"What a hoot that was. Thanks for suggesting that we shadow them today."

"They were a little louder than I thought they'd be," Sterling said, reaching up to tuck a strand of her hair behind her ear.

She tipped her head to the side and gave him one of her long, measuring stares. The kind that he was always positive that he couldn't live up to. Her cheeks were a little red from the sun.

"Are you around kids a lot?" she asked, pulling her sunglasses from the top of her head and putting them on.

"No. My sister has a couple but I only see them at holidays."

He took her hand in his and led the way back up to the resort. "Have you ever thought of having kids?"

"*Once*. But I'm pretty selfish—I don't know that I'd want to change my life to fit someone else's. You know what I mean?"

Did he ever. He'd always been so focused on the future and what he wanted that his ex-wife had said he was missing the present. And to her the present was kids and family. The very reason he and Sherri hadn't stayed together was that he was more focused on his career than on the relationship.

It was ironic that with Alexandra he was starting to want the things he once eschewed. Of course, he was ten years the wiser. And he'd accomplished a good number of the things he'd wanted to so long ago.

"According to my sister, the reward you get from having a child's love is more than compensation for what you give up."

"How old are her kids?"

"Thirteen and eight."

"Boys, girls?"

"One of each. They are both pretty wild and funny. They e-mail me all the time."

"That sounds nice."

He never thought about it as *nice*. He always thought of it as another obligation that he had to make sure he didn't shirk. But the kids were funny, e-mailing him, he was sure, at his sister's insistence because otherwise he wouldn't come home.

"I guess it is."

He didn't want to talk about families or kids. "Have you thought about the job offer?"

"It's only been a few hours."

"Not long enough to make up your mind?" But he knew it wasn't. She was thorough and would probably spend a lot of time researching and maybe even talking to the competition to see if she was getting the best deal.

"No. And the merger's not a done deal yet."

But it was and she knew it. Even Alexandra had to admit he'd met each of her concerns with a solution that wouldn't change the resort she'd loved so much.

He remembered the look on her face when they'd stood under the portrait of her father-in-law and deceased husband. He hoped to hell that the look had been a letting go. Saying good-bye to the dream that in the beginning even she'd said hadn't been hers.

But he wasn't going to bring Marcus up again. He didn't want to think any more about the man who'd won Alexandra's love and really defined her life. Dammit, Sterling thought, he wanted to be responsible for setting a new course in Alexandra's life.

One where they were together.

He'd known from the moment he'd seen her that she was different but now he knew how different. Making love to her, romancing her, and holding her in his arms at night had changed him, had sharpened that need in him to have things he'd never really wanted before.

She made him want to be a better man for her. Made him want to bring her home to meet his family. Made him want . . . to never let her go.

"Want to come to dinner at Dan's with me tonight?" she asked.

No, he wanted to take her back to the yacht he'd rented the other night and make love to her in the moonlight. To pretend that they could sail away from her fears and the problems she thought were between them. "Sure, what time?"

"Seven. You can meet me in the front office and we'll ride over together."

"Sounds good. Are you free this weekend?"

"Free to do what?"

"To take a sailing trip with me down to Miami. I have to check on the progress of the resort down there."

"Oh, I don't know if I should be away that long."

"The Haughton House can run without you for two days, honey."

"Don't be condescending," she said, turning away from him and walking up the path at a clipped pace.

Why did he always feel with Alexandra as if he took one step forward and two back? No matter what move he made, she always interpreted it in the worst possible way.

He ran to catch up with her, drawing her off the main path. "I wasn't being condescending and you know it. If you don't want to go with me, say no. But don't use work as an excuse. We are way past that."

She bit her lower lip and he knew that he'd pushed hard, maybe harder than he should have.

"You're right. I'll think about taking the trip. Do I have to let you know today?"

"By Wednesday. If you're not going with me, I'll probably fly down. Actually we could fly down and then bring my yacht back up here."

"I'm not sure. I never travel."

"Never?"

"Well, I went to Greenville when the twins graduated from East Carolina University, but otherwise, no—unless you count that trip to Myrtle Beach."

"I don't. That's not traveling. Are you afraid to fly?"

She shook her head. "I don't want to talk about it."

One of the lifeguards called her name and she walked over to deal with her employee. He watched her go. Every time he thought he had her figured out, he found another layer that she was hiding behind.

It was one of those nights that was never going to end. There had been an emergency when one of their guests had a heart attack in his room. They'd called 911, the ambulance had taken the man and his wife to the hospital, and Alexandra had ended up comforting two of the girls who'd been in her scavenger hunt group that afternoon.

But death and dying wasn't easy for her, and she'd been hard-pressed to find the words to reassure Rebecca and her sister Marlie. Sterling had stepped into the middle of it with his comforting presence and by volunteering to accompany her and the girls to the hospital.

She hated the feeling that came from being in an emergency room—she hadn't been in one since the night Marcus had died. She hadn't been able to visit her folks at the hospital when they'd both been sick.

She was breathing too heavily, just sitting in the parking lot. "Where are our mom and dad?"

Rebecca, the eight-year-old with wide blue eyes, had not stopped crying since the moment her father had been taken away on a stretcher.

"They are inside," Alexandra said, swallowing hard against her own panic. She could do this. She had to do this. She couldn't drop two little girls off at the ER entrance and just drive away . . . could she?

NO. She couldn't. She parked the car and looked over at Sterling, who was watching her like he knew something was going on but was not quite sure what it was.

"Come on, girls, let's go find your parents."

She opened her door and climbed out of the car. The night air was hot and heavy and for a minute she couldn't breathe. It had been a night just like this when she'd come here with Marcus.

She swayed on her feet, and Sterling was there, wrapping an arm around her shoulder before she fell. "Sorry. I think I'm hungry."

"Why don't you wait in the car," he suggested, opening the driver's side door and pushing her onto the seat. "I'll take care of finding the girls' parents and getting them situated."

She nodded mutely, watching him leave. But she hated that she was sitting there. Hated that she'd given in once again to this stupid weakness that she'd thought she'd gotten past. A weakness that made her feel incompetent.

Something she should have gotten past a long time ago. It

was a secret that no one knew about her. Not Priscilla or Burt or the boys. She'd been so careful about never trying to come and visit her parents while the Haughtons were with her. Careful that no one knew the one fear she hadn't been able to shake.

She looked down at her right hand where the wedding set was and knew that she clung too hard to certain parts of her past. She'd let go of a lot of it and moved on, but this . . . this was one of the last things she'd clung to.

She should think about not wearing the rings anymore. They were a connection to a woman that she scarcely remembered. A time that she needed to put firmly in the past. She got out of the car, locking the doors and walking carefully across the parking lot. She took a deep breath and walked straight into the ER, finding Sterling and the little girls at the nurses' desk.

With two crying little girls desperately clinging to his hands, he calmly asked the nurse a few questions. Very much the executive in charge of the situation. She'd never seem him at anything other than his competent best. Was there anything he couldn't do? He glanced up when she approached. "Thom's being operated on and Julie is in the ICU waiting room."

"Can the girls go up there?" Alexandra asked the nurse.

"Yes, they can. Their mother is expecting them," Nurse Hurboltz said.

"Do you need any information for insurance or anything?" Alexandra asked, thinking like a businesswoman and not a freaked-out-oh-my-God-I'm-in-a-hospital person. The atmosphere was a sense-memory trigger and she started shaking until she felt Sterling's hand on her shoulder. Just that touch brought her back to the present—and him.

"Mrs. Randall has already taken care of it," said the nurse.

They escorted the two girls to their mother, and as soon as they were delivered, Alexandra wanted to bolt out of the hospital. Job over, she thought. But as a hotelier she knew she couldn't just leave Julie Randall alone here. "Can we call anyone in your family?"

"I've made a few calls. My parents are taking the first flight out they can."

"Let Eugene at the concierge desk know when they will be arriving and he'll pick them up at the airport. When you are ready to go back to the hotel, just call and we'll send a car. Do you need anything sent over?"

She shook her head, looking dazed. Looking like a woman whose world was slowly crumbling. Alexandra knew exactly how she felt. She wrapped her arm around Julie and hugged her for a minute.

"It'll be okay. I'm going to send one of the women from the kids' club over to help you out with the girls, okay? Don't feel like you are alone, Julie. Everyone at Haughton House is here for you."

She nodded, and they left a few minutes later. As soon as they were outside, Alexandra found her breathing was a little erratic. She was gulping in huge draughts of air and she couldn't get enough.

Sterling put his hand on the back of her head and pushed her head down. "It's okay, honey."

A few minutes later she felt a calm numbness come over her and she stood. "I think you should drive back. I want to talk to the staff and make sure they know that whatever the Randalls need, we'll give them."

"Are you okay?"

"Sure," she said. She couldn't dwell on the fact that had just been brought home to her. *Life was precarious at best.* Death didn't just take young men who were on the verge of their lives; it also stole family men with obligations. It took husbands and fathers, and she glanced over at Sterling—it most definitely could take him.

She shivered a little deep inside because she'd been feeling safe. Like she didn't really have anything to lose because she'd been careful about the people she cared about. But Thom

Randall could easily be Brad or Dan or, God forbid, Priscilla or Burt.

He could also be Sterling, who was coming to mean more to her each day. Coming to mean too much. Dammit, too much. How had she let this happen?

"I can't go to Miami with you," she said out of nowhere. She knew it was abrupt and that he'd read all kinds of things into her comment but she didn't care.

She had to end this now before she got any more involved. Before the affection and lust she felt for him turned into something deeper.

"Let's talk about this later. When you're not still so upset."

"I'm not upset, Sterling. I'm not overreacting to a tense situation. I'm a mature woman making a decision."

He didn't say anything else but she felt the weight of his silence in the car as he drove back to the resort. She couldn't blame him, but she wished she was alone. She needed to be alone—now. She needed some time to regain her equilibrium, something she couldn't do while he was sitting next to her in her car.

His expensive aftershave filled the small area so that every breath she took reminded her he was right there. Right next to her, waiting and watching. Wanting something from her that she promised herself she'd never give another man. Something she had a feeling she was going to end up feeling for him whether he knew it or not.

She closed her eyes and tried to forget everything that had happened, but when she felt his hand on hers, prying her tightly clenched fist apart, she knew she couldn't. That it was too late to back away from Sterling, because he'd already carved a place for himself in her inner circle. In that protected place in her heart and soul where she kept the people she cared for.

How the heck had this happened? It was just sex, he was just a great lover. A vacation fling and nothing more. But her words felt like a lie and she knew better than to believe them.

Chapter Fifteen

Dan, Jessica, and Brad showed up at Haughton House less than an hour after Sterling had called to tell them Alexandra and he weren't going to make it for dinner. She didn't want to talk to her brothers and had immediately gone into superefficient, Amazon-businesswoman mode, leaving Sterling to take care of assuring the boys that she was okay and send them on their way. He noticed an odd tension between Brad and Jessica but didn't dwell on it. He had his hands full figuring out what was going on inside Alexandra's head.

He found Alexandra alone in her office on the phone. Her voice was flat and cold. She was running on adrenaline and not the good kind.

He couldn't crack her shell no matter what he said or did. He didn't like the glazed look in her eyes and had seen enough people in shock to know that she wasn't quite back to normal. Seeing her reaction tonight and watching her work through her own fears had only made him admire her more than he already did.

She'd taken charge of her fear and worked right through it, comforting Julie Randall and making arrangements for the other woman so that all Julie had to do was wait for her husband to come out of surgery.

But it was taking a toll on her, and Sterling wanted nothing more than to carry her to his suite and hold her in his arms. Reassuring himself that she wasn't slipping away from him, even though he knew that she was.

"Come on, honey, it's time to call it a night."

"I'm not leaving the resort tonight. I'll ask Perry at the front desk to find me a vacant room."

"You don't need a room—you're sleeping with me."

"Sterling—"

"Don't argue with me. You aren't going to win this fight. Not tonight."

She gazed up at him and the confusion in her eyes almost broke his heart. He wanted to tell her not to worry, that he'd protect her, but he knew that she wouldn't believe him. That life had already shown her that no one could protect her from these kinds of emergencies.

He lifted her out of her desk chair and carried her through the deserted lobby and down the long hallway that led to his suite. She rested her head against his shoulder and didn't say anything else to him. He wasn't sure that was a good thing. Maybe an argument with him would give her something else to focus on.

"This changes nothing," she said, when he opened the door to his room and set her on her feet.

He didn't answer her because he wasn't going to argue. Tonight had changed a lot in his mind and she had to realize it, too. He went into the bathroom and ran the water in the garden tub. He used the bubble bath that was in a container on the countertop provided by the hotel. The scent of magnolias filled the room; he turned off the bright overhead light, leaving just the small, recessed one over the tub.

Alexandra still stood in the doorway where he'd left her. He drew her into the room and slowly undressed her and then lifted her into the tub. He rolled a pillow up and propped it behind her head. "I'll be right back."

He called down to room service and ordered a cold dinner for two, asking them to serve it on the veranda so that they would have food waiting for them whenever they were done in the bath.

He grabbed the candles he'd bought the day before, anticipating a time when they'd make love in his big Jacuzzi tub. He set them up on the countertop in the bathroom and lit them all before undressing and joining her in the tub.

He lifted her up and slid down between her and the rim of the tub so that she was cradled in his arms. He pulled her back against him, lowering his head to kiss her shoulder.

"I hate hospitals," she said after a while. Her voice was still flat and unemotional. Like she was in some kind of stasis.

"I'm not fond of them, either. The last time I was in one was when Colby gave birth to my nephew. So it wasn't an unhappy time," he said.

He'd never lost anyone important to him. Never really let himself care enough about anyone outside his family to allow an accident or death to touch him. The thought of one of his sisters or brothers-in-law going through what Thom Randall was experiencing scared him a little.

"That sounds nice. I've never been to the hospital for a birth. Only for deaths," she said quietly.

"Your husband and parents?" he asked. She'd had a lot of grief in a relatively small amount of time. More grief than she obviously knew how to handle. But she had been handling it. She'd liberated herself from her fears.

"Just husband. I couldn't go in when my parents were there. They weren't in there at the same time but I couldn't make myself go in."

She tipped her head back, staring at the flickering candles on the countertop. He held her hand loosely in his, her right hand where she still wore the wedding set that Marcus had given her.

"My mom and I had a fight about it. My dad got really sick toward the end but it was barely a year after Marcus had died. And I . . . I'd had a kind of breakdown."

"That's understandable. You were young, right?"

"Twenty-two. And so spoiled. I'd never lost anything that mattered to me before. My mom was so angry that I wouldn't go with her to visit him in the hospital, but every time I tried to I couldn't cross the threshold. I would get one foot inside the hospital and freeze."

She must have hated that. She was so strong—she'd carved a life for herself out of her own fears and to be unable to conquer that one must have been hard for her.

"When my mom was sick, she didn't even go to the hospital. She wanted me by her side and she'd seen how hard it was for me with Dad. I guess she kind of enabled me by staying home."

"Or maybe she just loved you too much to put you through that. Was she sick?"

"They both had cancer. My dad smoked two packs a day for most of his life."

Cancer was a hard way to die. One of the partners at Pack-Maur's wife was under hospice care for ovarian cancer. Just watching the struggle that Louis Martel went through made him realize how hard it must have been for a young woman to lose both of her parents to the disease.

She tipped her head back, looking up at him with those wide brown eyes of hers, imploring him to do something. Reaching up, she drew his head down to hers, opening her mouth under his and inviting him to kiss her.

He did his best to make her forget. Or maybe that was his own ego that told him he could make her forget her fear and her pain. Forget the emotional upheaval that she'd experienced tonight.

He got them both out of the tub, dried her off slowly, lingeringly, caressing her without obvious attention, but arousing all the while. Then he wrapped her in a big, thick Haughton House terry cloth robe before drying himself off.

He carried her through his suite of rooms out onto the veranda, where the dinner he'd ordered was waiting. She pushed the Cobb salad around on her plate and barely touched her sweet tea.

"Come on," he said, drawing her to her feet and leading her back into the suite. He took her through the living area and into his bedroom.

Alexandra wrapped herself around Sterling's warm body and didn't want to open her eyes. She just curled closer to him, resting her head on his chest right over his heart. His heart beat under her ear and she kept her eyes closed, not ready to wake up and face the day. Not after last night.

She curled her arms around his chest as she felt his hands sweep down her back and draw her more fully against his body. She knew this was going to have to end. Heck, it would probably end when she walked out of his hotel suite door today. Because she wasn't going back to that place she'd been emotionally last night.

She'd had other emergencies in her years at the resort, none of them as serious as Thom Randall's, but not one of them had affected her as deeply as the one last night. She closed her eyes, remembering the way Julie had looked.

That grief in her eyes and the lost, sinking feeling. Alexandra didn't need to talk to the other woman to know exactly how she felt. It was the kind of emotion that a woman would always remember.

And Sterling was the kind of man who could make her feel that way again. She'd been falling for him since the moment he'd asked her to make him a martini. It was crazy, really. She'd spent the last ten years doing her damnedest not to fall for anyone, and this man, the one she shouldn't have even been tempted by, had somehow found a way to make her feel again.

His hand tightened on her ass and she lifted her head, looking down at him. He watched her with an intense awareness that made her suspect he might already know more about what was going on in her head than she wanted him to.

"Sterling—"

He wrapped his hand around the back of her neck and drew

her down toward him, his mouth opening lazily on hers and tasting the words that she was trying to get out. She forgot all about talking as he rolled her under his body and covered her completely.

Safety and security swamped her as he wrapped his arms around her, rocked his mouth over hers, and settled himself between her legs, their naked skin rubbing against each other. In the early morning light it was too easy to read the expression in his eyes. Too easy to acknowledge that he wasn't letting her go without leaving his mark on her. Too easy to just push her own common sense aside and give herself up to his lovemaking.

He cupped her head in his hands, rubbing his lips over hers and then licking a trail down the side of her neck to a spot just at the base of her neck. He sucked on her skin until she arched into him. Wanting, searching for more from him. He lifted his head; his lips were swollen from all the kisses they'd shared.

He brushed his thumb back and forth over her lower lip until she bit on the tip of it and sucked it into her mouth. He continued his trail of licking and suckling kisses down to her breasts. He kissed her everywhere. Didn't leave one inch of her torso unexplored. She was so sensitized from his kissing, she felt she was going to explode.

Her nipples were tight buds and her breasts felt too full. He scraped his teeth up and down the sides of her breasts and then cupped them in both his hands. He massaged her entire breast with his fingers and his palm.

She ran her nails down his back, lingering at the scar on his hip, her fingers moving over it and remembering the story he'd told her about it. She looked into his gray eyes, which were anything but cold this morning. She skimmed her hand around his hip to his cock, taking it in her hand and stroking him from base to tip.

She circled her finger over the tip at the end of each upstroke. Bracing himself with his arm, he levered up to give her greater access to his body. She loved the way he responded so openly to her caresses. He made love to her like she was the only woman in the world he wanted.

She skimmed her fingers into her own wetness and rubbed it on his erection. She kept caressing him until she felt a spurt of moisture at the tip of his cock. She caught it with her fingers, drawing her hand up to her mouth and licking her finger.

He bent down and opened his mouth over hers. Their tongues tangled, the mingled taste of both of their bodies in her mouth. He lowered himself over her again.

He continued his downward journey on her body, skimming his lips over her ribs and then tracing the line of each one with his tongue.

"I can't get enough of you, honey. You taste so good," he said, his words trailing off as he moved lower down to her belly.

She couldn't get enough of him, either, though she'd never say it out loud. He made her feel so wonderful, like she was the most beautiful woman in the world. Like she had no flaws and was perfect the way she was. Not anyone else's version of perfect, just the perfect Alexandra. The right woman for him.

He lingered over her belly button, glancing up at her over the length of her body. She swallowed hard and pulled him back up over her. She reached out blindly for the condom packet on the nightstand and grabbed one, tearing it open and fitting it over him in one smooth motion.

He tested her with his fingers and then shifted his hips and entered her in one smooth movement. She held on to his hips, urging him to be still when he would have started thrusting. Their gazes met and held and she took a deep breath, so that the mingled scents of their skin and sex were embedded deep in her senses. So that she'd never forget this moment with the rising sunlight streaming through the partially opened curtains.

The softness of the mattress beneath her back—and the hardness of his body over hers. When he started to thrust, she lifted her hips to meet his. Slid her hand down between their bodies and caressed his balls with her fingers. Then slipped her hand a little lower, pressing on his perineum. His hips jerked harder against her. He reached down, pulling her hand away from him.

He pushed her legs back against her own body, to give him greater access to her. His thrusts were fiercer now, and she couldn't do anything but hold onto him and his hips and let the feelings he generated wash over her.

Every nerve in her body reached mass-critical and pulsed with her orgasm, but he only grunted her name and changed the angle of his penetration.

Riding her hard through her climax until she felt it build again. It was too much—she couldn't do it again; she wanted to slide down on the bed and close her eyes. But he was relentless, using his cock, his mouth, his hands to build her once again toward the pinnacle and this time following her over.

Her orgasm was even more intense than the first. He called her name as he emptied himself into her, collapsing against her chest. She wrapped her arms around his shoulders, one hand in his hair as he rested his face between her breasts. His breath sawed in and out of his open mouth, warming her chest and sending goose bumps all over her highly sensitive skin.

He glanced up at her and she tried to close her eyes and look away. Tried to give herself a place to hide. But she knew it was too late for that. Too late to run from this man who'd seen her so clearly, even when she was at her best with all her armor in place.

He cupped her face in his hands and kissed her with an exquisite tenderness that rocked her, body and soul. She clung to him even though she didn't want to. She held him closer to her, wrapping her arms and legs around his body as the sweat dried on his back.

She held him like that until she felt him drift off to sleep and then quietly extracted herself from him and his bed. She dressed in yesterday's clothing and walked quietly from his suite.

* * *

Sterling rolled over when he heard the quiet closing of the door. Cursing savagely under his breath, he got to his feet. How long could he keep chasing her? Why was it that every time he felt like they got a little closer, she ran as fast as she could?

He showered, shaved, and dressed for the day, ignoring the candles that littered the vanity in the bathroom, though they seemed to mock him. Seemed to remind him that he was pursuing a woman who wanted none of the romance he had to offer her.

Karma was a bitch. When his wife had wanted romance, he'd ignored it, focusing instead on his career—and he'd lost her. He never really missed Sherri, never felt more than a fleeting sense of regret that their marriage hadn't worked out, but he missed Alexandra.

His cell phone rang.

"It's Powell."

"Sterling, it's Burt Haughton."

Of course it was. "What can I do for you, Burt?"

"My golf buddy is sick and I was hoping I could interest you in a game."

The last thing Sterling wanted to do was play golf with Burt but with his personal life such a wreck it seemed prudent to focus on business. And it made perfect business sense to join the older man for a round of golf this morning.

"Sounds good, Burt. What time do we tee off?"

"As soon as you can get down to the country club."

Sterling hung up the phone, grabbed his clubs, and was on his way to the country club less than five minutes later. As he crossed through the lobby he glanced at Alexandra's office. He sensed she wasn't there. Good thing, he thought. He was tempted to confront her.

And he wouldn't be the easygoing man he'd attempted to be during his courtship of her. He rubbed the back of his neck. She was so much trouble. Too much trouble. Life was hard enough without chasing after a woman who wanted nothing to do with him.

The valet brought his car and he put the top down to drive to the country club. It was a bright, sunny summer day, the kind of day where he didn't want to have to worry. But he did.

Alexandra. No matter how he tried to nurse his anger, he knew that he wasn't really mad at her for leaving the way she had. He was angry because she still didn't trust him. He was angry because no matter that he'd been wooing with honesty, she was still afraid of him. He was angry because he didn't know how much longer he could keep it up.

He pulled into the country club and met Burt in the restaurant that overlooked the golf course. Burt stood as soon as Sterling entered, shouldering his clubs and walking over to meet him.

Sterling shook the older man's hand. "Good morning."

"Glad you could make it on such short notice."

Sterling was glad once they were outside and playing. Burt didn't use a golf cart, preferring to walk between holes. It made for a longer game and left more time to chat. At the second hole, Burt gave him a serious look that made the hair on the back of Sterling's neck rise.

"What happened with Alexandra last night?"

"One of the guests had a heart attack and the wife accompanied him to the hospital in the ambulance," Sterling said, trying to be objective and talking about the entire incident like it was a report he was writing for the insurance company.

"That doesn't sound too bad."

"The couple had two little girls that couldn't ride in the ambulance. Alexandra and I had to take them to the hospital."

Burt didn't say anything else. They played through that hole and as they were walking to the third, he turned to Sterling.

"How did she do at the hospital?"

"She went in. I took the girls inside to meet up with their

mom, but a few minutes later Alexandra came in and took over. She represented Haughton House like you'd expect her to."

"I could give a crap about the resort's reputation," Burt said.

His esteem for the other man rose as he heard the underlying affection in Burt's voice. "It was rough for her."

"It would be. She should have called Priscilla and me."

"Asking for help is just not her style."

Burt gave him a knowing look. "You know that girl better than I'd have expected after only a few days."

Sterling was aware of the fact that his relationship with Alexandra would seem like it was going too fast to others. But to him it felt almost as if too much time had passed, that there were too many days in the future that they'd spend apart unless he could convince her to take a chance on him.

"She's not that hard to understand if you just watch her."

"Why do you want to understand her?"

Sterling shrugged. What he felt for Alexandra was complex and personal. There was no way in hell he was going to share that with Burt Haughton.

He took out his driver and put the ball on the tee. This conversation was veering into personal territory, and he wouldn't want to discuss his feelings with his own dad, much less Alexandra's father-in-law. He swung at the ball and watched it fly over the landscape, thinking how easy life was on the golf course.

There was a clear goal for him to see and he could correct any missteps with an extra stroke. So different from life and his relationship with Alexandra. No matter how he analyzed it, answers were few and far between.

Burt put his hand on Sterling's shoulder.

"Is she giving you a hard time?"

"Yes. But I don't want to discuss it."

"To be honest, I don't either. Just know that she only runs from people she really cares about."

"But not the Haughtons," Sterling said, realizing it was true. She did keep a barrier in place between her and everyone else but that inner circle of her deceased husband's family. He'd been with her enough to realize that she had no close girlfriends that she called and hung out with. She was a very private person.

"I think we're a leftover from that period in her life when she was more gregarious. She feels safe with us, or as safe as she does in any relationship."

He arched one eyebrow at the older man. While Burt was a nice man and obviously loved his family, those comments didn't sound like something he'd say.

He shrugged. "At least that's what Priscilla says."

Sterling grinned at the older man. "Your wife is one smart cookie."

"I know it, but I'm careful not to let her realize it. Despite the Southern-lady charm, she's got a will of iron and the need to dominate. If I told her she was smarter than I am, I'd never hear the end of it."

Much like Alexandra. He realized that Priscilla had influenced the woman Alexandra was today probably more than the Haughtons realized. Nothing was resolved playing golf with Burt, but at the end of the game when Sterling left the country club he'd realized one thing.

There was no escaping what he felt for Alexandra. If he had to keep chasing her, catching her and letting her go, he would. Whatever it took until she realized that he wasn't going anywhere without her.

Chapter Sixteen

The dinner party was a bust, so when Brad suggested they all stop by Friday's for drinks and potato skins, Dan immediately said yes. Seeing Alexandra, all pale and white, an ultraefficient Amazon but with that fear, was something that Jessica didn't understand.

Dan was tense, as was Brad, and she knew there was more to this evening than she saw. "What was going on with Lexi?"

"She has a thing about hospitals."

"Why?"

"Because she held our brother's dying body in her arms in a hospital," Brad said.

Dan put his arm around her, rubbing her arm and soothing her, though she doubted she'd ever be soothed. Brad wasn't going to go back to the likeable guy he'd been in the beginning. Did it have something to do with their older brother's death? Or was he just an asshole?

"I'm sorry. I didn't know."

"It's okay, baby. I haven't seen Lexi like that in a long time. I thought she'd put the hospital thing behind her when her parents were sick."

"Obviously she didn't," Brad said. He ordered another round of drinks.

Jessica didn't feel like drinking. She felt like going home with Dan and holding him in her arms. She felt like pretending that it was just the two of them in this world. She felt like finding a place where she could wrap him in her love and that would be enough.

"Enough of this topic. It's too dark for a late night."

Brad arched one eyebrow at his brother and Jessica felt a sinking feeling in the pit of her stomach. But Brad didn't say anything, and she thought that maybe she was a bit paranoid where Brad was concerned. Dan wrapped his arm around her, pulling her more firmly against the side of his body.

He was so big and warm, and strong. She felt so safe with him, which was silly because she'd always looked inside herself for that feeling. Never depended on anyone else until he'd moved into her life.

He bent his head to kiss her and she rose up to meet him. The kiss was sweet and tender, but lined with heated promises that would be kept later on when they were home alone.

His fingers flittered over the dolphin charm at her belly button. He loved to play with her charm and she squirmed closer to him.

"Jesus, Dan, we're in a public place," Brad said.

"You don't have a problem with it when you're the one," Dan said, lifting his head and glancing over at his brother.

"But I'm sitting over here alone."

"You don't have to be alone. Jessica's friend Molly is more than interested in you."

Which was true, but Brad had said that he wasn't interested in dating her friends. That was totally fine with her. At first she'd thought it would be great if he got together with Molly, because Dan and he were very close, and having her best friend hook up with Brad would have been more than nice.

But the jerkier he acted toward Molly, the less she wanted to see that happen.

"Nah, she's not my type."

"What is your type?" she asked. For the life of her, she couldn't figure out how two men who were twins could be so different.

"The same as Dan's here."

"What's your type, Dan?" she asked, blatantly fishing for a compliment. Something sweet that would soothe the worry that his brother always raised in her.

He rubbed his thumb over her lower lip. "You are my type, but you're one of a kind, so Brad is out of luck."

She smiled up at him. This was what mattered. Not his family's approval or how she dressed. This look in his eyes that said *forever*. Even though forever had not been something she'd wanted with any other guy.

"That's not what you said when we first saw her," Brad said, finishing his second beer with a long swallow.

"Really? What did you say?"

Dan glanced at his brother with a smile that was pure troublemaker. "I said you looked like my type of girl."

She smiled up at him. "I *am* your type of girl."

Brad signaled the waitress for another beer. "That's right—you seemed like our type of girl—single, stacked, and ready for sex."

Jessica just stared at Brad, unable to believe what he'd said. "Did you mean that?"

"Baby, it's just a joke between me and Brad," Dan said.

But it didn't feel like a joke to her because she had slept with Dan the first night they'd met. She hadn't slept with any other guy on the first date but she had with him because he'd seemed so into her.

They'd left the club when it closed and walked on the beach for hours, just talking and kissing until she'd realized that there was something different about him. Something that made her invite him to come home with her.

She swallowed hard, telling herself that she wasn't going to cry.

"Why would you say that?" she asked, edging away from him. Dan had tossed her his car keys when they'd left the resort, letting her drive to the restaurant so she wasn't stranded here.

"I didn't even know you, Jess. It's just something stupid we say to each other. It has nothing to do with you."

But it did, and she didn't want to try to explain it to him. She left the booth before he realized what she was doing and went out into the parking lot, leaving him behind.

Alexandra dressed in a very conservative pants suit and felt a measure of calm go through her as she smoothed her unruly hair back into a chignon. She refused to dwell on any of the emotions that were just beneath the surface today. She clenched her hands into fists and closed her eyes.

Concentrating instead on making this day just another one like any other, she drove to her office and checked her calendar. But instead of finding her normal level of comfort in her routines, she felt . . . lost.

Walking away from Sterling had been the only thing she could do. She hoped he'd just let her drift away from him. She had checked out the on-line job offerings of two other hotel conglomerates as soon as she'd gotten back to her home this morning.

Working at Pack-Maur wasn't going to be something she could do if it meant having Sterling as her boss. There was no way she could work with him on a daily basis and not be involved with him personally. And Priscilla had been right on the money yesterday when she'd said that merging Haughton House was a smart business move. So that meant she was going to have to do something different.

Moving on was never easy; actually, she'd never moved on, but staying with Sterling anywhere in the vicinity wasn't an option.

She rubbed her eyes with the heels of her hands, feeling a headache building. She was tired from last night. She wanted nothing more than to go back to Sterling's suite and crawl back into his bed. And that was so dangerous.

The promises she'd made to herself long ago were the one thing she counted on to get her through each day. And she liked the life she'd carved, she reminded herself. She had a life most would envy and she wasn't ready to give that up for a man. For the emotional roller coaster that came from being involved in a personal relationship with her lover.

It was one thing to have an affair, but last night when she'd been stripped bare emotionally and he'd held her in his arms and made love to her, she knew that they'd gone way beyond just having an affair.

It was too late to try to pretend that she didn't care about him. She knew she did. How had this happened?

He'd swept into town on Friday night and knocked her off course. She didn't want to get back on the same path she'd been on for so long. Priscilla had been right when she said it was time to start living again. But it was hard, so hard to do when she was afraid of getting hurt again. She'd managed to keep her affairs light and breezy for the last eight years, but in one night Sterling had changed all that.

There was a knock on her door; she sat up straighter in her chair, putting on her game face. "Come in."

The door opened and Brad walked in. He looked a little ragged and tired this morning. His eyes were bloodshot and his clothes were unkempt. Not at all how the young man usually looked.

"Are you okay?" she asked, worried that something bad had happened.

"I don't know," he said in a dazed tone that made her heart race.

"What happened?" she asked.

He sank down into one of the guest chairs. "I started a fight between Jessica and Dan last night after we left the resort."

"Oh, Brad."

He leaned forward, putting his head in his hands. She got up and went around to him, resting her palm on his shoulder. "Tell me what happened."

"I think I drove her away from him, Lexi. That was my goal, but when she left . . ."

She didn't want to think about what had happened after she'd left. She'd seen Dan with Jessica and knew the two of them shared a deep love connection that wasn't a fleeting emotion.

"Where is Dan?"

"I just left him at my apartment—he was totally broken up all night. I've never seen him like that. Oh, hell—what did I do?"

Alexandra wondered the same thing. "Tell me what happened. We'll figure out a way to fix this."

"God, I hope so. Jessica won't take Dan's calls or even see him."

"Did you go to their place after ya'll had been drinking?" she asked. It was two in the afternoon, but she could tell that Brad had been on an all-nighter.

"No, we went before we started drinking. If I can't fix this, I don't think he'll ever forgive me."

"Tell me exactly what you said."

Brad refused to look at her, staring at his shoes instead. "When Dan first saw Jessica he said she was his favorite type of girl . . ."

Alexandra flinched because she knew what the boys always said after that line—a girl who was stacked and sweet and ready for sex. "You told her that?"

"I was—oh, hell, Lexi, I was a total ass. Dan thought it was funny at first but then when he saw the way she took it, it just went downhill. You know he can't explain his way out of any situation."

"Yes, I know that," she said. "Let me call Jessica and see if she'll talk to me. You go get Dan cleaned up and have him here at the resort at six for dinner."

"Thanks, Lexi. I knew you'd know just what to do. I couldn't go to Mom and Dad because they really like Jessica . . ."

"And you don't want them to know what you did."

He looked up at her, his blue eyes filled with regret. "Exactly."

She sighed, her heart aching for him. She didn't have a clue what to do. But she knew someone who would know. Someone who understood romance and courtship better than anyone else she knew. "You need to apologize to Jessica and Dan."

"I will. I didn't realize how deeply he cared about her. I never realized that love could hurt that bad until I saw him last night."

Brad left a few minutes later, and Alexandra picked up the phone to call Jessica—but Brad's words echoed in her mind. Love did hurt; she knew it better than anyone. And she realized that was what she was running from. Not Sterling and the changes he brought with him, but the fear of experiencing something deep and meaningful and feeling the pain that could go with it.

Sterling was surprised when his cell rang and it was Alexandra. He'd expected her to keep a low profile and quietly try to ease herself out of his life. But then, she always did the unexpected.

"Hey, honey," he said, happier than he wanted to admit that she'd called him. He'd done a lot of thinking on the golf course with Burt and he still wasn't any closer to figuring out what to do next with Alexandra.

"Sterling. Listen, I know I owe you an explanation but I need your help first."

He wanted her explanation, but it could wait until they were together. He needed to see her face and look into her eyes when she told him whatever it was she thought he'd buy as an explanation for walking out on him after a night of soul sex. And that he realized was what really pissed him off this morning.

It wasn't that she'd left, because he knew her well enough to know that she backed off every time he got past another one of her emotional barriers. No, what ticked him off was the fact that he'd laid his soul bare making love to her and showing her that he was her man—and she'd still snuck out the door without a word.

"Sterling? Are you still there?" she asked.

"Yes, you wanted a favor?"

"It involves Dan and Jessica. Last night they apparently had the mother of all fights and Dan needs some advice."

"Why me?"

"You know more about wooing a woman than any other man I know."

"It's not transferable, Alexandra. What works with you, won't work with her."

There was silence on the line for a long time. He bit back a curse, realizing she wasn't going to respond to him. That really pissed him off, because he thought that if he'd shown her anything, he'd shown her how deeply he cared for her. Shown her that he wasn't just here for a vacation fling.

"Okay, what do you need?" he asked.

"Will you call Dan and talk to him about how a man should treat a woman he cares for?"

"I'm not sure I should be handing out any advice—I'm having some relationship problems myself."

She sighed. "I don't want to do this over the phone."

"Okay. What's Dan's number?"

She rattled it off. "Make sure he's dressed nice and at the resort at six tonight. I made him a reservation at Oceania Dining Room."

"I'll do it."

"Thank you, Sterling. I know my family's problems aren't yours," she said.

But he wanted them to be. And her calling him for help made him realize she might realize that, too. And he wasn't doing this for her family. He was doing it for their relationship.

"I want you to meet me at 6:30 at the marina. Same berth as last time," he said.

"I . . . okay. I'll be there."

He hung up the phone and called Dan. The younger man was a complete mess, and Sterling felt every one of his forty years as he talked to him. He was also a little bothered that he could still feel the same way at forty as Dan did at twenty-seven.

That one woman could bring a man's life such joy or this kind of depression was something he'd hoped to control, something he'd planned for. Seducing Alexandra had been his plan. Making her fall for him, getting her into his life without ever showing her how he really felt.

"Take a shower and get cleaned up. I'll be at your place in twenty minutes and we'll come up with a plan of action."

He didn't want to have to fix Dan's problems—actually, he knew couldn't. He'd give the younger man some advice, probably the same advice that Burt would give him. "Why didn't you call your dad?"

"I said something that would piss the old man off. He has rules about how a man should act with a woman."

"What did you say?" he asked, because for the life of him he couldn't imagine Dan saying something crass to the girl he loved.

"Something stupid. Brad and I always joke around about girls before we actually meet them. Kind of an ego thing with us."

Sterling didn't need to hear any more. "You said this to her?"

"Yeah, I know I'm an ass. I'm really not good when it comes to talking to people. I try to say the right thing but it just comes out wrong."

Sterling was usually pretty smooth on his feet, but around Alexandra he always felt like he was running out of control. "This is going to be a big-scale apology, right?"

"Yes."

"How serious are you about this girl, Dan?"

"She's my life, man. I have to fix this."

She's my life. Dan sounded so sure of himself as he said those words, and Sterling envied the younger man that. At forty he looked at life and relationships with a jaundiced eye. And the eternal planner in him had a backup strategy in case something didn't work out.

Was that what he was doing with Alexandra? Not giving a hundred percent in case it didn't work out? Keeping a part of himself in reserve?

"You need to tell her that."

"I can't. I mean, I really can't. What if she laughs—or worse, gets that shocked look on her face?"

"What if . . . you have to take a chance on love, Dan. You're young—if she reacts that way, she's not the woman for you and it might be time to move on."

"I don't think it is."

"You'll never know until you step out there and lay it all on the line."

"I think I need another drink," Dan said.

"Drinking isn't a good idea if you want her to believe what you're saying."

When the call to Dan ended, Sterling pulled the car off the road and made several calls to get the ball rolling on his evening with Alexandra. Helping Dan wasn't going to be easy, and he needed every detail in place before he saw Alexandra.

He glanced at his watch. He had less than four hours to get Dan to the Haughton House, along with the right apology gift and, of course, the right words.

Cyrano had nothing on Sterling Powell . . . except maybe a gift for romantic language and a large nose. He didn't know

Jessica, so he'd have to rely on Dan's impressions. Growing up with two sisters had given Sterling an insight into the feminine psyche that few guys had.

His girlfriends had always seemed so pretty and together, not like his sisters, who were a mess at home. They'd been so unsure of their appeal to boys, but one day he'd seen Mackenzie at the beach with a crowd of boys. She'd been totally poised and flirtatious and she'd just ruled those boys in a way that made him doubt what he'd seen at home.

It had been a moment of truth he'd carried with him from that day on. Girls were just as unsure of themselves as guys were, only for some reason they never showed it when they were around men. He had no idea what the right thing was for Dan to do to win Jessica back. But he knew that honesty and sincerity would go a long way.

And he wanted Dan to succeed so that Alexandra would have one more reason to look at him and think he was the kind of man she wanted by her side.

Chapter Seventeen

Alexandra was beyond tired when she got to her house after five. She had a resort to run and she'd managed a few small crises throughout the day. Gotten Julie Randall's parents situated in a room and sent flowers from the resort to Thom Randall. He was recovering, and the doctor she'd talked to saw no reason why he wouldn't make a full recovery.

There was a large cardboard box leaning against the doorframe of her house. She unlocked the door and pushed it open before bending to pick up the package. She knew who it was from without even looking at the card. Sterling was making it impossible for her to reinforce the barriers she always used to keep men at bay.

She closed her front door and sank to the floor, leaning back against the glass-and-wood door. She opened the box and found four smaller, gaily wrapped boxes inside. She propped the largest box on her legs and slowly removed the wrapping. She wished he wouldn't give her gifts, but as she pulled open the box and pushed the tissue paper to the side, she was glad to have this one.

She stood up and took all the gift boxes into her bedroom. Then she pulled the silky dress from the open box—it was a turquoise-print, halter-topped sundress, brighter than anything she'd normally choose for herself. She held it up to her body, staring at her reflection in the mirror.

With her boring beige pants suit underneath, it looked like

. . . well, not like her. Not like the woman she'd always been. She put the dress back on the bed. Shrugging out of her jacket, she sat in the middle of her bed, digging out another box.

The long, narrow one was almost a giveaway. Shoes. She pushed the lid off and saw a pair of white spiky heels with a pretty turquoise stone across the toes. She kicked off her sensible loafers and slipped on the unpractical shoes that she'd probably only be able to wear with the dress he gave her.

She glanced down at her unpainted toes sticking out of the sexy, one-of-a-kind sandal and felt something shift inside her. Did she really want to let Sterling be a part of her life?

She reached back into the box and pulled out the two remaining gift-wrapped boxes. She opened the larger of the two—one that looked like a dress-shirt box. She opened it, finding a white thong and matching strapless bra in the bag, along with a smaller package of stick-on, belly-button jewels.

She shook her head, opening the last box, which contained . . . a teardrop turquoise simply set and held on a quarter-inch white gold chain. She had never been so seduced by a man—and he was not even in the room with her!

Sitting in the middle of her safe, Laura Ashley decorated room with all the gifts he'd sent surrounding her, she realized he saw a different woman when he looked at her. She wore the charm bracelet he'd given her on her right wrist. She glanced at it. At the sweet memories it evoked, and realized something as she looked farther down her own arm at the wedding set she always wore: Sterling dominated her life in a way that Marcus never had.

She felt unsure of herself, which she didn't like. Sexy undergarments, even the clothing, she could handle. It was the feelings he'd evoked with them that gave her pause.

She took the undergarments and the dress into her bathroom, hanging the dress on the hook over the door to her closet before turning on the shower. She showered quickly and toweled dry.

Then she got out the package of gems for her belly button . . . she wasn't sleeping with him again. Hadn't she decided that this morning when she'd walked out of his room? But as she fingered the silk of the dress, she knew that chances were she'd give in and have sex with Sterling one more time. At least one more time.

She placed one of the gems in her belly button and felt a low-level arousal spread outward from the little piece. She stepped into the thong underwear, staring at herself in the mirror. The underwear was cut higher on the sides than her swimsuit so she had a tan line.

She decided it was a good thing she had a bikini wax regularly as well. She put on the strapless bra before blow-drying her shoulder-length hair and putting on the dress.

She stepped into her sandals when the doorbell rang. It was six o'clock. She wanted to give Brad a call and make sure Dan and Jessica were okay before she turned her phone off for the evening.

The doorbell rang again and she hurried through her small house to answer the door. A florist delivery woman was standing there.

"These are for you," she said, handing her a large bouquet of wildflowers.

She set the flowers on the table in the entryway and then gave the woman a tip before she left. She closed the door and turned to the flowers. They were pretty and fragrant. She opened the card. *I was your Cyrano, now be my Roxanne.*

The card was signed only with an *S* at the bottom. She had to thank him, really thank him, for his help with Dan. Both of the boys had called her to thank her for sending him over, saying only that he'd helped.

She picked up the phone and called Brad.

"Hey, Lexi."

"Brad, did Jessica and Dan go in for dinner yet?"

"No, they are at the bar talking. But their table is ready."

"How's the night going?"

"Looks good from here. I apologized for my part in last night's fiasco and told Jessica that, well, if Dan is serious about her, I'm ready for another sister."

"Good, Brad. I'm glad you were able to say that."

"I thought about you a lot this afternoon, Lexi. About how different all our lives would be without you, and I realized another sister-in-law might not be a bad thing. You saved my ass today."

"Glad to know that I helped."

"It's more than that. You know we all love you, Lexi."

"Thanks, Brad."

He hung up after saying good-bye and she realized something she hadn't thought of before—how much fuller her life was with the boys and Priscilla and Burt in it. Love didn't only have a potential for great joy and pain—it also brought more people into your family. People you could lean on when things got rough.

Sterling wasn't sure that Alexandra wouldn't stand him up, so when the limo driver called to let him know that he had her in his car, he felt a bolt of relief. He put the finishing touches on their dinner.

This night was either going to be the culmination of all of the seduction he'd done since they'd met or the ending of their relationship before it had a chance to begin.

He had Chicago playing on the Bose speaker system—"Color My World." It was just part of a mix that Brad had shared with him, not anything he wanted to dwell on too closely, but she *had* colored his world. In ways he didn't want to think of. She'd given him something to focus on that wasn't just his job. And he had the feeling that even if she decided to go her own way, that the color she'd brought to his life would never fade.

She'd shown him that there was more to life than just PackMaur, but he knew that he might be back to his cold, lonely life of eighty-hour workweeks and no personal life if she walked out the door.

But he was determined to make sure she didn't. His gut instinct had been to kidnap her. Blindfold her and take her to his private plane and fly her to Miami. Not take the blindfold off her until he had her tied naked to his four-poster bed in the high-rise condo he owned there.

But that would probably land him in jail with some serious charges leveled against him. And he doubted his board of directors would be inclined to keep employing him after that.

He checked his look in the mirror, smoothing back his hair and straightening his collar. He wasn't sure she'd wear the clothing he'd sent her but he hoped she did. He wanted to pamper her the way she'd once dreamed of being taken care of. He wanted to make her his princess.

The limo driver called him when he was pulling into the marina parking lot, and Sterling left the yacht and walked to the parking area. He checked the room one more time to make sure he had everything where he wanted it.

This night needed to be more than a romantic fantasy. It had to be all that he had to offer her, an example of what real life could be in their relationship.

He got there just as the chauffeur opened the door. He saw the spiky, high-heeled shoes he'd sent her emerge first, and then those silky, long legs of Alexandra's. Soon she was standing next to the white stretch limo, large sunglasses covering half her face, A big leather bag held in one hand, and a small package in the other. A wrapped gift box.

It didn't look like any of the ones he'd sent. He wondered what it contained. The clothing he'd selected looked even better on her curvy body than he'd anticipated. He went to her side, bending to steal a kiss but lingering over her mouth when she cupped his jaw and opened hers wider.

He caressed her neck and jaw, held her with just that one hand on her body and his mouth moving on hers when what he really wanted to do was wrap her in a bear hug. To pull her closer to his hungry body and keep her wrapped up in him.

She'd been gone for too long. One day apart was too much time alone. He missed her while he'd filled his day with her family. The Haughtons were nice enough, but Alexandra was the one he wanted. She was the one who consumed him. The one who made him believe that she'd be hard to get over.

Harder than any other woman he'd ever made love to. The limo driver cleared his throat and Sterling lifted his head, giving the man a hard stare. He excused himself and climbed back into the limo.

What he felt for her was so personal. So deep and uncontrollable that he wanted to always have her in his arms. And that was what bothered him most about this morning and listening to her leaving—the fact that he really needed her to stay. That something had changed inside him, and he didn't know if he was going to be able to find his way back to the man he used to be.

He slipped his arm around Alexandra's waist, tucking her under his shoulder as they walked toward the marina and the yacht he had docked there. He didn't want to let her go. When he had his hands on her, everything felt less like some kind of fantasy and so damned real.

"Thank you," she said, her voice breathless and soft. She wrapped one arm around his waist but didn't look up at him. Just held him with that one arm, her hand right over his scarred hip. The scars that had always served as a reminder of what an idiot he could be.

"For?"

She tipped her head back and her hair fell over the arm of his shirt and open collar. It was cool and silky-smooth against him. He still hadn't felt it all over his body like he wanted to. He slid his hand against the back of her head, twisting the loose strands of her hair around his palm.

Leaning down, he kissed her while holding her head back so

she could deny him nothing. She always kept him at arm's length, and tonight he didn't want to be a beggar. Begging for something that she didn't want to give outright and freely.

He felt like a beast with her arms around him and forced himself to draw back to let go of her and her hair. He was a civilized man, and it didn't matter if she chose to run away. He knew that he couldn't keep her if she didn't want to stay.

What the hell were they talking about? He realized the reason why he kept kissing her was twofold. He couldn't be around her and not want to taste her lips, but he also didn't want to give her a chance to explain her actions of this morning.

He knew that whatever she said, he wasn't going to take it like a civilized man. And maybe that's why he was acting like a rutting male with his runaway mate. He wanted to hold her down and make her acknowledge what they'd had together. What they could still have together.

But he needed to do it when he was in the position of power.

He lifted his head, and rubbed his lips over hers one last time, leading her down the dock toward the yacht.

"I was thanking you for all the beautiful gifts you gave me. The clothing, this necklace, helping with Dan."

"You're welcome for the clothing and necklace. Dan already thanked me . . . about a million times. I even had Brad pull me aside and thank me. I told them we were even."

"Even for what?" she asked.

"For dragging you out to the marina on the Jet Skis. Otherwise I think I would have spent a lot longer coaxing you to get to know me."

"Oh, Sterling," she said. There was pain and longing in her voice. Not acceptance and hope.

"Don't say anything else," he said, taking her hand and leading her onto the yacht. "Let me get a drink before we have the conversation that we've put off all day."

She nodded. "I was sincere about appreciating your help. Dan and Jessica are so right for each other."

Sterling agreed with her. "They aren't the only ones who belong together."

"You might be right, but they at least have a chance at actually living together happily. The way a married couple should."

He'd steamed the salmon fillets in the oven with tomatoes, onions, garlic, and a few herbs. It was a recipe that his mom had taught him when she'd come to Atlanta and realized that once his divorce from Sherri was final, he'd been eating rice and a steak every night. He'd made couscous as a side and grilled some asparagus on the grill pan.

But the way Alexandra was staring at the plate, he didn't doubt she'd noticed the food. He refilled his wineglass but had a feeling that chardonnay wasn't going to be enough tonight. She'd placed the small, gift-wrapped box on the table next to her plate and hadn't made a move to touch it since she'd started eating.

She put her fork down and crossed her hands together. She still wore that wedding set on her right hand. He couldn't believe how much he resented that piece of jewelry. It didn't matter that she wore the clothes he'd given her from the skin out—at least, he hoped it was from the skin out.

"Dinner is good."

"Then why aren't you eating it?" he asked. He knew he should be all suave and urbane, but he couldn't find that part of himself tonight. He was one hundred percent raw testosterone. He felt a little crazy.

"Not hungry, I guess. It's been a really long day."

He reached across the table and took her hand in his, rubbing them over her wrist where the charm bracelet he'd given her was. She smiled at him then, but it was one of those sad smiles that made his gut clench and his hands shake.

He pulled his hand away from hers and stood up, taking the plates to the galley and leaving them on the countertop. She turned toward him and he knew that whatever else, this night was going to be the final chapter in the courtship he'd been conducting.

Before she could speak, he walked back over to her and pulled her to her feet. "Don't say it. Not yet. I have to believe that you wore the clothing I sent for a reason. Tell me why."

"It is all so pretty and feminine. You're the first man in a long time to look at me and see more than a driven businesswoman. I couldn't resist wearing it."

"All of it?" he asked, stroking his finger down the side of her face. God, she was like an addiction. Was he going to be her fool? Was that what this was all about?

Not him convincing her to move their relationship to the next level. Convincing her to move to Atlanta with him.

"Yes."

"But you're still going to leave, aren't you?" he asked. They both knew the way this evening would end, he wasn't the kind of man who hid from the facts or the truth. He met it head-on and fought for what he wanted. But there was no fighting the decision and determination he read in Alexandra's gaze.

"From the beginning I've tried to tell you that this thing between us couldn't be anything more than sex."

"Just sex?" he asked.

He wasn't going to let her hide or pretend or make up stories that she'd feel better telling herself at night. What had happened between the two of them was about so much more than sex.

"Yes, only a physical lust thing."

But her lower lip trembled as she said it and he knew that she was hoping that he'd let this go. Let her go. Let her hide behind the lies that she'd said so easily. Except she'd promised him truth, and, like a fool, he'd believed her.

"Prove it."

"What? How can I prove it's just sex?"

"By taking off your dress for me and doing a sexy little striptease."

He felt like an ass as he called her bluff, and even though she didn't have a poker face and he could see how raw those words made her feel, she cocked her hip to one side and shook her head. Let her hair brush against her bare shoulders as she walked to the middle of the living room area.

"Where's your iPod?"

"Why?"

"I need the right music to dance to."

He gestured to the iPod and Bose speaker system on the built-in bookcase. Soon Marvin Gaye's "Let's Get It On" was playing. The slow and steady rhythm and sensual lyrics filled the room.

He remembered the first night they'd been here together. Making love to her for the first time. He saw those memories in her eyes as well, as her hips swayed to the music and she moved closer to him. She danced for him, beckoning him a little closer with each of her movements.

He didn't remember standing and walking over to her, but soon she was in his arms. He held her closer than he should have. Listened to the music and let the memories that he now knew were going to have to last a lonely lifetime play through his mind.

He just held her in his arms this last time, knowing that he couldn't let her prove that he meant nothing other than some incredible sex to her. He was the one who needed more from her.

She was shuddering in his arms, her head resting on his shoulder as she held him with her arms tight around his waist.

"You're right," she said, her words whispered against his chest. "It was more than sex."

"I know. We said no lying. That's why I pushed you," he said, speaking into her hair, feeling he'd taken a gamble that might just pay off.

"This isn't about truth or sex or anything like that, Sterling. This is about surviving."

She pushed out of his arms and he let her go. He tried to play it cool as he walked across the room and turned the music off. Let the silence fill the room they stood in. She crossed to her large leather bag, picking it up.

He thought she'd leave then, just walk out of his life as easily as she'd walked into it. And he knew that even though the merger with Haughton House would go through, that Alexandra was leaving his life.

She had her arms wrapped around her waist and he wasn't sure anymore why he was so determined to force her to admit something that it was clear she wasn't going to.

It no longer felt like she was the winner and he the loser in the challenge they'd had going between them. Instead it felt like maybe it was a draw . . . some kind of lose-lose situation where neither one of them was ever going to recover.

"Honey," he said, walking toward her.

She put her hand up. "Stay there. It'll be so much easier to do this when you're across the room."

"Do what?"

She kicked off the shoes and then removed the dress, letting it fall to her feet. He saw that she had one of the gems nestled in her belly button, and though he saw the sadness in every line of her body, he couldn't help himself—he was still aroused by her partially clothed body.

She unfastened the bra and then stepped out of the thong. She stood there for a moment, beautifully bare and exposed to him.

"Honey . . ."

"No. I'm not your honey, Sterling. Although for a few moments, I actually thought that I could be, but I can't." She reached into the bag and pulled out a handful of fabric. It wasn't until she'd slipped it over her head that he realized it was a dress. She put her feet into some small black slip-on shoes and then walked toward him.

"I'm so sorry, but I can't accept any of your gifts. I'm not the woman you need in your life."

She took the bracelet off and handed it to him. Placed it in his shirt pocket. He stood there like a man who'd been struck dumb. Actually, he'd been struck numb. Too numb to move or do anything other than watch her leave. Until she reached the gangway that would take her up to the deck and out of his life forever.

"Coward," he said. "You're a fraud, Alexandra Haughton, and don't think I will keep that a secret."

Chapter Eighteen

Alexandra knew he meant the words as an insult or a dare and she knew that turning around and confronting him was the worst possible action, but she did it all the same.

She was trembling from the inside out, and only by clenching her hands into fists was she able to not show that weakness. It was like the emotions—all the emotions she'd suppressed from the moment Marcus had died ten long years ago were swimming to the surface and swamping her.

She felt anger, rage, and an infinite sadness that she wasn't strong enough to stay and fight for Sterling. But she wasn't strong enough and she never would be. He wanted more from her than she was ready to give.

But he deserved more than her walking out on him without a word. She knew that this morning and she knew it now.

"Yes," she said, pivoting to face him. Trying not to see the remains of the dinner he'd fixed or the pile of pretty clothes he'd given her. "I am a coward and I'm not going to stop running and hiding."

"So don't stop running. At least slow down a little."

But she couldn't. He didn't understand it, and frankly, some days neither did she. She only knew that last night had skated too close to her dark fears of what life held for those who reached for the brass ring. How happiness was somehow meant to be illusive and forever out of her reach.

Oh, damn. What if she'd doomed Dan and Jessica to the same fate by helping them in their romance?

"If you leave, then the job offer goes. You'll be outsourced when the merger goes through."

She shook her head. "I think we both know that working together would be impossible now."

"Yes, I do know that."

He said nothing else and she wrapped one arm around her waist, wondering why this hurt so badly. She'd compartmentalized him. She didn't care about him. *Liar.* When had lying become her staple?

He crossed the distance between them, lifting her off the steps and onto the floor. "Why won't you admit we have a chance at a future together?"

"Because we don't." She knew that with the kind of bone-deep certainty that she couldn't ignore. The future—*her* future—was one that would be spent alone. She'd have Priscilla and Burt in her life, and the boys and whoever they risked loving. But for her she'd just keep to her single path.

If the Haughton House wasn't a part of it, that was okay. She'd come to terms with losing that part of her life. But she needed Charleston and the Haughtons. She didn't want to need Sterling, too.

"You mean we can't because you're too busy clinging to the past." The words should have sounded harsh but instead they came out softly, understandingly. Like he'd seen all the way to her naked soul and come back with the answers.

And he *had* seen her naked. Not just her body—that she could have handled easily and walked away from. He'd seen her heart and soul. Her fears, her vulnerabilities, and whether he acknowledged it or not, he'd seen her caring and affection.

"I'm not clinging to it. Not the way you mean," she said, trying to explain to him something she wouldn't have to any other person. She owed no one explanations for the life she lived or the way she lived it. But Sterling had gotten closer to her than any other man ever had. Even Marcus, and that was why she was sprinting for the door and not planning on stopping.

"Then explain it to me, Alexandra. Because from where I'm standing, it's not clear."

She wanted to hide, wanted to make herself so small that she'd escape the anger and oh, God, the pain she saw in his eyes. She didn't want to be responsible for hurting him.

Words weren't coming to her. Even in her head, where it was always full of things to do and say. She was numbingly cold. Standing there watching him, seeing the pain that he was trying to hide, she knew that she had to find something to say, but didn't have any idea of where she should really start.

"I'm not clinging. Really I'm not. I know that you think I wear these rings to remember but that's not true."

He reached between them, picking up her right hand, holding it in front of her face so she could see the platinum wedding set that Marcus had given her so long ago.

She couldn't explain the jewelry to anyone else. Even Priscilla had given up asking her why she still wore it. It wasn't some kind of lingering love for her deceased husband. What they'd had together was a sweet memory that she'd always cherish but she wasn't living in the past with him.

She'd moved on. Had really had no choice but to move on, and until she'd met Sterling she thought she'd found some kind of normal life. Only having him in her world had made her realize how shallow her life was. That what she thought was living was really just a demanding job and a kind of safety in routine.

"I wear them as a reminder. As a sort of safety belt for myself to remember that love can really hurt. That the reward is not worth the risk."

He slid his hand up her arm, cupping the back of her head and using his hand to tip her head up toward his. He was so tall and strong, she thought. There was never a moment when she hadn't seen him totally confident and sure of himself. From the first moment they'd met, on the phone before she'd had any idea of the masculine beauty he possessed, she'd known that Sterling Powell was a man who took life by storm.

"Love isn't always worth the risk. I know if we asked Julie Randall she'd say she'd take the years together with Thom even if he wasn't with her for the future," he said, rubbing his thumb over her bottom lip.

She wanted to believe him. Wanted to just surrender to Sterling and this moment. To curl up in his arms and let life throw its best and worst at them.

But once she curled up there, she knew she'd be devastated to ever have to live without him. She knew that it was a kind of sickness, the way she wanted some guarantee from the universe that it couldn't give.

"Then Julie Randall is a stronger woman than I am. Because I couldn't live with losing the man I cared about again." It was the truth. The first moment of clarity she'd had in a long time. A moment where she understood that she'd always care about Sterling. Oh, hell, why hedge it for herself? She loved him. She didn't understand how or why, because it was so much more than the seduction. It was more than the romance he'd wooed her with.

"Are you saying that you care for me?" he asked, a bit of sarcasm in his tone.

She didn't begrudge him his nasty tone. She'd be a lot worse if he was the one leaving her. The one reluctant to take a chance on spending a lifetime together.

"Yes, Sterling. I care for you. Probably more deeply than even I realize. When you held me in your arms last night, I felt whole and complete in a way I never have before."

He dropped his hand and walked away from her, and it hurt more than she thought it would. But she knew that if she had even a fifty-percent chance of surviving the next few years as her life morphed from safety and routine, then she had to do it on her own. Not in his arms, where she wanted to just curl up and stay forever.

"Then why are you insistent on leaving today?"

One more step up the stairs and he was just going to pack it in and stop trying to get through to her. But she'd stopped and now they stood face-to-face, and he saw the glimmer of tears in her eyes and felt an answering tug in his heart.

He didn't want to be responsible for making her cry. He didn't want to be the kind of man who, in lieu of getting what he wanted from a woman, lashed out at her and left her an aching mess of emotions. He'd never been that man and he wouldn't be now.

There was just that damned feeling in his gut that made him believe that if he let her walk out of his life he wasn't going to find another woman to take her place. It had been different when Sherri had left, because he'd been young, barely thirty, and life had seemed so full of possibilities. Like he had a lifetime stretching in front of him.

Plenty of time to accomplish his business objectives before focusing on the personal ones, because he had time. But the clock was ticking more rapidly now, though that wasn't the reason he wanted Alexandra. He wanted her because he knew that the chances of him finding another woman who fit his life so perfectly were slim.

There wasn't another woman out there waiting for him. There was just her, and he realized suddenly that the chase wasn't what this was all about. This was about capturing her and holding her in his arms every night for the rest of his life.

She was so beautiful as she stood there with the muted light from the open dining and living room spilling over her. He didn't know the right thing to say or the right action to take. Had no idea what reassurances he could give her that would convince her to take a chance on them.

On him, really. Because if she showed one moment of indecision, he'd scoop her up in his arms and take her to bed. Make love to her until she couldn't think of anything, much less walk away. He'd keep her in his bed until he had her promise to stay.

Dammit, why had he thought dinner and romance were the way to win her tonight? From the beginning it had been the almost electric spark of awareness and desire between them that had given him the edge.

"I asked you a question," he said, his voice sounding raw and rough to his own ears. Where was the smooth operator who never let anyone see him sweat?

But he knew that guy was gone. And he had no chance of finding him while she was poised with one foot in his life and the other on the runway.

"Why am I leaving tonight?" she asked, but he could tell she'd done it to stall for time. She knew exactly what he'd asked her and exactly the answer he wanted.

"Yes, honey. The truth this time."

She caught her hair back from her face with one hand and she looked too young and almost scared when their eyes met. Which made no sense—she had to know he'd give his life to keep her safe.

"Trust me, honey."

He felt like he'd loved her forever and not just for a few days. He'd seen the future in her eyes when he'd held her under him in bed. When he'd made her body his and merged their souls together.

And he sensed she'd felt that as well. It was the reason she was running. She would have stayed for sex. She would have been more than willing to commit herself to a red-hot fling, but anything more serious than that made her want to circle the wagons and protect her flank.

And he had no idea how to convince her that he wasn't her enemy. That he'd protect her better than she could ever protect herself.

"Trusting you is hard, Sterling, because I want promises you can't give."

"What promises?"

"Promises that if I stay with you I'll never be alone."

Oh, those kind of promises. He understood her fears, had held her last night through one of the worst ones. She'd been abandoned. Not by uncaring or unloving parents or husband. But by doting and loving people. People she'd counted on to stay by her side. And she wanted . . .

"That's impossible. You know that. You're too much a realist to expect me to make a promise like that."

She nodded and he knew then that was why she was leaving. She'd recognize any assurances he gave her for the lies they were. She was expecting him to back down and let her leave because she wanted things neither of them could ever guarantee.

"I know it's not realistic. But it doesn't change the fact that I've made a life based on those promises."

"Do you expect all the Haughtons to outlive you?"

"No. I don't, but it was too late for them. I got through my parents' deaths," she said, her voice hollow.

"Life isn't meant to be lived in a shell, Alexandra. You have so much waiting for you. So much more than you can have on your own."

She shook her head and he knew then that it was over. Really over. That no matter what he said, she'd made up her mind. And he'd had enough encounters with her in the boardroom to know that there was no changing her mind.

"Keep the clothes—I have no use for them."

"I can't. I don't want any lingering reminders of our time together."

Her words hurt him unexpectedly. As if hearing that she wanted no trace of him left in her life wouldn't hurt. He wanted to lash out at her, cut her as deeply as she'd cut him, but he didn't.

He wanted to be her Superman. He wanted to make the

promises she needed to take a chance on them. But he had the feeling of inevitability about this evening. About this relationship which had burned hotter than a meteor flying through space in a bright burst of heat and speed.

"Do you think it'll be that easy to forget?"

She shrugged. "I hope so."

He hoped that it wasn't easy. He hoped that every night for the rest of her life he was a lingering memory in her bed next to her. He hoped that she'd feel the pain of leaving him for a long time.

"I'll drive you home," he said.

"I can call a cab."

"Do you really want to stand out there for the world to see, waiting on a cab?"

She looked small and fragile, too vulnerable to be the tough-ass businesswoman he knew her to be. And this was it, he realized. The woman that she was running from being. The woman that she didn't want the world to see.

"I never meant to hurt you. From the first I warned you that I was empty inside. That I had no place for a man who wanted more than sex from me."

He rubbed the back of his neck, realizing that he was the one responsible for the aching in his gut. For the mess that this had become. She had warned him but he always knew what was best. He always was able to overcome every obstacle and find the path to what he wanted.

"I know you did. But foolishly I thought I could prove you were wrong."

Nearly two weeks later, Alexandra found herself outside the downtown Atlanta corporate offices of Pack-Maur. She didn't know what kind of reception she'd get when she walked into the building but she had no other address for Sterling.

One of his vice-presidents, James Burton, had followed up

with her last week with a very generous job offer. She'd told him she'd consider it but her mind, for once, wasn't on her job.

It had been on Sterling. She'd believed that by telling him that she wasn't going to let herself care for him, she'd mitigated the feelings of insecurity she felt by loving him. But she'd been wrong.

And no matter how she tried to figure out a way around it, she realized that she wasn't going to be able to fall back into her comfortable routine. Or even make a new one for herself.

James Burton was very nice to her and showed her around the building. When they ended the tour at what would be her new office if she took the position with his company, she finally asked the question that had been on the tip of her tongue since she'd arrived.

"Is Sterling in the office?"

"No. He's on an extended vacation."

"Oh. I don't suppose you'd tell me where?"

"Why do you want to know?"

"Um . . . listen, I can't tell you things that I haven't even discussed with him. But there is no way I can come to work here with him every day until I straighten out the mess I made of our personal lives. Will you please tell me how I can get in touch with him?"

She didn't want to have to tell James that Sterling refused to answer any of her cell phone calls. Maybe she was being an idiot and this was the worst idea of her entire life.

"Never mind. I'll let you know my decision about the job offer by the end of the week."

She brushed past him, walking down the hall. "Ms. Haughton?"

She glanced back at him.

"He's in California with his family. If you have a minute, I'll give you his address."

She felt a huge swelling of relief until she realized she was going to have to leave the South. As dumb as it sounded, she'd never left the area, but she'd come to realize in their time apart that there was nowhere she wouldn't go for Sterling.

One day later she found herself in a first-class cabin on a direct flight from Atlanta to Los Angeles International Airport. Priscilla, Burt, Brad, Dan, and Jessica had all wished her luck on her journey. Dan had more than made up for the hurt he'd caused Jessica and they were now engaged.

Brad was going to be the best man. When they'd talked a few days before she'd finally decided to come to Atlanta, she'd realized her brother-in-law had been hiding the same way she had. Both of them hoping their family would stay the same. Both of them afraid of any more changes.

When the plane landed, she almost went to the counter and booked a flight straight back to Charleston. She needed her safety, but more than that, she needed Sterling. Not in some weak-kneed, can't-live-without-him-way, but in a life-will-be-richer-with-him-by-my-side way.

She tried his cell phone again, hoping he'd pick up, and was surprised when the phone was answered.

"Sterling Powell's phone."

"May I speak to Sterling?"

"He's not here. Can I give him a message?"

"No message."

She hung up and pulled off the 5 onto the shoulder. What the hell was she doing, showing up on his front step without an invitation. But then she remembered the night he was waiting for her at her house when she'd gone out with Jessica. At the time she hadn't considered what a big risk he'd taken. Hadn't realized that she'd let him take all the risks.

She slowly eased back onto the interstate and realized she was going in the wrong direction. Soon she was parked in front of the Powells' home. And she really hoped that Sterling had returned in the hour it had taken her to drive from the airport.

She got out of the rental car and walked up on the porch,

wishing she'd stayed on the yacht that night or maybe invited him to stay at her place. Anything that would have kept him by her side instead of sending him away. Even as she'd done it, she knew she'd regret her actions.

She rang the doorbell and heard the sound of footsteps approaching and almost bolted back to her car. It was only the fact that the last two weeks had confirmed for her how hard it was to live without the man she'd fallen in love with that kept her feet planted.

"Can I help you?" asked the man who opened the door. He looked like an older version of Sterling. His hair had started to gray around the temples and he had laugh lines around his eyes.

"I hope so—I'm Alexandra Haughton. I'm looking for Sterling Powell. I was told he was here."

"Alexandra? From Charleston?"

She flushed at the way he'd asked that. What had he told his family about her? "Yes, sir."

"I'm Darius, Sterling's father."

"Pleasure to meet you, sir."

"He's out back. Come in."

She followed him through the house, which was a multilevel ranch decorated in a clean and modern style. Darius walked out onto the deck but she paused in the doorway. Sterling was sitting in a lawn chair next to an in-ground pool. Or at least she thought he was. Two kids were on top of him, tickling him and laughing.

She watched as he stood up with the kids. She knew the moment he saw her, the moment he noticed her standing in the doorway, because he was distracted from the kids long enough for them to push him into the water.

He scooped both of them up around the waist and brought them into the pool with him, then stroked to the side and pushed himself up and out of the pool.

"You have a guest," Darius said, handing Sterling a towel.

"What are you doing here?"

"I couldn't forget you."

He took her arm and led her away from his family. She'd noticed two women sitting at the redwood picnic table before he drew her away from the pool and into a walking path through the garden.

Sterling had been dodging phone calls from Alexandra since he'd left Charleston. He didn't trust himself enough where she was concerned not to settle for whatever little crumb she threw his way. So he'd decided a clean break would be the best. But here she was. Looking tired and nervous and like she'd slept in her clothing.

She looked nothing like the well-put-together woman he'd come to know, yet at the same time she looked so beautiful that it almost hurt to look at her.

"What are you doing here? Really."

"First I want to apologize. You offered me your heart and I acted like it didn't matter. Like what we had together wasn't anything I was interested in. But as soon as you drove away . . . I realized I'd made a mistake."

She stopped walking and put her hand on his shoulder to draw him to a halt. "I thought I'd found a way to insulate myself. To protect myself from every feeling of pain I had experienced when I lost Marcus and my parents. I thought that if I could keep people in compartments, I wouldn't ever have to hurt like that again."

He stared down into her wide brown eyes, saw them fill with tears, and knew he was goner. He didn't care why she was back. If she was back for a relationship that she wanted to call just-sex, he'd take it. Because the last few weeks had been long and lonely without her. And he believed that with enough time he could convince her to love him.

"But I hurt anyway, Sterling. I missed you so badly that at first I didn't realize that days were going by and I wasn't eating or leaving the house. I was falling back into my pattern of grief."

She framed his face with her small hands, holding it between them and leaning up to kiss him. A soft, sweet, forever kind of kiss that he hoped like hell he wasn't mistaking.

"I love you," she said, her voice hoarse and breaking on the words. "I'm so scared of caring for you the way I do, but I can't live without you. Actually, I probably could but I don't want to."

He pulled her more fully against his body in a hug so tight that when she drew back, her clothing was wet from the dunking he'd taken in the pool earlier.

"Do you mean it, honey?"

"I do. I'm so sorry that I was afraid to take the chance before. But if you still want me, I think we can make a new start of things. I'm considering the job offer at Pack-Maur, so we'd be living and working in the same city."

"I love you, honey. You know that, don't you?"

She nodded. He still saw the fear that she'd probably always have that came from caring for someone, but she'd made a heck of a first step. Coming all the way to California for him.

"How was the flight?" he asked her.

"Long. I hated it. There was nowhere to move and the flight attendant took my BlackBerry when I was checking e-mail."

"Why were you checking e-mail on the flight?"

"That's a long time to go without checking in with the office. And until the merger goes through, I'm still in charge of the Haughton House."

"If you want to keep running it, I could probably commute to Charleston every weekend."

She swallowed hard. "Thank you. That's the most romantic gesture you've made for me yet. But I'm ready to leave my safe little nest. I'm ready to start a new life with you."

He kissed her with all the desire and longing that had been building since she'd walked out on him. He held her in his arms, carrying her to the bench. He kept kissing her as she sat on his lap and they talked about the future. About how they saw their lives together.

He could never make himself let go of her for the rest of the day and evening, and that night, when they were finally alone in his old bedroom, he made love to her. Holding her in his arms afterward he realized he'd found the peace and the home he'd always wanted.

"Why are you so scared of me?" Sebastian asked softly.

She shifted away as if she planned to move down a step and then bolt. He couldn't let that happen, not before he understood what had brought on this outburst.

"Wilhelmina, talk to me." He placed a hand on the wall, blocking her escape down the stairs.

She glared at him with more anger and more of that uncomfortable fear.

"You can bully your mortal conquests," she said, her voice low. "But you can't bully me."

Sebastian sighed. "My earlier behavior to the contrary, I don't want to bully you. Or anyone."

'You can't seduce me, either," she informed him.

"I don't . . ." Seduce her? Was that what all this was about?

"Do you want me to seduce you?" he asked with a curious smile. Maybe that was the cause for her crazy outburst. She *was* jealous.

She laughed, the sound abrupt and harsh. "Hardly. I just told you that you *didn't* want to seduce me?"

"No," he said slowly. "You told me *I can't.* That sounds like a challenge."

Irritation flared from her, blotting out some of the fear. "Believe me, I'm *so* not interested."

He raised an eyebrow at her disdain. "Then why do you care about me being with that blonde."

"That blonde?" she said. "Is hair color the way you identify all your women? It's got to be a confusing system, as so many of them have the same names."

He studied her for a minute, noting just a faint flush colored her very pale cheeks

"Are you sure you don't want me to seduce you?" he asked again, because as far as he could tell, there was no other reason for her to care about the identification system for his women.

She growled in irritation, the sound raspy and appealing in a way it shouldn't have been.

Sebastian blinked. He needed to stay focused. This woman thought he was a jerk, that shouldn't be a draw for him.

"Why did you say those things?" he asked. "What have I done to make you think I'm so terrible?"

Her jaw set again, and her midnight eyes locked with his. "Are you going to deny that you're narcissistic?"

He frowned. "Yes. I'm confident maybe, but no, I'm not a narcissist."

She lifted a disbelieving eyebrow at that. "And you are going to deny egocentric, too?"

"Well, since egocentric is pretty much the same as narcissistic, then yes, I'm going to deny it."

Her jaw set even more, and he suspected she was gritting her teeth, which for some reason made him want to smile. He really was driving her nuts. He liked that.

He was hurt that she had such a low opinion of him, but he did like that fact that he seemed to have gotten under her skin.

"I think we can also rule out vain, too," he said, "because again that's pretty darn similar to narcissistic and egocentric." He smiled slightly.

Her eyes narrowed, and she still kept her lips pressed firmly together—their pretty bow shape compressed into a nearly straight line.

"So you see," he continued, "I think this whole awful opinion that you have formulated about me might just be a mixup.

What you thought was conceit, which is also another word for narcissism," he couldn't help adding, "was just self-confidence."

His smile broadened, and Wilhelmina fought the urge to scream. He was mocking her. Still the egotistical scoundrel. Even now, after she'd told him exactly what she thought of him. He was worse than what she'd called him. He was . . . unbelievable.

"What about depraved?" she asked. Surely that insult had made him realize what she thought.

"What about it?" he asked, raising an eyebrow, looking every inch the haughty, depraved vampire she'd labeled him.

"Are you going to deny that one, too?" she demanded.

He pretended to consider, then shook his head. "No, I won't deny that one. Although I'd consider myself more debauched, than depraved. In a very nice way, however."

He grinned again, that sinfully sexy twist of his lips, and her gaze dropped to his lips. Full, pouting lips that most women would kill for. But on him, they didn't look the slightest bit feminine.

What was she thinking? Her eyes snapped back to his, but the smug light in his golden eyes stated that he'd already noticed where she'd been staring.

She gritted her teeth and focused on a point over his shoulder, trying not to notice how broad those shoulders were. Or how his closeness made her skin warm.

He shifted so he was even closer, his chest nearly brushing hers. His large body nearly surrounding her in the small stairwell. His closeness, the confines of his large body around hers, should have scared her, but she only felt . . . tingly.

"So, now that we've sorted that out," he said softly. "Why don't we go back to my other question?"

She swallowed, trying to ignore the way his voice felt like a velvety caress on her skin. She didn't allow herself to look at him, scared to see those eyes like perfect topazes.

"Why are you frightened of me, Mina?"

Because she was too weak, she realized. Because, despite what she knew about him, despite the fact that she knew he was dangerous, she liked his smile, his lips, those golden eyes. Because she liked when he called her Mina.

Because she couldn't forget the feeling of his fingers on her skin.

She started as his fingers brushed against her jaw, nudging her chin toward him, so her eyes met his. Golden topazes that glittered as if there was fire locked in their depths.

Once again she was reminded of the ill-fated moth drawn to an enticing flame. She swallowed, but she couldn't break their gaze.

"You don't have to be afraid of me," he assured her quietly.

Yes, she did. God, she did.

Here's a peek at Alison Kent's
seductive new novel
BEYOND A SHADOW.
Available now from Brava!

She sighed heavily, shook her head. "What I wouldn't give for a real vacation. Christmas break is coming up, but I set aside that time to finish up the renovations to this place I've been putting off for too long."

He thought back to his earlier assessment that she wasn't happy with her life in Comfort Bay, and knew he'd been right. The fact that she put off such simple repairs as faulty wiring reflected her discontent. "If the upkeep is too much for you, why don't you share your place with a friend?"

"It's not that easy," she said, grabbing another screw. "The people here have roots. They grow up here. They marry here. They stay. I came for the peace and quiet, and had my life turned upside down."

He understood roots. He understood tradition. He did not understand why she remained if being here made her unhappy and restless for change. She did not strike him as a woman to let a failed marriage stop her from living her life.

He watched the flex and roll of her shoulders as she worked to tighten the screw. "What keeps you here then, if you don't have roots? Have you become that attached to the people and the town?"

She turned, angling her body into the shadows and hiding her face. "I told you this morning. My friends, my students. I adore my job."

The better part of valor demanded he let the subject drop.

"I can only hope mine will be equally satisfying. And that I don't disappoint the Maples."

"Well, you get points for being handy with a flashlight. There," she said, finishing with the final screw. "That will do until tomorrow."

"Is there no one in town to make such repairs?"

She nodded. "Dale Potter. But he's only one man in a small town that seems to be falling down around his ears with an unfortunate regularity."

"Then it seems I might be your best bet."

"Would you need access from inside?"

"I might."

She glanced over her shoulder at the window as if taking stock of her valuables. "I can leave the place unlocked, I guess. Or you can get the key from Molly."

"If you are not comfortable with me being here without you, I could wait until the evening when we are both finished with work for the day."

"I don't mind you being here, no. But I'll go ahead and call Potters to see when Dale can get out here. If it's going to be weeks, I'll take you up on the offer, okay?"

"Okay," he said, and reached up to help her down.

He had not intended to do anything more than offer his hand, but she turned to toss her screwdriver into the toolbox at his feet, and he grabbed for her as she leaned. It was an instinctive move, thinking she had misstepped and was going to fall, his hands going to her waist to steady her.

But she had not misstepped. And she did not fall. She remained standing where she was, where he held her on the ladder, his hands on her T-shirt beneath her open sweater, her abdomen inches from his face. The screwdriver clattered against the porch. He listened as it began to roll, knowing he needed to release her.

Instead, he slipped his hands lower, finding the small strip of skin where her shirt rose above her jeans and inching his thumbs along the hem, circling one around her navel and breathing her in. The feel of her flesh, her scent . . . it took nothing more. The moment ceased to be about discovering and exploiting any weaknesses in her loyalties. It became, instead, about wanting her.

But he would not force her; he would never force her. And so he bowed his head and prepared to step back. She stopped him. First with a small earthy whimper. Then by cupping one hand to the back of his head and pulling him near. He buried his face against her, gripping her waist, and she held him there as if her want mirrored his.

He felt her skin heat. He heard the rapid beat of her heart. He opened his mouth against her and tasted her on his tongue. His body tightened. His cock began to swell with the rush of his blood. And his reasons for being here vanished beyond the shadows.

Take a look at Jennifer Apodaca's upcoming novel
THE SEX ON THE BEACH BOOK CLUB.
Available next month from Brava!

She was sure that Wes knew Cullen's last name. All she had to do was convince him to tell her. Holly hurried through the cool night and reached the bookstore just in time to see Wes come outside, turn around, and lock the door.

Slowing her pace, she walked up. "Hi." Damn, he was still sexy in that overbearing male way.

He pulled his key out of the lock, then turned his gaze on her. "Change your mind?" He glanced down at the book in her hand. "Want me to return Cullen's book?" He added a grin that should be labeled as dangerous.

Holly leaned against the side of the bookstore and shrugged. "I have time to kill. Thought I'd see if you still wanted to get a drink. Unless"—she opened her eyes wide—"you really are afraid that I'm a stalker with murder on my mind."

A small smile tugged at his mouth as he shoved his keys into his pants pocket. "If not murder, then what—sex?"

Oh yeah. Wait, no! God, she was weak tonight. Maybe it was her bad week. She decided to change tactics. "I asked you out for a drink, Brockman. All you have to say is that you aren't interested." She turned and started to walk away.

"Does that work?" he called after her.

She'd only gone a couple feet and turned back. "What?"

"The offensive. Does it work?"

She couldn't help smiling. "Most of the time. But then I don't usually have to beg men for their company."

He directed his gaze in a slow examination down her body, clad in a burgundy tank top and form-fitting jeans, then back to her face. His green eyes darkened. "Tell me more about this begging."

Down, girl. What was it about him? She shot back, "For that, you'd have to buy the drinks."

He stepped closer, throttling his voice down to a dangerous rumble. "Sex on the Beach?"

She swore the ocean roared in her head. Her hormones surged up into huge waves of longing, washing over her. "You're offering me sex on the beach?"

His grin widened, crinkling his gorgeous eyes. "The drink. What did you think I meant?"

Her thighs tightened in response. *Get a grip, Hillbay—it's just a reaction to a handsome man and a long dry spell of no sex.* Holly was all for sex, but on her terms. She always kept her emotions in check. She was the cool one—the one that walked away when the relationship had played out. It was time to take back the power. She said, "That information will cost you more than the price of a drink."

He didn't hesitate. "Name your price."

"Steak." She was hungry. And food might keep her from thinking about sex.

"Done. You can follow me in your car."

She was practically dizzy from the pace he set. Or maybe that was pent-up lust breaking free. "Follow you where?"

"My house. On the beach. I'll make the drinks and we'll grill some steaks out on my deck and watch the waves. Or maybe listen to the waves, since it's dark out." His grin suggested more than wave-watching.

She thought about that, but in the end, Wes had what she wanted. Information on Cullen.

Not sex.

She lifted her chin. "I'll follow you. I can spare an hour or so."

He nodded like it was no more than he expected.

Annoyed, she said, "I'm not sleeping with you."

He moved up to her until she felt the brush of his breath. "No?"

She felt a tremor in her belly that spread wet heat. *Keep control of the situation*, she reminded herself. "I don't go to bed on the first date."

He reached down and picked up her free hand in his larger one. "Kiss on the first date?"

She should put a stop to this. But the feel of his hand wrapped around hers was warm and sensual. She opened her mouth to tell him they weren't dating, but ended up saying, "If I like the man."

He ran his thumb over her palm. "You like me. Make out?"

Regaining her wits, she jerked her hand away. "Ain't gonna happen, book boy."

His face blanked at the nickname, then a grin spread out over his face. "Why don't we go to my house and take these rules of yours for a test drive?"

She was playing with fire. She knew it but couldn't stop herself. Wes was not the man she expected when she walked into his bookstore. There was so much more, and she had a strange compulsion to peel back the layers and find out just who this man was.

Could she do that and keep her clothes on? Or maybe do it naked, but keep her emotions in check?

She was going to find out. "Lead on, book boy."